Outstandi...

A HEAD FUL...

WINNER OF THE 2015
BRAM STOKER AWARD

Named One of the Best Books of 2015 by
NPR, the A.V. Club, Tor.com, and LitReactor

"*A Head Full of Ghosts* scared the living hell out of me, and I'm pretty hard to scare."

—Stephen King

"Paul Tremblay's terrific *A Head Full of Ghosts* generates a haze of an altogether more serious kind: the pleasurable fog of calculated, perfectly balanced ambiguity."

—*New York Times Book Review*

"*A Head Full of Ghosts* is such a wonderfully wild novel. Disturbing and destabilizing, haunting and heartbreaking, this is a horror story that also plays with the history of horror tales in a way that's simply marvelous. Paul Tremblay is an excellent writer, and this book is such a fun ride."

—Victor LaValle,
author of *The Devil in Silver*

"Progressively gripping and suspenseful—[Tremblay's] ultimate, bloodcurdling revelation is as sickeningly satisfying as it is masterful."

—NPR Books

"*A Head Full of Ghosts* doesn't end just because you close the book. Some horror, it bleeds through the pages, gets onto your hands, stays with you. You'll be thinking about this one long after you've read it."

—Stephen Graham Jones, author of *Demon Theory* and *Mongrels*

"A genuinely scary, postmodern homage to classic horror that invokes Stanley Kubrick and Shirley Jackson in equal measure, but also manages to innovate on nearly every page. [It] is unlike any horror novel you've read, and yet hauntingly, frighteningly familiar."

—Sara Gran, author of *Claire DeWitt and the City of the Dead* and *Come Closer*

"Crackling with dark energy and postmodern wit . . . [this] superb novel evokes the very best in the tradition—from Shirley Jackson to Mark Z. Danielewski and Marisha Pessl—while also feeling fresh and utterly new. Deeply funny and intensely terrifying, it's a sensory rollercoaster and not to be missed."

—Megan Abbott, author of *The Fever* and *Dare Me*

A HEAD
FULL OF
GHOSTS

Also by Paul Tremblay

THE PALLBEARERS CLUB
SURVIVOR SONG
GROWING THINGS AND OTHER STORIES
THE CABIN AT THE END OF THE WORLD
DISAPPEARANCE AT DEVIL'S ROCK
SWALLOWING A DONKEY'S EYE
IN THE MEAN TIME
NO SLEEP TILL WONDERLAND
THE LITTLE SLEEP

PAUL TREMBLAY

A HEAD FULL OF GHOSTS

A NOVEL

wm

WILLIAM MORROW

An Imprint of HarperCollinsPublishers

Grateful acknowledgment is made to Future of the Left for permission to reprint an excerpt from "An Idiot's Idea of Ireland," words and music by Future of the Left © 2013.

Grateful acknowledgment is made to Charlotte Perkins Gilman for the excerpt from "The Yellow Wallpaper," © 1892.

Grateful acknowledgment is made to Bad Religion for permission to reprint an excerpt from "My Head Is Full of Ghosts," words and music by Bad Religion © 2013.

First William Morrow premium printing: September 2022
First William Morrow paperback printing: May 2016
First William Morrow hardcover printing: June 2015

Print Edition ISBN: 978-0-06326981-1
Digital Edition ISBN: 978-0-06-236325-1

Art used throughout © by gualtiero boffi /Shutterstock, Inc.
Cover design by Nadine Badalaty
Cover photograph © Nina Sinitskaya/Getty Images

For Emma, Stewart, and Shirley

My memory, she was first to the plank, and the
B-movie played in the aisle.
    —Future of the Left, "An Idiot's Idea of Ireland"

It is so pleasant to be out in this great room and
creep around as I please!
                                —Charlotte Perkins Gilman,
                                    "The Yellow Wallpaper"

Do you wanna know a secret? Will you hold it
close and dear? This will not be made apparent,
but you and I are not alone in here.
                    —Bad Religion, "My Head Is Full of Ghosts"

PART ONE

CHAPTER 1

"THIS MUST BE so difficult for you, Meredith."

Best-selling author Rachel Neville wears a perfect fall ensemble: dark blue hat to match her sensible knee-length skirt and a beige wool jacket with buttons as large as kitten heads. She carefully attempts to keep to the uneven walkway. The slate stones have pitched up, their edges peeking out of the ground, and they wiggle under her feet like loose baby teeth. As a child I used to tie strings of red dental floss around a wiggly tooth and leave the floss dangling there for days and days until the tooth fell out on its own. Marjorie would call me a tease and chase me around the house trying to pull the wax string, and I would scream and cry because it was fun and because I was afraid if I let her pull out one tooth she wouldn't be able to help herself and she'd pull them all out.

Has that much time really passed since we lived here? I'm only twenty-three but if anyone asks I tell them that I'm a quarter-century-minus-two years old. I like watching people struggle with the math in their heads.

I stay off the stones and walk across the neglected front yard, grown wild and unbounded in spring and summer, now beginning to retreat in the new cold of autumn. Leaves and weedy fingers tickle my ankles and grab at my sneakers. If Marjorie were here now, maybe she'd tell me a quick story about worms, spiders, and mice crawling underneath the decaying greenery, coming to get the young woman foolishly not keeping to the safety of the pathway.

Rachel enters the house first. She has a key and I don't. So I hang back, peel a strip of white paint off the front door, and put it in my jeans pocket. Why shouldn't I have a souvenir? It's a souvenir that so many others have helped themselves to by the looks of the flaking door and dandruffed front stoop.

I didn't realize how much I missed the place. I can't get over how gray it looks now. Was it always this gray?

I slink inside so that the front door is a whisper behind me. Standing on the scuffed hardwood of the front foyer I close my eyes to better see this initial snapshot of my prodigal return: ceilings so high I could never reach anything; cast iron radiators hiding in so many of the corners of the rooms, just itching to get steaming angry again; straight ahead is the dining room, then the kitchen, where we mustn't ever linger, and a hallway, a clear path to the back door; to my right the living room and more hallways, spokes in wheels; below me, under the floor, the basement and its stone and mortar foundation and its cold dirt floor I can still feel between my toes. To my left is the mouth of the piano-key staircase with its white moldings and railings, and black stair treads and landings. The staircase winds its way up to the second-floor in three sets of stairs and two landings. It goes like this: six stairs up, landing, turn right, then only five stairs up to the next landing, then turn right again and six stairs up to the second-floor hallway. My favorite part was always that you were completely turned around when you reached the second floor, but oh, how I complained about that missing sixth stair in the middle.

I open my eyes. Everything is old and neglected and in some ways exactly the same. But the dust and cobwebs and cracked plaster and peeling wallpaper seem faked somehow. Passage of time as a prop to the story, the story that has been told and retold so often it has lost its meaning, even to those of us who lived through it.

Rachel sits at the far end of a long couch in the almost-empty living room. A drop cloth protects the couch's upholstery from anyone careless enough to sit on it. Or perhaps Rachel is the one being protected, with the cloth saving her from contact with a moldy couch. Her hat settles in her lap, a fragile bird that has been bullied from its nest.

I decide to finally respond to her nonquestion, even if it has expired.

"Yes, this is difficult for me. And please, don't call me Meredith. I prefer Merry."

"I am sorry, Merry. Maybe our coming here is a bad idea." Rachel stands up, her hat flutters to the floor, and she hides her hands in her jacket pockets. I wonder if she has her own paint chips, or strips of wallpaper, or some other pieces of this place's past hidden in her pockets as well. "We could conduct the interview elsewhere, where you would be more comfortable."

"No. Really. It's okay. I willingly agreed to this. It's just that I'm—"

"Nervous. I totally understand."

"No." I say *no* in my Mom's lilty, singsong. "That's just it. I'm the opposite of nervous. I'm almost overwhelmed by how comfortable I feel. As weird as it sounds, it's surprisingly nice to be back home. I don't know if that makes sense, and I normally don't carry on like this, so maybe I am nervous. But anyway, please, sit, and I'll join you."

Rachel sits back down on the couch and says, "Merry, I know you don't know me very well at all, but I promise that you can trust me. I will treat your story with the dignity and care it deserves."

"Thank you, and I believe you will. I do," I

say and sit on the other end of the couch, which is toadstool soft. I'm thankful for the drop cloth now that I'm sitting. "It's the story itself I don't fully trust. It's certainly not *my* story. It does not belong to me. And it's going to be tricky navigating our way through some of the uncharted territories." I smile, proud of the metaphor.

"Think of me as a fellow explorer, then." Her smile, so unlike mine, is easy.

I ask, "So, how did you get it?"

"Get what, Merry?"

"The key to the front door. Did you buy the house? Not a terrible idea at all. Sure, giving tours of the infamous Barrett House didn't quite financially work out for the previous owner, but that doesn't mean it can't work out now. It'd be great promotion for the book. You or your agent could start the tours again. You could spice things up with readings and book signings in the dining room. Set up a gift shop in the mud room and sell clever and ghoulish souvenirs along with the books. I could help set up scenes or live action skits in the different rooms upstairs. As—how was it worded in our contract again?—'creative consultant,' I could supply props and stage direction. . . ." I lose myself in what was supposed to be a light joke, which goes on way too long. When I finally stop babbling, I hold up my hands and fit Rachel and the couch between the frames of my thumbs and fingers like an imaginary director.

Rachel laughs politely the whole time I'm talking. "Just to be clear, Merry, my dear creative consultant, I did not purchase your house."

I am aware of how fast I am talking but I can't seem to slow down. "That's probably smart. No accounting for the deteriorated physical condition of the place. And what is it they say about buying houses and buying other people's problems?"

"Per your very reasonable request that no one else accompany us today, I managed to persuade the very kind real estate agent to lend me the key and the time in the house."

"I'm sure that's against some sort of housing authority regulations, but your secret is safe with me."

"Are you good at keeping secrets, Merry?"

"I'm better than some." I pause, then add, "More often than not, they keep me," only because it sounds simultaneously mysterious and pithy.

"Is it okay if I start recording now, Merry?"

"What, no notes? I pictured you with a pen at the ready, and a small black notebook that you keep proudly hidden away in a coat pocket. It would be full of color-coded tabs and bookmarks, marking the pages that are research bits, character sketches, and random but poignant observations about love and life."

"Ha! That's so not my style." Rachel visibly relaxes and reaches across and touches my elbow. "If I can share a secret of my own: I can't read my own scribbles. I think a large part of my motivation for becoming a writer was to stuff it in the faces of all the teachers and kids who made fun of my handwriting." Her smile is hesitant and real, and it makes me like her a whole lot more. I also like that she doesn't color her pepper-gray hair, that her posture is correct but not obnoxiously so, that she crosses her left foot over her right, that her ears aren't too big for her face, and that she hasn't yet made a remark about what a creepy, empty old house my childhood home has become.

I say, "Ah, revenge! We'll call your future memoir *The Palmer Method Must Die!* and you'll send copies to your confused and long since retired former teachers, each copy illegibly signed in red, of course."

Rachel opens her jacket and pulls out her smartphone.

I slowly bend to the floor and pick up her blue hat. After politely brushing dust from the brim I place it on top of my head with a flourish. It's too small.

"Ta-dah!"

"You look better in it than I do."

"Do you really think so?"

Rachel smiles again. This one I can't quite read. Her fingers tap and flash across the touch screen of her phone and a bleep fills the empty space of the living room. It's a terrible sound; cold, final, irrevocable.

She says, "Why don't you start by telling me

about Marjorie and what she was like before everything happened."

I take her hat off and twirl it around. The centrifugal force of the rotations will either keep the hat on my finger or send it flying across the room. If it flies off, I wonder where in the whole wide house it will land.

I say, "My Marjorie—" And then I pause because I don't know how to explain to her that my older sister hasn't aged at all in fifteen-plus years and there never was a *before everything happened.*

CHAPTER 2

THE LAST FINAL GIRL

Yeah, it's just a BLOG! (How retro!) Or
is THE LAST FINAL GIRL the greatest blog
ever!?!? Exploring all things horror and
horrific. Books! Comics! Video games! TV!
Movies! ~~High school!~~ From the gooey gory
midnight show cheese to the highfalutin
art-house highbrow. Beware of spoilers.
I WILL SPOIL YOU!!!!!

BIO: Karen Brissette
Monday, November, 14, 20 _ _

**The *Possession*, Fifteen Years Later:
Episode 1 (Part 1)**

Yes, I know, it's hard to believe that
everyone's favorite (well, my favorite)
reality TV crash 'n burn *The Possession*
originally aired fifteen years ago.
Damn, fifteen years ago, right? Oh those
heady days of NSA surveillance, torrent,
crowdfunding, and pre-collapse economy!

You're going to need a bigger boat for my
grand deconstruction of the six-episode
series. There's so much to talk about. I
could write a dissertation on the pilot
alone. I can't stand it anymore! You can't
stand it anymore! *Karen, stop teasing
ussssssss!!!!*

Insert authorial voice here: As late as the
mid-2000s a midseason replacement in the
fall/holiday season meant the show was being
dumped. But with the success of *Duck Dynasty*
and many other cable networks' so-called
"redneck reality" TV shows, any time slot
could be the time for a surprise hit reality
show.

(aside: these "redneck reality"—a bourgeois
term if there ever was one—shows filled the
lack of blue-collar sitcoms or dramas . . .

remember *Green Acres* or *The Dukes of Hazzard*, nah, me either)

The Discovery Channel bet big on *The Possession*, though at first glance it didn't exactly fit the redneck mold. The show was set (yes, I'm using the word *set* as I'm treating the show like fiction, and that's because it was, like all the other *reality* TV, fiction. Duh.) in the well-to-do suburb Beverly, Massachusetts. Too bad the Barrett family didn't conveniently live in the town next door, Salem, where, you know, they burned all them witches back in ye olde days. I hereby request the sequel be made and set in Salem, please! I kid, but they might as well have set *The Possession* in a town that infamously tortured "improper" young women to death, right? But I digress . . . So, yeah, at first glance, the show had no rednecks, no backwaters, no ponds with snapping turtles, no down-home, folksy wisdom, or dudes in giant beards and overalls. The Barretts were a stereotypically middle-class family at a time when the middle class was rapidly disappearing. Their fading middle-classness was a huge part of the show's appeal to blue-collar folks and the down-and-outers. So many Americans thought and continue to think they're middle class even when they're not, and they are desperate to believe in the middle class and the values of bourgeois capitalism.

So here came this 1980s sitcom-esque family (think *Family Ties*, *Who's the Boss?*, *Growing Pains*) who were under siege from outside forces (both real and fictional), and where *The Possession* nailed that blue-collar sweet spot was with John Barrett, an unemployed father in his early forties. The family's financial situation, like so many other folks, was in the shitter, shall we say. Barrett had worked for the toy manufacturer Barter Brothers for nineteen years but was laid off after Hasbro bought out the company and closed down the eighty-year-old factory in Salem. (Salem again! *Where are all the witches at?*) John wasn't college educated and had worked at the factory since he was nineteen, starting out on the assembly lines, then working his way up through the place, climbing that toy ladder until he was finally in charge of the mail room. He'd received thirty-eight weeks of severance pay for his double-decade of servitude, which he'd managed to stretch out into a year and a half of living wage. There was only so much stretching the Barretts could do to maintain two daughters and a big house and real estate tax bill and all the hope and promise and yearning that comes with the middle-class lifestyle.

The pilot episode opens with John's tale of woe. What a brilliant choice by the writers/producers/show-sters! Opening with one of the many supposed possession-reenactments would've been too cliché, and frankly, too goofy. Instead they gave us grainy black-and-white photos of John's old factory in its days of prosperity, photos of the workers inside happily making their foam and rubber toys. Then they cut to a montage with the images flickering by almost subliminally quick: DC politicians, angry Occupy Wall Street protestors, Tea-Party rallies, unemployment charts and graphs, chaotic courtrooms, ranting talking heads, crying people filing out of the Barter Brothers factory. Within the first minute of the series, we'd already witnessed the new and all-too-familiar American economic tragedy. The show established a sense of gravity, along with an air of unease by using only realism and by first introducing John Barrett: the new and neutered postmillennial male; a living symbol of the patriarchal breakdown of society and, gosh darn it, he symbolized it well, didn't he?

Ugh, I didn't intend to introduce this series of blog posts about THE series with politics. I promise I'll get to the fun gory horror stuff eventually, but you have to indulge me first . . . BECAUSE KAREN SAYS SO!!!

If *The Possession* was going to emulate so many of the archconservative possession movies and horror movies that had come before it, then it was going to do so while standing on those sagging shoulders of *the man of the house*. The message was already clear. Daddy Barrett was out of a job and consequently the family and society as a whole was in full decay mode. Poor Mom, Sarah Barrett (stalwart bank teller), only gets a brief background check in the opening segment. Her being the sole breadwinner in the family isn't mentioned until later in the pilot when she offhandedly mentions her job during one of the confessional (see what they did there????) interviews. Sarah is barely a prop in the opening as we see a montage of wedding photos and pictures of the two daughters, Merry and Marjorie.

In the photos everyone is smiling and happy, but ominous music plays in the background . . . (dun, dun, DUN!)

CHAPTER 3

I TELL RACHEL that there is no starting point or ground zero for what happened to Marjorie and our family.

If there was, the eight-year-old me was not aware of it, and the almost quarter-century-old me cannot find it with the supposedly clear lens of hindsight. Worse, my memories mix up with my nightmares, with extrapolation, with skewed oral histories from my grandparents and aunts and uncles, and with all the urban legends and lies propagated within the media, pop culture, and the near continuous stream of websites/blogs/YouTube channels devoted to the show (and I have to confess to reading way more online stuff than I should). So all of it hopelessly jumbles up what I knew and what I know now.

In a way, my personal history not being my own, being literally and figuratively haunted by

outside forces, is almost as horrible as what actually happened. Almost.

Let me give you a small example before we
really start.

When I was four my parents attended two
church-sponsored Marriage Encounter weekends. I've learned from second-third-fourth-hand
accounts that Dad insisted they go with the hopes
of getting them through a rough patch in their
marriage and to rediscover God in their relation-
ship and lives. Mom, at the time, was no longer
Catholic or practicing any religion at all and was
very much against the idea, but she still went.
Why she went is subject to total speculation as
she never told me or anyone else why. That I'm
talking about it now would totally embarrass her.
The first weekend went well enough with their
A-frame cabin, walks in the woods, their group
discussions, and dialogue drills; each couple
would take turns writing down and then sharing
their answers to questions concerning their marriage, with those questions framed within the
context of some biblical lesson or text. Apparently the second weekend didn't go so hot, with
Mom walking out on Marriage Encounter and
Dad when he reportedly stood before the entire
gathering and quoted an Old Testament verse
about the wife having to submit herself to the
husband.

Now, it's certainly possible that story about
Mom's weekend walkout is an exaggeration based
on a couple of facts: My parents did leave the sec-

ond weekend early and ended up staying a night in a Connecticut casino; while Dad famously found religion again when we were older, he (and we) did not attend church, Catholic or other, for many years prior to the attempted exorcism. I mention these facts in the interest of accuracy and context, and to point out that it's possible his quoting the Bible didn't actually happen even if enough people believe it did.

But I am not saying it isn't probable that Dad quoted the offending verse at Mom, as it sounds totally like something he'd do. The rest of that particular story is easy to imagine: Mom storming away from the retreat cabin, Dad running to catch up with her, begging for forgiveness and apologizing profusely, and then to make it up to her, taking her to the casino.

Regardless, what I remember of those Marriage Encounter weekends is only that my parents went away with the promise that they'd be back soon. *Away* was the only word the four-year-old me remembered. I had no concept of distance or time. Only that they were *away*, which sounded so weirdly menacing in an *Aesop's Fables* way. I was convinced they went away because they were sick of my eating pasta without spaghetti sauce. Dad had always grumbled about his not believing that I didn't like the sauce while he added butter and pepper to my macaroni elbows (my preferred pasta shape). While they were away my dad's younger sister, Auntie Erin, babysat Marjorie and me. Marjorie was fine but I was too scared and freaked out to keep to my normal sleep routine. I built a meticulous fortress of stuffed animals around my head while Auntie Erin sang me song after song after song. What song didn't really matter, according to my aunt, as long as it was something I'd heard on the radio.

Okay, I promise I will generally not footnote all the sources (conflicting or otherwise) of my own story. Here in the pre-beginning, I only wanted to demonstrate how tricky this is and how tricky this could get.

To be honest, and all the external influences aside, there are some parts of this that I remember in great, terrible detail, so much so I fear getting lost in the labyrinth of memory. There are other parts of this that remain as unclear and unknowable as someone else's mind, and I fear that in my head I've likely conflated and compressed timelines and events.

So, anyway, keeping all that *in* mind, let's begin again.

What I'm not so delicately saying with this preamble is that I'm trying my best to find a place to start.

Although, I guess I already have started, haven't I?

CHAPTER 4

I HAD A playhouse made out of cardboard in the middle of my bedroom. It was white with black outlines of a slate roof and there were happy flower boxes illustrated below the shuttered windows. A stumpy, brick chimney was on top, way too small for Santa, not that I believed in Santa at that age, but I pretended to for the benefit of others.

I was supposed to color the white cardboard house all in, but I didn't. I liked that everything on the house was white and that my blue bedroom walls were my bright sky. Instead of decorating the outside, I filled the inside of the house with a nest of blankets and stuffed animals, and covered the interior walls with drawings of me and my family in various scenes and poses, Marjorie often as a warrior princess.

I sat inside my cardboard house, shutters and

door shut tight, small fold-up book light in my hand, and a book spread across my lap.

I never cared about the pigs and their silly picnic. I wasn't interested in the dumb banana mobile, the pickle car, or the hot dog car. Dingo Dog's reckless driving and Officer Flossy's endless pursuit annoyed me to no end. I only had eyes for that rascally Goldbug even though I'd long ago found and memorized where he was on every page. He was on the cover, driving a yellow bulldozer, and later in the book he was in the back of goat-Michael-Angelo's truck and he was in the driver's seat of a red Volkswagen Beetle that dangled in the air at the end of a tow truck's chain. Most of the time he was just a pair of yellow eyes peering out at me through a car window. Dad had told me that when I had been very little, I'd work myself into a lather if I couldn't find Goldbug. I'd believed him without knowing what "a lather" was.

I was eight years old, which was too old to be reading Richard Scarry's *Cars and Trucks and Things That Go* as my parents constantly reminded me. What I was or wasn't reading was once a big deal and the main source of familial Barrett angst before everything that happened with Marjorie. My parents worried, despite my doctor's assurances, that my left eye wasn't getting stronger, wasn't catching up to her socket sister on the right, and it was why I wasn't excelling in school and didn't show much interest in reading books more appropriate for my age. I could and did read just fine, but I was more interested in the stories my sister and I created together. I'd placate Mom and Dad by carrying around various "chapter books," as my second-grade teacher, Mrs. Hulbig, called them, pretending to be reading beyond my grade level. More times than not my pretend-reads were from this endless series of corny adventure books, each with its simple-minded plot essentially outlined in the title and usually involving a magical beast. Answering Mom's *what's the book about* question wasn't difficult.

So, I wasn't actually reading and rereading *Cars and Trucks and Things That Go*. My quiet and private refinding of Goldbug was a ritual I performed before Marjorie and I would write a new story in the book. We'd added dozens and dozens of stories, one for almost all of the random bit players in Richard Scarry's world, each story written in the actual pages of the book. I certainly can't remember all the stories, but there was this one we wrote about the cat driving a car that had gotten stuck in a puddle of molasses. The brown goop leaked out of a truck with its tank conveniently marked MOLASSES in big black letters. On the cat's face I'd drawn a pair of blocky black-framed glasses that were just like the ones I wore, and I'd drawn those same glasses on all of the other characters for which we'd created stories. In the space around the cat and between the molasses truck, and in my small, careful handwriting (but with terrible spelling),

I'd transcribed the following story: "Merry the cat was late for work at the shoe factory when she got trapped in the sticky molasses. She was so mad her hat flew off her head! She was stuck all day and all night. She was stuck there in the middle of the road for days and days until a bunch of friendly ants came and ate all the molasses. Merry the cat cheered and took the ants home with her. She built them a huge ant farm so they would stay. Merry the cat talked to them all the time, gave them all names that began with the letter *A*, and she always fed them their favorite food. Molasses!"

The stories in my Scarry book were short and weird and had oddly happy or reassuring endings. Marjorie was the main source of the stories and she named all the animal characters after me, of course.

After finding Goldbug in the last scene, I scooped up the book into my arms, exploded out of my cardboard house and out of my room, and ran down the long hallway to Marjorie's bedroom. I ran with bare and heavy feet, slapping my soles against the hardwood floor so she could hear me coming. It was only fair to give her a warning.

During that fall, new privacy protocols had been established. Marjorie had begun shutting her bedroom door, which meant "Merry, stay out or else!" The door generally was shut when she did homework and in the morning when she dressed for school. Marjorie was fourteen and a freshman. This new high schooler now took much longer to get ready in the morning than her previous youthful middle schooler had. She monopolized the upstairs bathroom, then cloistered herself in her room until Mom, standing expectantly in the foyer, would yell up the stairs that we were going to be late for school and/or some unnamed appointment because of her and that Marjorie was being very snotty and/or selfish. The selfish bit always made me giggle because Mom invariably would be yelling too fast to keep up with her own words and it would sound like she loudly proclaimed Marjorie was being very *shellfish*. I was secretly disappointed when Marjorie would storm down the stairs with her normal hands instead of giant pincer claws.

With this being a lazy Saturday afternoon, I was not expecting to find her bedroom door shut. I respected Marjorie's closed-door policy as much as any little sister could be expected to, but Marjorie surely had to have heard my bounding down the hallway.

I stood nearly panting outside Marjorie's grand door, which was the only door in the place that was original to the old house. Solid oak, darkly stained to match the floors, it was wall thick, built to withstand barbarous hordes and battering rams and little sisters. So unlike my cheapo, pressed sawdust door that my parents let me decorate and desecrate how I pleased.

Oak, schmoak. Since it was Saturday, I was within my well-delineated and negotiated rights to knock on Marjorie's door, which is what I did. I then cupped my hand around my mouth and the keyhole and yelled, "Story time! You promised me yesterday!"

Her high-pitched giggle sounded like she couldn't believe she was getting away with something.

"What's so funny?" I frowned hard and everything inside me sank into my toes. The door was blockaded because this was a joke and she wasn't going to make a new story with me. I yelled, "You promised!" again.

Marjorie then said in her normal voice, which wasn't as helium-high as her laughter, "Okay, okay. You may enter, Miss Merry."

I did a quick little dance I'd seen on *SpongeBob*. "Yeah! Woo!" I shifted the book so its top was tucked under my chin and partly pinned against my chest by my elbows. I didn't want to drop the book to the floor, that was bad luck for the book, but I needed both hands free to turn the doorknob. I finally bullied my way in, grunting and ramming my shoulder against the stubborn, monolithic door.

Because I was convinced that I was going to grow up to be exactly like Marjorie, entering her room was like discovering a living, breathing map of my future, and a map with consistently shifting geography. Marjorie was always rearranging her bed, dresser, desk, assorted bookcases, and milk crates filled with the most current accessories of her life. She even would rotate her posters, calendar, and astronomy decorations on the walls. With each permutation, I'd remodel the interior of my cardboard house to match hers. I never told her that I did that.

On this Saturday her bed was wedged tight into one corner and underneath her only window. The curtains were gone and only a thin, lacy white treatment remained. Her posters hung crookedly, overlapped, and clustered haphazardly on the wall across from her bed. The rest of the walls were bare. Her dresser and mirror were shoved into another corner, with her bookcases, nightstand, and milk crates filling the other two corners so that the middle of the room was wide open. The room's floor plan was an X without the crossing part.

I slowly tiptoed in, careful not to trigger any unseen trip wires that might set off Marjorie and her increasingly unpredictable mood swings. Any perceived transgression on my part could spark an argument that would end with either my crying and running to my cardboard house or with Dad's brutish method of mediating (i.e., his yelling the loudest and longest). I stood in the center of her room's centerless X, and my heart rattled like a quarter loose in a dryer. I loved every second of it.

Marjorie sat cross-legged on her bed, in front of the window so that she was silhouetted by the graying light. She wore a white T-shirt and her new, soccer-team-issued sweatpants. They were Halloween-orange with the word *Panthers* stenciled in black along the side of one leg. Her dark brown hair was pulled back in a tight ponytail.

She had a large book open on her lap. By large, I don't mean thick like a dictionary. The book spanned the width of her crossed legs. The pages were splashed with color, and they were tall and wide, about the size of the pages in my Scarry book that I still held against my chest like a shield.

I said, "Where'd you get that?"

I didn't really have to ask. It was obvious that Marjorie had a kid's book in her lap, which meant that it was one of mine.

Marjorie sensed the twitching and grinding in my head and started talking thirteen thousand miles per hour. "Please, please, please, don't be mad at me, Merry. I had this amazing story just suddenly come to me, and I knew it wouldn't quite fit in your book. I mean, we already have a molasses story in your book, right? So, okay, I just gave part of the story away, that it's another molasses story, but this one is *so* different, Merry. You'll see. And, anyway, I figured maybe the Scarry book was full and it was time to start a new book so I went into your room, and, Merry! I found the perfect book! I know it was not fair of me to go into your room without asking when I know that if you did the same to me I'd be so mad. I'm sorry-sorry, little Merry, but wait until you hear it and see what I drew." Marjorie's face was a giant smile; all white teeth and all wide eyes.

"When did you go into my room?" I didn't want to start a fight, but I had to know how she did it. Knowing where Marjorie was at all times in our house was my business, and if her door was shut, I always had one satellite-dish ear aimed toward her room, listening for the door to creak open.

"I snuck in while you were playing in your house."

"No you didn't. I would've heard you."

Her smile avalanched into a smirk. "Merry. It was easy."

I gasped with my then usual hammy over-actor exuberance, dropped my book, and balled my hands into fists. "That's not true!"

"I heard you talking to yourself and to your stuffed animals, and so I tiptoed in, holding my breath to make me lighter, of course, and I walked my fingers through your bookcase, and after, I even stood over your house and looked down the chimney. You were still talking to yourself and I was a big, horrible giant consider-ing whether or not to crush the peasants' house. But I was a good giant. Rawr!"

Marjorie leapt off her bed and stomped around the room saying, "Fee fi fo ferry, I smell the stinky feet of a girl named Merry."

I yelled, "Your feet are stinky!" and I laughed, roared my own righteous roar, and scampered around and through her too-slow giant arms and poked her in the sides and slapped her butt. She eventually scooped me up in her arms and fell backward onto her bed. I scuttled behind her and wrapped my arms around her neck.

She reached behind but couldn't get hold of me. "You're too squirmy! Okay, okay, enough. Come on, Merry. It's story time."

I shouted, "Yay," even though I felt played. She was getting off way too easy for sneaking into my room and stealing a book, and worse, listening to me talk to myself.

Marjorie pulled the book back onto her lap. It was *All Around the World*. Each page featured a busy cartoon version of a real city or foreign country. I hadn't read or thought about that book in a long time. It was never a favorite of mine.

I grabbed at the book but Marjorie roughly pushed my hands away. "Before you see what I drew, you have to hear the story first."

"Fine. Tell me!" I was all revved up, twitching in my skin.

"Do you remember when we went down to the aquarium and the North End in Boston this summer?"

Of course I remembered: First we went to the aquarium where Marjorie and I pressed our faces against the glass of the three-story-tall, tube-shaped tank, waiting for one of the snaggletoothed sharks to swim by and scare us. Later, when Mom and Dad wouldn't get me a rubber octopus, I pouted and jellyfished around the gift shop, my arms and legs all slippy-sloppy. Then we walked to the North End and ate dinner at some fancy place with black tablecloths and white linen napkins. On the way back to the parking garage we found this dessert place that was supposed to be the best in the city. Mom ordered us cannolis, but I didn't want one. I told her they looked like squished caterpillars.

Marjorie said, "Well, this story happened like almost one hundred years ago in the North End. Back in the old days, they kept all their molasses in giant metal storage tanks that were fifty feet tall and ninety feet wide, as big as buildings. The molasses was brought in by trains, and not trucks like in your book." Marjorie paused to see if I was paying attention. I was, though I wanted to ask why they needed all that molasses given that the only time I'd seen the stuff was in the Scarry book. I didn't ask. "It was the middle of winter, and for more than a week before the accident, it was really, really, super cold, so cold people's breath-clouds would freeze and then fall out of the air and smash to bits on the ground."

"Cool." I pretended to breathe some of that ice breath.

"But after all that cold, Boston got one of those weird warm winter days it gets sometimes. Everyone in the North End was saying, 'My, what a beautiful day,' and, 'Isn't it the most perfect, beautiful day you've ever seen?' It was warm and sunny enough that all kinds of people left their apartments without their coats and hats and gloves, just like little ten-year-old Maria Di Stasio, who was only wearing her favorite sweater, the one with holes in the elbows. She played hopscotch while her brothers were being cruel to her, but it was a regular everyday cruel so she ignored them.

"There was a rumbling sound that everyone in the city heard but didn't know what it was, and the rivets on the sides of the molasses tank shot out like bullets, and the metal sides peeled away like wrapping paper, and the sticky, sweet molasses poured out everywhere. A giant wave began to sweep through the North End."

"Whoa." I giggled nervously. This giant molasses wave was exciting for sure, but there were so many things wrong with this story. Marjorie was using a particular place and time, and using people instead of the goofy-looking animals of the Scarry book, and using people who were not named after me. Plus, the story was too long already and I'd never be able to write this all in the book. Where would I fit it?

"The wave was fifteen feet high and it crushed everyone and everything in its path. The wave bent the steel girders of Atlantic Avenue, tipped railcars, swept buildings off their foundations. Streets were waist deep in molasses, horses and people were stuck, and the more they wriggled and struggled to get free, the more they got stuck."

"Wait, wait—" I stopped her. What was going on with this story? I was normally allowed some input. I'd voice my displeasure or shake my head and Marjorie would back up and change the story until it was more to my liking. Instead of asking her to start over, I asked, "What about Maria and her brothers?"

Marjorie lowered her voice to a whisper. "When the tank exploded, Maria's brothers ran for safety and she tried to run too, but she was too slow. The wave's shadow caught her first, sprinting up the backs of her legs, then up the length of her favorite sweater, and then over her head, blotting out the sun, blacking out the most beautiful day ever seen. Then Maria was caught and crushed in the wave."

"What? She died? Why are you saying this? That's a terrible story!" I jumped off the bed, and scampered to pick up the Scarry book off the floor.

"I know." Marjorie sounded like she was agreeing with me, but her smile was back and so were her wide eyes. She looked proud, like she just told the greatest story ever.

I slunk back to the bed and sat across from Marjorie. "Why would you make up something like that?"

"I didn't. It's a real story. It happened. Maria and twenty other people really died in a molasses flood in Boston."

"That's not a real story."

"Yes, it is."

"No, it isn't!"

"Yes, it is."

We repeated this quid pro quo for another two measures before I relented.

"Fine. Who told you about this?"

"No one."

"You found it on the Internet, right? Not everything you read on the Internet is true, you know. My teacher says—"

"You can find the molasses flood on the Internet, it's there, I checked. Most of it is there, anyway, but that's not where I heard it."

"Where, then?"

She shrugged, then she giggled, then she stopped, and she shrugged again. "I don't know. I woke up yesterday and just sort of knew the story, like it was something that's always been there in my head. Stories are like that sometimes, I think. Even real ones. And I know this one was a horrible, terrible, no good story, but I—I can't stop thinking about it, you know? I wonder what it was like to be there, what it was like to be Maria, to see and smell and hear and feel what she felt that second right before the wave got her. I'm sorry, I can't explain it well, but I just wanted to tell you, Merry. I wanted to share it with you. Okay?" Her voice was getting gravelly like it did when she was doing homework and yelling at me to leave her alone. "You okay with this, Miss Merry?"

"I guess." I didn't believe her and didn't know why she was trying so hard to make me believe that she hadn't first found the story online. I was eight now and not a gullible little baby anymore. When I was really little, she'd tell me that her room rearranged itself at night when she was asleep, and she'd be dead serious when she said it, pretending to be upset and freaked out, and then I'd get upset and freaked out with her, my emotions amping up and in danger of redlining, but she had the knack to stop me the moment before the flood of tears would come and would say, "Okay, jeez, I was only kidding. Chill, Merrymonkey." I'd hated when she called me "Merrymonkey."

"Hey, look at what I drew." Marjorie scooted over to where I was sitting and opened *All Around the World* and rested it on both our laps. The city page was Amsterdam but she'd mangled and re-formed the letters to roughly read Boston. She'd drawn a giant cylindrical tank with a vicious, jagged gash in its front, and out spilled brown marker all over the city. Marjorie had drawn Richard Scarry–esque cats and dogs wearing sport coats and ties, and they were stuck in the molasses, thrashing around. The molasses wave crested above a doomed train, its passengers, made to look like cats and dogs, screaming in horror.

I wanted to punch Marjorie, punch her stupid smiling face. She was making fun of me and my silly book and its silly stories. Still, I couldn't look away from the page. It was terrible and would give me nightmares, and yet there was something wonderful in its terribleness.

Marjorie said, "Look. There's Goldbug," and she pointed at a small yellow figure with

X-ed-out eyes and stick-figure arms and hands reaching out of the molasses flood to no one and everyone.

I shut the book without saying anything. Marjorie put the book on my lap and then rubbed my back. "I'm sorry. Maybe I shouldn't have told you this story."

I was quick, too quick to say, "No. Tell me anything. Tell me all your stories. But tomorrow, can I get a story like the old ones? A story that you made up?"

"Yes, Merry. I promise."

I slowly slid off the bed, purposefully looking away from Marjorie and to the wall and the cluster of posters. I hadn't really noticed when I first came in the room, but they were hung so that they overlapped one another. Only certain pieces of the assorted singers, athletes, and movie stars were visible; disembodied hands, legs, arms, hair, a pair of eyes. In the middle of all those collaged body parts, everything seemed to focus on a mouth that was either laughing or snarling.

"Hey, what do you think of the posters?"

I was done with this. I had both books in my arms and they were impossibly heavy. "Lame," I said, hoping it would sting her a little.

"You can't tell Mom or Dad because they'd lose their minds, but when I woke up, my room was like this, I swear, and when you look at the posters in the mirror—"

"Shut up! You're not funny!" I ran out of her room, not wanting her to see me crying.

CHAPTER 5

MY STUFFED ANIMAL companions became my sentries, strategically placed around the room. I turned my cardboard house so the mail slot faced my bedroom door. I spent the rest of that weekend in the house, looking out through the slot, totally convinced that Marjorie would be back to apologize, or to prove that she could sneak in whenever she wanted, or to steal my books again, or something worse, like her coming into my cardboard house to rearrange my drawings in the awful way she'd done with her own posters. I was good at imagining the somethings worse.

With each passing minute that she didn't come into my room, I grew more frantic and paranoid and convinced that she was indeed coming. So I rigged my bedroom to try to catch her in the act. Wouldn't she be in trouble with Mom and Dad then, given how much of a surly-teen stink she put up whenever I went near her room. I took the belt from my fuzzy purple robe that I never used and tied the ends to a bedpost and the doorknob. The belt had just enough slack that my bedroom door opened so only someone my size could wiggle safely through. I also balanced an empty plastic orange juice jug on top of the slightly open door so that it leaned against the door frame. If the door opened beyond the constraints of my robe belt, the jug would crash to the ground, or better yet, on the door opener's head. No way would Marjorie sneak in without getting stuck or making enough of a ruckus to be heard by me.

I didn't feel 100 percent safe so I built motion-detecting surveillance cameras and a laptop computer out of cereal boxes. I spent Sunday morning conducting quite a few background checks on one Miss Marjorie Barrett. Oh, the things I found.

Despite Marjorie's promise to tell me a real, made-up story the following day, I would make her wait this time. I would make her come to me. So I stayed in my room and only ventured out for food and bathroom breaks.

Still not satisfied, I built a tower of books with *All Around the World* and *Cars and Trucks and Things That Go* as part of the foundation. To remove either book without everything crashing down would be impossible. I tried it twice and earned a bruise on my thigh from one of the falling books.

When I woke up Monday morning, Marjorie was already in the shower and my parents were loudly stumbling and mumbling about the house. I slowly sat up and a folded piece of paper tumbled off my chest.

I flung the covers off me and checked for security breaches. The robe belt was still tied and the empty orange juice jug was in place. My stuffed animals were still on watch. I scolded them for falling asleep on the job. I checked my cameras and laptop. Nothing. My tower of books was intact, but *All Around the World* was gone, stolen, and replaced with *Oh, the Places You'll Go* by Dr. Seuss. Did she just yank the book out and stuff in the replacement without the tower falling? Did she patiently break down the book tower piece by piece to get to the book and then rebuild? Maybe I forgot to put the book back after one of my structural integrity tests, but no, *All Around the World* wasn't anywhere else in my room.

I stormed into my cardboard house and I opened the folded note she'd left on my chest. Surely, it was from Marjorie and not Mom or Dad, though Dad was an occasional trickster if he was in a good mood.

It was written in green crayon.

I sneak into your room when you are asleep,
Merry-monkey. I've been doing it for weeks
now, since the end of summer. You're so pretty

when you're asleep. Last night, I pinched your
nose shut until you opened your little mouth
and gasped.

Tonight it's your turn. Sneak out to my
room, after you're supposed to be in bed, and
I'll have a new made-up story ready for you.
Pictures and everything. It'll be so much fun!
Please stop being mad at me and do this.

xoxo
Marjorie

CHAPTER 6

WE ATE DINNER in the kitchen, never in the dining room. Our dining room table, as far as I could tell, was not for dining, but for stacking the clean and folded laundry we were supposed to bring upstairs to our rooms and neatly put away, which we never did. The piles of folded clothes would grow to dizzying, unstable heights and shrink into sad little leaf piles of socks and underwear after we'd cherry-picked what we wanted to wear.

Mom made spaghetti and sighed loudly in the general direction of my father because he was still in the living room, sitting in front of the computer. We all heard the traitorous keyboard keys clacking away. Dinner was ready five minutes ago. Marjorie and I sat with our full steaming plates of pasta; hers topped with red sauce, mine with melted butter, pepper, and a blizzard of grated cheese. Mom said that we weren't allowed to start eating until "*he* showed up." Our not eating was supposed to be some sort of punishment for him.

I grabbed my stomach, swayed in my chair, and announced, "I'm gonna die if I don't eat! Come on, Dad!"

Marjorie was all slumped and disheveled, lost in her sweatshirt. She whispered, "Shut up, monkey," to me, apparently low enough that only I heard her, because Mom, who was standing right behind us, didn't admonish Marjorie.

Dad tiptoed into the kitchen and poured himself into a chair. I was always shocked by how quietly graceful he could be for such a large man. "Sorry. Just had to check a few emails. Didn't hear back from any of the places I'd hoped to."

Dad had lost his job more than a year and a half ago. When he graduated high school he'd started working at Barter Brothers, a New England–based toy manufacturer. By the end of his nineteen-year tenure he was in charge of the corporate office mail room. Barter Brothers hadn't been doing well for years and Dad managed to survive a few layoffs, but didn't survive the sale of the factory, and he was cut loose. He hadn't found another job yet.

Mom said, "I'm sure it could've waited until after dinner." She was extra agitated tonight. Surely a carryover from earlier, when she and Marjorie had come home from wherever it was they were. Marjorie ran upstairs to her room before the front door shut. Mom threw her keys on the kitchen table and went out back to smoke three cigarettes. Yes, I counted them. Three meant something was wrong.

Our kitchen table was round, a light shade of brown that had never been in style, and its legs were as wobbly and unsteady as an old dog's. So when Dad did a quick drum roll with his hands, our plates and glasses bounced and clinked together.

He said, "Hey, maybe tonight we should say grace."

This was new. I looked to Mom. She rolled her eyes, pulled her chair in tighter to the table, and took a large bite of garlic bread.

Marjorie said, "Seriously, Dad. Grace?"

I asked, "What's grace?"

Mom said, "You get to explain that one."

Dad smiled and rubbed his dark wirehair beard. "You don't remember? Has it been that long?"

I shrugged.

"It's something we used to do all the time in my family. Someone at the dinner table says a few words about how thankful we are for the food and for everyone in our lives, right? It's like a prayer."

Marjorie grunted a laugh and twisted her fork, entangling it deep in her red spaghetti.

"This isn't technically a dinner table, Dad. It's just a kitchen table," I said, proud to have found a loophole in this grace thing. I was good at finding loopholes.

Mom said, "Why are you bringing this up now?"

Dad held up his surrender hands and stammered through a nonexplanation. "No reason. Just thought it would be nice, you know? Just a nice family thing to do at dinner."

Mom said, "It's fine," in that way of hers that meant it wasn't fine. "But starting a new dinner tradition is a big deal. It's something we can all discuss later."

I said, "Yeah, we can have a family meeting about grace." Big family decisions and to-do's were supposed to be discussed during family meetings. Generally, we only seemed to have family meetings to share bad news, like when Grampy died and our dog Maxine had to be put to sleep. Or we had meetings to try to enact a new set of chores for Marjorie and me. Democracy was a pretense in those new-chores family meetings, where Marjorie and I would get the honor of choosing from a list of options that never included anything we really wanted to do, like sit on the couch, watch TV, read books, make up stories. The meetings never quite worked out the way any of us wanted them to.

Dad said, "That's a fantastic idea, Miss Merry." He loudly sucked in one long piece of spaghetti for my entertainment.

"I think it's a bad idea." Marjorie managed to hide most of her face behind her untied hair and her oversized sleeves.

"You always say my ideas are bad!" I said,

looking to pick a fight. I patted my leg to make sure I still had Marjorie's confession letter in my front jeans pocket. I hadn't been able to analyze it with my cardboard laptop yet, but no matter. I had written proof that she'd been sneaking into my room and stealing things. I would surely use it if she continued being mean to me.

Mom said, "Relax, Merry, she's not talking about you."

"So, what's a bad idea, Marjorie? Please, explain," Dad said. We knew he was angry because he was obviously trying to act not angry.

"All of it."

Mom and Dad shared a look across the table. Marjorie had managed to get my parents on the same team again.

"Did you have practice today?"

"Nice change of subject, Dad."

"What? I'm just asking."

"I had an *appointment*."

"Oh. Right. Sorry." Dad's not-anger deflated instantly, and he shrank in his chair. "How did that go?"

I had no idea at the time what they were talking about, which made me very nervous.

"Just awesome." Marjorie didn't change her posture or position, but her voice lessened and drifted far away, like she was on the verge of sleep. But then she turned to me and said, "Dad wants us to say grace so that we'll all go to heaven someday."

I patted her letter again and made a mental

note to tighten the security in my room. Perhaps I could put baby powder on the floor around the door to track any footprints that weren't mine.

Dad said, "That's not fair. Now look, Mom's right, we can talk about this later—"

"Rub-a-dub-dub, thanks for the grub," Marjorie said, then scooped half of her spaghetti into her mouth, comically distending her cheeks with pasta, but no one was laughing. Spaghetti and sauce leaked out of her mouth, down her chin, and onto her plate.

Mom and I said, "Marjorie, don't be disgusting," and "Ew, gross," at the same time.

"Hey, listen, I've always tried to respect you guys and not force my beliefs on you, so—"

"By trying to get us to say grace, right?"

"So!—You will respect mine!" Dad's volume escalated until it was louder than his drumming hands had been earlier. Dad had a bullhorn hidden inside his chest, one that rattled the walls and shook the foundation. He put his head down and harpooned his pasta.

I couldn't read Mom. Usually she'd get all over Dad for yelling and he'd be quick to apologize to us all. In our group silence Mom sat with her hands folded under her chin, and she watched Marjorie.

"Hey, Dad, I actually talked about heaven today. At my appointment." Marjorie wiped her face with the back of her hand and then winked at me.

Dad had stopped taking me to church when

I was four years old. My only memories were of boredom, wooden benches, and the big hill out behind the church on which we used to go sledding. So heaven was this vague, uneasy, almost cartoonish concept, a confusing cultural mashup of puffy clouds, harps, winged angels, golden sunlight, a giant hand that may or may not belong to a giant man with a flowing white beard named God. It was this exotic place kids at school would sometimes talk about, telling me their dead grandparents or pets were there. I didn't understand it, what it was, why it was, and I didn't really want to.

Marjorie asked Dad, "Can I ask you what I asked Dr. Hamilton?"

"Sure." Dad moved food around on his plate like he was the petulant child being scolded.

"You believe in heaven, right?"

"Yes, I very much do, Marjorie, and—"

"Hold on, I didn't get to my question yet. So, in heaven, do you believe that the ghosts or spirits or whatever of your loved ones are there, waiting for you to share in eternity?"

"Yes, but—"

Marjorie said, "Wait," and giggled. "I'm still not to my question, yet. How do you know for sure that in heaven, the ghosts of the people you love are real?"

"I'm not sure what you're asking."

"I'm asking how would you know if you were really talking with the ghost of your father, of Grampy, say, and not some demon totally faking

it? What if that demon was perfectly impersonating Grampy? That'd be pretty horrible, yeah?
Picture it: You're in heaven with who you think
is Grampy. The ghost looks like him and talks
like him and acts like him, but how can you be
sure it's really him? And as more and more time
passes you realize you can never be sure. You can
never be sure that any of the other ghosts around
you are not all disguised demons. So your poor
soul is forever in doubt, expecting that in any
one moment of eternity there will be some terrible, awful, horrible change in Grampy's face as
he embraces you."

Marjorie got up, clutching her glass of water
to her chest. Her chin was stained red with spaghetti sauce.

Sitting around the small circle of our kitchen
table, I looked at Mom and Dad and they looked
at each other as though they didn't recognize
anyone. No one said anything.

Marjorie slowly walked out of the kitchen.
We listened to her footfalls, to her progression
deeper into the house and then upstairs to her
room, and we heard her door click shut.

CHAPTER 7

A COMMERCIAL FOR a local car dealership woke me up at 11:30 P.M. Someone was shouting: *No one can beat our prices, so come on down!* I'd put my alarm radio under my pillow so my parents wouldn't hear it when it went off.

The hall and bathroom lights weren't on, which meant that my parents had turned them off and gone to bed already. Their room was across the hall from Marjorie's room and their door was shut. Past those rooms and at the other end of the hall was the sunroom and a streetlight dotted its bay window.

The hallway floor was cold on my bare feet, so I walked on my heels and with my toes bent up backward. I didn't bother to bring the Scarry book with me. Marjorie's door was slightly ajar and low-volume ambient music and soft light spilled out of her room. I didn't knock. I gently pushed her great door open.

She said, "Shut it behind you, quietly."

I did, and I twisted the knob with the care of a safecracker.

Only her dim night lamp was on, spotlighting Marjorie's bed. I still had to squint and blink until my eyes adjusted.

"Quick, tell me do you think my room is the same as it was last time or has it been rearranged?"

I looked around carefully. By "carefully" I mean that I didn't stare because I was afraid of staring too long, of seeing too much, of seeing the poster formation with all the overlapping body parts and the mouth and its teeth in the middle.

I said, "It's the same."

"Maybe it is the same. I don't know. Maybe the room changed when you left. Maybe yesterday my rug and bed were on the ceiling. Maybe my room changed and changed and kept on changing, and then the room changed back right before you came in. Maybe your room is like mine and changes all the time too, but only in secret so you don't notice."

"Stop it. I'm going back to my room if you keep talking like this."

Marjorie sat on her bed with an open book in her lap. She was still dressed in her sweats, and her chin was still stained red with spaghetti sauce. Her hair was dark, greasy, and heavy, weighing down her head.

She said, "Come on, I'm just teasing. Come sit next to me, Merry. I have your new story."

I dutifully sat next to my sister and said, "I didn't like your letter, you know." I imagined Marjorie sneaking into my room and pinching my nose shut while I slept, and it scared me. Then I imagined doing the same right back to her, and it was thrilling. "You can't sneak into my room anymore, or I'll tell Mom. I'll show her the note." I felt brave saying such things, and my bravery puffed up my chest as it lightened my head.

"Sorry. I don't know if I can promise you anything like that." Marjorie turned her head abruptly from side to side, as though she was listening for the sounds of my parents walking out of their room and into the hallway.

"That's not fair."

"I know. But I have your new story." She opened the book on her lap. It was my book, of course, the one she stole from my room: *All Around the World*. She flipped to a page with a cartoon New York City. The buildings were brick red and sea blue, and they crowded the page, elbowing and wrestling one another for precious space. The streets and sidewalks, and the people on the streets and sidewalks, were scribbled over with green ropey lines. She must've used the same green crayon with which she wrote my note.

She said, "New York City is the biggest city in the world, right? When the growing things"—Marjorie paused and ran her hands over the green lines she'd drawn in my book—"started growing there, it meant they could grow anywhere. They took over Central Park, poking through the cement paths and soaking up the park's ponds and fountains. The stuff just came shooting up, crowding out the grass and trees, and the flower boxes in apartment windowsills, and then filled the streets. When people tried cutting the growing things down, they grew back faster. People didn't know how or why they grew. There was no soil under the streets, you know, in the sewers, but they still grew. The vines and shoots broke through windows and buildings, and some people climbed the growing things so they could break into apartments and steal food, money, and HD TVs, but it quickly got too crowded for people, for everything, and the buildings crumbled and fell. They grew fast there, like a foot an hour, just like everywhere else." She kept on talking about how in the suburbs the growing things swallowed up everyone's pretty lawns and gardens and their driveways and sidewalks. And in the country and the farms, the growing things overran the corn, wheat, soy, and all the other crops. They couldn't stop the growing things so people poured and sprayed millions of gallons of weed killer, which didn't work. People quickly grew desperate and dumped bottles of Liquid-Plumr, lye, and bleach. None of it worked on the stuff and all the chemicals and poisons leached into the groundwater and poisoned everything else.

I was tracing the green loops on the New York City page, my head filling with those snaking vines and thorns and leaves, when I noticed that Marjorie had stopped talking and was now staring at me.

"There's more. Ask me something."

I knew what she wanted me to ask so I did. "What about us? How do we beat the growing things?"

Marjorie closed the book and turned off a reading lamp clipped to her headboard. It was so dark it was like nothing was there in the room with us. Only the nothing was actually something because it filled my eyes and lungs and it sat on my shoulders.

Marjorie pushed my head down onto her lap. Her legs smelled like sweat, and she petted my head roughly and ran her fingers through my hair, catching strands in her mood ring and yanking them out.

She said, "Toward the end of it all, there were two girls left, living in a small house on the top of a mountain. The house looked just like the cardboard house in your room. The girls' names were Marjorie and Merry. They alone lived with their father. Their mother had disappeared when she went to the grocery store weeks before when the growing things first attacked their town.

"They hadn't enough food anymore and their

father wasn't right. He spent most days locked in a room by himself. Poor Marjorie wasn't right either. She was sick. Malnourished. Dehydrated. She heard whispering voices that told her terrible things. She tried to stay in bed and sleep until everything was okay, but it didn't work. Only brave little Merry was still herself.

"On the last day, their father left the house to go find food. He told Merry not to open the front door no matter what and to stay out of the basement. Hours passed and Merry didn't know what to do because Marjorie was coughing and moaning and speaking gibberish. She needed food, water, something. Merry went down into the basement to look for some secret stash of food that they'd forgotten. Instead she found tips of the growing things poking out of the basement's dirt floor. She watched them grow and grow, and as they grew, they pushed up a large shape out of the dirt, and it hung off the growing things like a broken puppet. It was the body of their mother. Merry knew the horrible truth then, that their father had poisoned their mother and buried her in the basement, and that he'd been slowly poisoning Marjorie as well. It was the only explanation for Marjorie's sickness. Their wicked father had done it and Merry would be next.

"Merry ran out of the basement and upstairs to Marjorie and crawled in bed next to her. The growing things then began to break through the kitchen floor and into the rest of the house, turning everything green. That little cardboard house on the mountain creaked and groaned under the strain of the growing things that tore through the floors and walls and ceilings. But then there was a great knocking on their front door."

Marjorie paused and knocked lightly but insistently on my head. Not hard enough to hurt, but hard enough so it sounded like she was knocking inside my head.

"Merry tried to ignore the pounding on the door. Instead, she asked Marjorie two questions: 'What do we do if it isn't Dad outside the door? What do we do if it is?' "

I sat up and rolled out of Marjorie's lap and onto the floor, landing on my knees. My crash landing was loud and my teeth smashed together. I stood up, wobbly, tears stinging my eyes.

I was going to shout *you are a horrible sister and I hate you!*

But then Marjorie said, "I'm not well, Merry. I don't mean to frighten you. I'm sorry," and her voice cracked and she curtained her face with her hands.

I said, "It's okay. But you'll get better, right? Then we'll tell normal stories, like we used to. It'll be fun."

"No. You have to remember that story about the two sisters. You have to remember all my stories because there are—there are all these ghosts filling my head and I'm just trying to get them out, but you have to remember the story about the two sisters especially. Okay? You have to. Please say, 'Okay.' "

Marjorie was just a shadow on her bed. She could've been a pile of blankets, twisted and discarded. I couldn't see her eyes or her spaghetti-sauce-stained chin.

When I didn't answer her, she screamed as though she were being attacked; so loud it lifted my feet off the floor and pushed me backward.

"Say, 'Okay,' Merry! Say it!"

I didn't. And I ran out of her room.

CHAPTER 8

I WANTED TO be a soccer player just like Marjorie, only an even better one. She had a good leg; Dad-speak meaning that she could kick the ball hard and far. But I had two good legs. I was shifty and fast and could already dribble past players older than me. Marjorie was a sweeper for her freshman team, which sounded so cool. I really didn't understand what that position was, other than it meant she was the special or most important defender. I didn't want to be a sweeper though. I wanted to score goals, and I pouted if the coach put me on defense.

We were early to practice and Mom said to wait in the car with her until the coach showed up. With my robin's-egg-blue soccer ball in my lap, I kept vigilant watch for coach's orange shirt. Mom rolled down the window halfway and lit up a cigarette. Smoking wasn't allowed near the field.

"How come Dad isn't bringing me to practice?" I knew the question would irritate Mom, but I was mad because she'd tied my hair back and I wanted to leave it loose. I always liked how my hair trailed behind me when I ran, like the tail of a kite.

"What, you don't want me here? Jeez, that's nice."

"No. I want you here. Just asking."

"He's going with Marjorie to her appointment."

"Don't you usually do that?"

"Yes. But the last one didn't go so well. The doctor thought it was a good idea if maybe we switched things up."

"What happened?"

Mom sighed, and instead of her expertly blowing smoke out of the side of her mouth and through the open window, it spilled out and fogged the car. "Honey, nothing happened, really. It was just Dad's turn to go with her."

She was lying. It was obvious, almost comically so. Her hiding whatever it was she was hiding from me gave me license to imagine all manner of doctor's office horrors. Not that I knew what kind of doctor Mom was talking about. Not that I knew there were different kinds of doctors. To the second-grader me, a doctor was simply a doctor; someone who made sick people well. I did, however, know enough to worry about

Marjorie having cancer or some horrible disease with a name I couldn't pronounce. I'll never have kids but if I were suddenly and inexplicably cursed to be a mother, I solemnly swear to answer any questions my child might have, tell my child everything, and to not withhold even one single nasty detail.

Fishing for information that wouldn't be forthcoming, I played the only card I had. "Mom, she's been acting really weird lately."

"Oh yeah? How?"

I wanted to cry that I even said anything. This was beyond tattling. This was betrayal of my sister, who, apparently, was terribly, terribly ill. But it didn't matter and I couldn't keep any of it in anymore, so I opened my mouth and let it all spill out. I told Mom about Marjorie sneaking into my room at night, taking my book, the molasses flood story, the note, the growing things, and how she said she had ghosts in her head. I embellished the growing-things story, telling her that Marjorie said they would start growing here at the soccer field while I had practice and that they would swallow all of us up.

Mom rubbed her forehead with one hand and then put the cigarette in her mouth with the other. "Thank you for telling me this, Merry. Please, tell me everything she does if it seems . . . I don't know . . . seems weird. Okay? It's going to help us. Going to help her." She shook her head and exhaled more smoke. "Marjorie shouldn't be scaring you like that."

"I'm not scared, Mom."

Mom opened up the center console and pulled out a red book that was about the size of her hand. There was a pen neatly tucked away inside and she quickly jotted down some notes.

"Oooh, can I have one of those?" I reached for the red notebook and Mom yanked it away from me.

"Merry, you don't just grab! How many times do I have to tell you that?"

"Sorry."

"Look. Sorry, I yelled. But you can't have this notebook. Dr. Hamilton wants me to keep a record of what's happening at home." She must've seen something break and crumble in my face because Mom rested a hand on my shoulder and said, "And I hope you don't think that any of what's happening with Marjorie is in any way your fault."

I didn't think any of it was my fault, but now that she'd said it, I was panicked. I grabbed fistfuls of Mom's collar and pulled myself up out of my seat, closer to her. I was going to tell her that Marjorie wasn't being all that bad, that I had exaggerated her tall tales, that I kind of liked them and wanted to hear more of them and maybe even make up some of my own. Instead, I said, "Please, please, please don't tell Marjorie I told you anything. You can't."

"I won't, sweetie. I promise." Her promise wasn't a real one. It was simply the dot at the end of her sentence.

I sat back down, still desperate to know what was really going on. "Well, I'm worried about Marjorie, even if you're not."

Mom smiled and stubbed out her cigarette. "Oh, of course, I'm worried, Merry. I'm very worried. But Marjorie is getting help and we'll get through this. I promise. In the meantime, be sure to be extra nice to your sister. Extra understanding. She's—She's very confused right now, about things. Does that make sense?"

It didn't make sense. But I nodded my head yes so fast I just about shook out of my hair braids and elastics.

We didn't say anything else until the coach pulled into the parking lot in his little red car. It looked like something Goldbug would hide in.

"There he is. Okay, have fun and listen to your coach."

"Mom, I can't go until you give me coaching advice like Dad does."

"What does he usually say?"

"Kick through the ball. Head up. And he says that you can't coach speed."

Mom laughed. "What does that even mean?"

"It means I'm fast and you can't coach me? I don't know!" I laughed too, but it was forced and manic.

"Okay. Go. Have a good practice, sweetie."

Mom kissed my forehead and stayed in the car. I jogged out onto the field and to a gaggle of my teammates. Olivia, our tallest and blondest player, pointed at me, held her nose, and said,

"Pew, Merry smells like smoke." Coach told her to be nice. During our one-on-one drills I kicked Olivia just above the protective barrier of her shin guard. She fell to the turf, screaming and clutching her leg.

The rest of my teammates yelled my name, begging for me to pass them the ball. I wouldn't. I dribbled the ball past the moaning and writhing Olivia as fast as I could because you couldn't coach speed.

CHAPTER 9

I SAT UP in bed. All I knew was that I was in the house, which was this dark, expansive space, and that Marjorie was somewhere else in the same house, maybe lost, maybe in hiding, and she was screaming.

I couldn't understand how Marjorie wasn't right there next to me with her hands cupped around her mouth, because she was so shockingly loud. She screamed like I've never heard someone scream, before or since. Her hyperactive pitch was layered and schizophrenic, imploding down into a singularity, then going big bang, expanding and exploding all over everything. These dizzying changes in her voice were instantaneous and hallucinatory, as if she were somehow atonally harmonizing with herself.

I shimmied past my slightly ajar bedroom door, careful to not trigger my security devices, and Marjorie's shrill voice echoed in the organ pipe of the hallway. My parents emerged from their room yelling Marjorie's name and futilely cinching closed their open robes as they plodded across the hallway. As scared as I was, I remember being angry at them; those bumbling caricatures of sleepy parents. How could they ever protect Marjorie and me? How could they ever keep us safe?

Mom saw me and pointed, rooting me to the spot at my end of the hallway, and shouted, "Go back to bed! I'll be there in a minute!"

I didn't go back to my room and instead curled up into a tight ball on the hallway floor. I made promises to Marjorie in my head. I promised her she could tell me any crazy-weird-scary-icky stories she wanted to tell me and I wouldn't tell Mom if she'd only stop screaming.

Dad banged on the door and twisted the knob. The door stayed closed and he called out to Marjorie, but he called out weakly. There was no way she heard him. Mom pulled in tight behind him and similarly cried out to Marjorie, using the words *honey* and *sweetie*, cajoling as though trying to trick her into eating broccoli. They didn't know what to do, how to proceed. They were scared too. Maybe even more scared than I was.

Then Dad finally pushed open her door and my arm-in-arm parents were awash in the bright, golden light of her room. There was a volcanic increase of volume that shattered everything in my head, which I tried to hold together with my little hands, but pieces slipped through. Pounding on the walls or the floor, or both, joined Marjorie's screams and it all echoed and multiplied until everything was pounding, thudding, crashing, screaming, and I heard and felt it all with my insides.

Dad yelled, "Jesus Christ, Marjorie! Stop it!" and disappeared into her room.

Mom stayed behind in the doorway and yelled all sorts of staccato instructions that were directed at Dad. "Don't! Easy! Gentle! John! Go easy! Don't touch her! Let her calm down first! She doesn't know what she's doing!"

I crawled down the hallway toward Marjorie's room, my palms and bare knees collecting grit and dust from the hardwood that hadn't been swept for weeks.

The pounding stopped. Marjorie was still screaming and hysterical but she'd calmed down just enough so that I could make out what everyone said.

Marjorie yelled, "Get them out of my head!"

Dad: "It's okay. You—You just had a bad dream."

"They're so old. They won't let me sleep. They're always there."

Mom: "Oh, Marjorie. Mom and Dad are here. Everything's okay."

"They'll always be there. There are too many."

Dad: "Shh, no one's here. It's just us."

"I can't escape them."

I was halfway to her room. Marjorie wasn't screaming anymore. She sounded calm, detached; speaking in that normal teenager tone where she barely mustered the energy to grunt an answer to annoying parental questions.

My parents were getting louder, growing more desperate.

Mom: "Please, honey. Climb down!"

"We can't escape them."

Dad: "Marjorie, come down from there! Now!"

Then Mom yelled at Dad for yelling at Marjorie, and Dad yelled at Marjorie to knock it off, and Marjorie began screaming again at the both of them, and everyone was screaming, and I thought it would never stop.

I leapfrogged into the doorway, still crouched low to the floor. And when I looked up and saw Marjorie, I started screaming too.

The next morning, Mom told me that Marjorie wouldn't remember any of what had happened because she was sleepwalking or something. And I asked her about the holes in the walls and Mom tried to joke, saying, "Yes, Marjorie was sleep punching too." I didn't get the joke. Mom explained that Marjorie was having some sort of night terror, which was a really strong nightmare that scared you so much it made your body seem awake to everyone else but you weren't really awake, and Marjorie was so scared that she punched holes in the plaster, probably trying to get away from whatever it was she was dreaming about. Mom assured me that Marjorie had the strength to punch holes in the walls, and that plaster, particularly the old and crumbly plaster of the second floor, wasn't very strong at all. I was supposed to find comfort in Mom's explanation, but I still couldn't quite wrap my head around what a night terror was, and I was equally concerned to hear that our walls were so weak. What kind of house had crumbly walls?

That night, standing in Marjorie's doorway, when I knew nothing of night terrors and old plaster, I saw Marjorie clinging to the wall like a spider. Her circular poster collage, her collection of glossy body parts, was her web, and she hovered over its center. Her arms and legs were spread-eagled, with her hands, wrists, feet, and ankles sunk into the wall as though it were slowly absorbing her. Marjorie squirmed and writhed in place, her feet at least my height above the floor. Dad had to look up at her and he tugged on her sweatshirt, demanding that she wake up and come down off the wall.

Marjorie's head was turned toward us. I couldn't see the side of her face because her hair was everywhere. She yelled, "I don't want to fucking listen to them anymore. I don't want to fucking listen to fucking anyone anymore! Fucking ever fucking again!"

Mom grabbed me by the hand and led me down the hall to my room. She shushed me the whole way, the sounds from Marjorie's room receding until we were at the end of the hallway. Mom powered my bedroom door open, busting through my tied robe belt that fell to the floor, a dead fuzzy vine. My plastic orange juice jug came tumbling down from the top of the door bouncing off Mom's head. She absently brushed a hand across her forehead and kicked the jug toward my open closet. I tried to explain what had just fallen on her head, but she shushed me again and hustled me into bed.

Mom lay down next to me. I cried hysterically, and repeatedly asked her what was wrong with Marjorie. She rubbed my forehead and lied to me, telling me that everything would be okay.

I turned away from Mom, but she still held me tight, winding and wrapping her arms and legs around me. I squirmed, trying to break free without knowing where I would go if I did escape. She hummed a lullaby into the back of my head. Marjorie's and Dad's screaming was now the soundtrack to some horror movie that was trying too hard, and somehow, eventually, everyone stopped yelling and screaming and humming, and we fell asleep.

Later, I woke with Mom still asleep in my little bed. All of the blankets were wrapped around her, and she had flipped over and faced the wall. The rise and fall of her back was gently rhythmic, up and down, up and down. I faced out toward the rest of my room and my little cardboard house. I couldn't remember when I'd last looked at the house. I couldn't remember if it had looked like this back when I'd originally gone to bed so many hours ago, or when I'd first awoken to Marjorie's screaming, or when Mom had brought me back to my room and hummed her song into the back of my skull.

I was calm; there would be no more tears from me. But I wouldn't fall back to sleep for the rest of the night as I tried to puzzle out when Marjorie had been in my room again and if she was in here while Mom and I were asleep. I groped around the bridge of my nose for signs of her pinching it shut.

My cardboard house's outer walls, the windowsill flower boxes, the slate roof, and even the chimney, were scarred with detailed vines and leaves drawn in sharp black outlines and colored in green with Magic Marker. Her growing things choked my house. In the window was a piece of paper with two Richard Scarry–style cats drawn so they were peering out of the window and at me. The cats were sisters. The bigger sister wore a gray hooded sweatshirt and looked ill, her eyes glassy and droopy lidded. The little sister was wide-eyed, determined, and had glasses on.

I got out of bed quietly and didn't wake Mom. I plucked the picture out of the window. Written on the bottom was the following:

> *There's nothing wrong with me, Merry.*
> *Only my bones want to grow through my skin*
> *like the growing things and pierce the world.*

It was even darker inside the cardboard house than it was in my room, like how deeper water is darker than the shallows. I backed away from the house but my traitorous eyes kept staring at the window. I wasn't sure if I was seeing things or not, but the shutters appeared to be moving slightly, as though the house were breathing. And I stared hard past the window and into the house, my eyes starved for patterns, desperate for data, clues, for something to process. The longer I stared and saw nothing, the more I could see Marjorie there, huddled, nesting in my blankets, waiting to reach through the window and grab me if I got close again, or maybe she was giggling to herself and spidering around the cardboard walls and ceiling, waiting to drop and sink her fangs into my neck. Or worse, maybe she was the victim trapped inside and she wanted me to help her. But I didn't know how to help her.

I told myself that maybe in the morning I would hang up the sister-cats inside the cardboard house. I folded the picture and put it in the top drawer of my bureau, next to the other note that Marjorie had written me. When I took my hand out of the drawer I noticed there was a green leaf with a curlicue stem carefully etched on the back of my hand.

CHAPTER 10

MOM AND DAD were having a talk in the kitchen.

Having a talk was another buzzword phrase in our house, one that meant something was wrong. More often than not their talks were controlled arguments that generally centered on housework (laundry piles still on the dining room table!) or the handling of us girls. Revelations gleaned in a typical talk: Dad didn't like the condescending tone Mom often used with us; Mom didn't like his yelling and its wildly inconsistent usage; Dad thought she was too quick to punish; Mom didn't like having her discipline edicts questioned in front of us. Initially acrimonious, their talks somehow managed to end like a pregame pep talk: rote promises to be rational in the face of our irrationality, a renewed commitment to presenting a unified front, team play, then hands in the middle: Go, parents, on three, ready, break!

On this afternoon they were trying to be quiet and discreet, or as discreet as you could be in our house. I hid under the dining room table and watched their feet, ankles, calves, and knees. Mom's legs twitched up and down when she talked, and swayed side to side when Dad spoke. His legs were still, as though they didn't know what they wanted to do. I wanted to roll up their pants legs and draw funny faces with huge, puffy red lips on their knees.

I traced the ghost lines of washed Magic Marker on the back of my hand. I'd scrubbed Marjorie's green leaf off as soon as I'd gotten up, and I regretted doing so.

Initially I could only make out some of what my parents were saying: snippets about doctors, appointments, prescriptions, health insurance, and one or all being too expensive. Most of the words, in and of themselves, didn't mean much to me. But I understood their tone, and the word *expensive*. They were very worried and so I was very worried, and hiding under the table spying on them was no longer any fun at all.

Then Dad said, "Hear me out on this."

Mom crossed one leg over the other. "Go ahead."

Dad rambled about being sorry for the last few weeks, that he hadn't been going out in the mornings and afternoons on job searches, but instead going to church to pray for a clear head and for guidance. He said that phrase numerous times as a measure of its importance. *For guid-*

ance. He said it so fast and so often it became one word in my head and it sounded like a mysterious, foreign land, a place that I would've asked Marjorie to write a story about if things were different, normal. He'd been meeting with a Father Wanderly and he'd been very helpful, calm, soothing, and there was nothing else going on there, he wasn't seeing him with a greater plan in mind, only seeing him forguidance forguidance forguidance. But now he thought Marjorie should meet with this Father Wanderly and talk to him, too.

"Jesus Christ!" Mom said.

I covered my mouth with my hand, feigning shock that Mom swore. I had to stop myself from jumping out from beneath the table, wagging a finger at her, and telling her not to swear. She usually only swore in the car when another driver was being a jackass (her favorite swear).

Dad said, "Wait a minute. I know how you feel about the church, but—"

There was no but. Mom's crossed-over leg started swinging out like a club. She whisper-yelled that their daughter was sick and needed real medical attention, and how could he suggest such a thing and no matter the cost—they'd sell the house if they had to—they would continue the appointments and follow the treatment.

And Dad, he stayed calm, saying, "I know," a lot, and that he just wanted to explore other options as well, that it couldn't hurt. Mom was having none of it. She claimed the last thing

Marjorie or anyone in the family needed, including Dad, was Father What's-his-face filling their heads with mumbo jumbo, which could most certainly hurt any chance she might have of recovery. Marjorie was already confused enough as it was.

I whispered "mumbo jumbo" to myself, testing out the words, making a mental note to use it whenever possible.

Dad said, "You don't know that. How could you possibly know that, Sarah?"

"That's my point! We can't go messing around with Marjorie and her treatment when we don't know if it would set her off, make her worse."

Dad sighed, and it was a long one; he'd sprung a leak. "You're going to be pissed, but I already, um, took Marjorie to see Father Wanderly."

"You what? When?"

"Yesterday."

"After her appointment?"

Dad didn't answer and even though I couldn't see their faces, I hid my face from them, just in case the dining room table split in half and fell apart around me, leaving me exposed and vulnerable. I needed to be safe from the looks they must've been giving each other.

Dad, finally, said, "No."

"What do you mean, 'no'? You couldn't have taken her before—" Mom paused and then her voice dropped down into her toes. "John, you didn't."

"I know, and I'm sorry, and I didn't do it on purpose. I swear to God. She was freaking out in the car on the ride over, just like the other night, only it was worse."

"You are such a—"

"You don't understand! The things she was saying and doing right there in the car!"

"You don't think I understand? Like I haven't been the one taking her to all the other appointments? Like I wasn't the one apologizing to the secretary and nurses every goddamn time? Like I wasn't the one getting spit on and scratched, John?"

"I—I didn't know what to do. She was going . . ." Dad stopped.

"Go ahead, say it. Crazy. Right? Your daughter was going crazy. So why not stop at church? Makes perfect sense to me."

"Marjorie was freaking out and I was crying, fucking bawling my eyes out right there in the front seat and she was laughing at me, growling, making animal noises, telling me that I wanted to do all kinds of sexual things to her, Sarah. My baby girl saying that stuff to me. She ever say that to you? Huh? And the church was on the way, it was right there, so I just stopped."

"I can't believe this."

"I just stopped and parked in front of the church, and it seemed to work, Sarah. She calmed right down. Father Wanderly came out and met us there in the car. He sat in the backseat and he had a great talk with her, and before we knew it an hour had gone by."

"You're telling me you missed her appointment, the one that Dr. Hamilton specifically requested you go to?"

"How much good has Dr. Hamilton been, huh? Seen any improvement yet? She's getting worse. I thought Father Wanderly could help her. Now I know he can help her. Help us."

"Have him help you find a job, have him help us pay our mortgage, then, but keep him the hell away from Marjorie."

They both started stuttering and yelling at each other, worse than ever. I couldn't take it anymore so I crawled away, weaving through the legs of the table and the chairs, then out of the dining room and into the front foyer. They must've seen me crawling out from underneath the table because they stopped arguing. I waved and gave them an all-teeth smile like I hadn't heard anything. They gave me matching weak smiles back and Mom told me to go upstairs, and that they were almost done.

I shrugged, because everything was cool by me. Everything they'd said jumbled and swirled in my head, and this Father Wanderly person my dad has been talking to, I wondered what he looked like. Was he young or old, tall or short, skinny or fat? Then I focused on more particular and peculiar details, like, what if he had big knuckles on his hands, or what if one leg was shorter than the other? Could he touch the tip of his nose with his tongue like my friend Cara could? Did he like pickles on his cheeseburger? Did his smile crinkle up the skin around his eyes? Would he yawn if he watched me yawn? What did his voice sound like that Dad would like him so much?

CHAPTER 11

MARJORIE'S DOOR MUST'VE been open because I heard her humming a song. It sounded like the saddest of sad songs with notes floating down the staircase and into the foyer like dead leaves; red, brown, and purple.

I reached up over my head and covered our front door's peephole with a finger, just in case someone was on the stoop trying to look in at us. I whispered through the door, "Who's out there?" but didn't hear anyone respond. I knocked twice for luck.

I zigzagged my way up the stairs, tapping the wall, then walking diagonally to tap the railing slats, while stepping on the black stairs as though they were the keys to a piano. On the first landing I said, "What's that song?" On the second landing I said, "Stop humming. You'll get it stuck in my head."

When I made it upstairs Marjorie was not in her bedroom, but was instead lounging in the small sunroom that overlooked the front yard. She was all folded up on the puffy loveseat and fiddling with her smartphone. She wore short red shorts and a black sports bra.

She stopped humming after I crash landed in the sunroom. "What is that song? Ew, put a shirt on!"

"What's ew? Girls wear this out jogging or to the gym all the time."

"I don't care. I don't like it." Giggling, I reached out and patted the pushed-up tops of her small breasts. I made *boing-boing-boing* noises, then said, "I don't want boobs. Ever."

"Merry!" Marjorie pushed my hand away, crossed her arms over her chest, and laughed, really and truly laughed for the first time in days, maybe weeks. I melted into relief and the blindest love. She was Marjorie again, my Marjorie: the one who hid under a blanket with me during scary parts of movies; the one who punched neighbor Jimmy Matthews in the nose after he'd dropped a dead fly down the back of my shirt; the one who made fun of Mom and Dad and made me laugh hard enough to snort after they'd yelled at me and sent me to my room because I'd dented the rusty old garage doors with my penalty kicks.

Marjorie said, "Well, sorry, monkey. Girls have boobs. You'll be getting them in a few years."

"I'm getting *those* in a few years?" I mock-screamed, covered my chest with my hands, and said, "Gross, no way!"

That made Marjorie laugh hard again. "Where did you come from? You're such a little goon sometimes."

"I know." I put my hands on one arm of the loveseat and jumped up and down, kicking my legs out behind me, dancing my little goon dance.

I asked, "How was school?"

"It was great. I didn't go."

"How come?"

"Oh, you know, I'm not feeling well."

"What's going to the sie-kie-a-trist like?" I carefully broke up the word into its parts so I wouldn't make a mistake.

Marjorie shrugged. "No biggie. He asks questions. I answer them like a good little girl. Then I leave the room and wait while he talks to Mom."

"Is he nice?"

"He's like wallpaper to me. Just there, you know?"

I pictured the psychiatrist covered in the yellow wallpaper of our sunroom.

I asked, "Why are you sitting in here?" Maybe Mom and Dad told her she couldn't spend so much time alone in her room anymore.

"No reason."

I thought about the holes in her bedroom wall and imagined them weeping dust and plaster. I didn't blame her if she'd rather be in the sunroom.

"Who are you texting?" I said it singsong. I said it like I knew the secrets of her teen life.

"Ugh. Just some friends, okay?" She wasn't looking at me anymore, but stared down at her phone's glowing screen.

"What friends? Do I know them? Do they have Boston accents? Do they like green M&M's with peanuts inside?"

"You can leave me alone now," she said, but there wasn't much oomph behind it. She wasn't really annoyed or mad, not yet. Not even close. I could still push her.

Trying to sound playful, I said, "This isn't your room, you know. I can be in here too if I want." Unlike her bedroom, or mine for that matter, the small sunroom felt like a safe place with its bright natural light amplified by the cheery yellow walls and its simple, cozy rectangular shape. No closets or beds or cardboard houses; no shadows and no places to hide. Here, in this neutral space, we were equals.

I asked, "Are you texting Father Wanderly?"

Her head snapped up, and everything in her face furrowed, folded, or curled, skin turning inside-out to reveal a totally transformed and snarling face. My little goon dance died and I let go of the arm of the loveseat.

Marjorie sighed heavily, as though she was the adult here. "Really, Merry, you don't know anything. Stop pretending you do."

"I do know things. I just heard Mom and Dad fighting about him and about you. They're still arguing right now, in the kitchen. Oh, Mom is so mad at Dad. You should hear her. Swearing and everything." I stopped talking, but I didn't really stop because my mouth kept moving, lips worming around silent words of self-affirmation: *I really heard them. I did.*

"You're doing the mouth thing again. Stop it. You're not a baby anymore."

When I was a preschooler, I moved my mouth after I finished talking. Mom thought it was cute. Dad said my mouth just couldn't keep up with everything that I had to say. Marjorie would speak half sentences and then mouth the rest at me. I knew she was only making fun of me but I would still focus on her moving lips, hoping that she was unknowingly giving away instructions on how to be a proper big girl. I used to overturn the wastebasket in the upstairs bathroom so I could stand on it, look in the mirror, and practice speaking, or practice stopping to speak without my lips stubbornly fighting for their phantom last words.

I thought I'd grown out of it. Horrified that my mouth had gone rogue again, I said, "I know. Sorry."

"I don't know what you heard Dad say, but I didn't talk to the creepy old priest, okay? I didn't say anything. I didn't even say 'hi' to him. He and Dad did all the talking and the stupid praying, and I just sat there in the car. I totally ignored them."

"Yeah, sure."

Our fun sunroom sister-time had deteriorated quickly into crumbling pieces so obvious and so there, just like the imperfections of the curling and stained yellow wallpaper on the sunroom walls were there if you looked long and hard enough.

"Shut up, Merry. And you better start minding your own business."

"But—"

"But nothing. Stop talking for one goddamn second. Listen." She didn't lean forward, she didn't move her body at all. Her posture remained relaxed with the phone in her hand and she sounded so matter-of-fact, which made it all worse. "I know you told Mom about our new stories, about the growing things. And what was that shit you made up about the growing things taking over the soccer field? I didn't say anything about that."

I slumped and shrugged at the same time. "I'm sorry." I fought to keep my lips still, to keep from saying or not saying *You shouldn't swear, Marjorie*. I don't think she ever realized or appreciated all the little things I tried to do for her.

"Mom told Dr. Hamilton everything you told her, you know. Now he wants to up my meds, turn me into a fucking zombie."

"I'm sorry! Please don't use those words. Marjorie—"

"Stop it! Just stop it! Listen to me. You tell on me to Mom again I'll rip your fucking tongue out."

I jumped backward and crashed into the wall behind me as though she'd struck me with a fist. We'd play-fought all the time. I practically used to go begging for her older sibling abuse as her ignoring me, her not caring that I existed within her vast universe would've killed me. I was the compliant recipient of a fair share of dope slaps, dead arms and dead legs, wrist burns, finger flicks, crow pinches, monkey bites, and twisted clam-ears, with maybe the worst being ponytail rodeo, but she never really hurt me. She'd never before threatened to really hurt me, either.

Marjorie kept texting, fingers crawling over the phone's keyboard screen while she talked at the same time. "I'll wait until you're asleep because you never wake up when I'm there. I'm in your room every night, Merry. It's so easy."

I imagined her standing over my bed, pinching my nose shut, drawing on my hand, hovering her face close to mine, breathing my breaths.

"Maybe the next time I'm there I'll reach into your mouth with pliers, no, wait, I'll just use my fingers, clamp them up real tight, turn my hand into a claw, and I'll pinch that fat, wriggling worm between my fingers and tear it right out of your skull, as easy as pulling dandelions out of the ground. It'll hurt worse than anything you've ever felt before. You'll wake up moaning around my hand, choking on blood, and seeing white stars of pain literally exploding in your head. And there'll be so much blood. You never realize how much blood there can be."

Even knowing what I know now, I'll never forgive Marjorie for what she said to me then, and I'll never forgive myself for staying in the sunroom and taking it all. I just stood there.

"I'll keep your tongue and put it on a string, wear it like a necklace, keep it close against my chest, let it taste my skin until it turns black and shrivels up like all dead things do. What an amazing fucking thought that is: your neverending tongue shrunken and finally stilled."

She kept talking and she kept talking. I thought she would never stop. Standing there, I felt the sun pour through the windows, setting and rising on my back. The sunroom had become a sundial measuring the geological age of my psychological torture.

"And your mouth, stupidly opening and closing, gaping like a fish drunk on too much air. You'd feel that loss. You'd learn the oldest lesson there is. The lesson of loss. We all learn it eventually. You'd feel that ragged stub of flesh cowering and hiding down by your molars. Or maybe your stupid flesh won't have learned anything and it'll wiggle and stretch toward the vowels and consonants forever out of reach."

I stood there as still and as silent as if my tongue had already been extracted.

"The flooding black river of blood will be the only thing to ever pour out of your mouth again. No more words. No one will listen to you. That's the worst part, Merry. You will not be able to speak ever again, which means you will never be able to tell anyone about what will happen next to you and everyone else in this house. All the awful, terrible, unspeakable shit that will happen to you, and it will happen to you, and to everyone else. . . . I know. I've heard about it and I've seen it. No one escapes."

Marjorie finally stopped talking and texting. She gently placed her phone on the side table and folded her hands in her lap.

Wide-eyed, I stood up, my back against the wall, and sobbed into my hands that bravely cupped my mouth.

Marjorie sighed again. "Oh, come on, I'm just kidding, Merry. Jeez. I would never do that to you. You know that, right?"

That made me cry harder, because I didn't know that. Not anymore.

"Okay, that was a mean joke, I know, but it wasn't that bad. Come here." Marjorie pulled out of her slouch, sat up, and patted an open section of the loveseat.

I stayed where I was, shaking my head. The sunlight flashed brighter outside and we both had to squint.

"Please, Merry. I am sorry."

Still crying the kind of tears that don't fall right away but instead build a wall on the lower lid, making everything blurry, I sidled over and sat down with my back to her, like I was supposed to.

Marjorie drew a capital letter between my

shoulder blades with her finger. "Guess the letter."

"*M.*" I was uncannily good at the back-letter-drawing game. Even in a state of emotional cataclysm.

"I shouldn't have said all that stuff to you, but I was very upset that you told Mom on me. I thought we were sisters, and that we had secrets."

"*E.*"

"How would you like it if I told Mom you came up here pawing my boobs, feeling me up?"

"*H?*" It wasn't *H*. I was flustered. I didn't know what she meant by feeling her up, but I knew her telling Mom about it wouldn't be good.

"No." She drew the letter on my back again, moving slower, adding more pressure.

"*R.*"

"Yes. What if I told Mom that you were teasing me, spying on me, following me around, generally making me crazy? I know she told you that you're supposed to be nice to me, to help out."

"*R.* I'm sorry about your boobs. Please don't tell Mom on me."

"I won't tell if you won't tell."

"Okay. *Y.* Merry." She'd written an easy word on my back to calm me down. It worked. I wasn't crying anymore, but my eyes felt heavier than ever.

"Then we have a deal, Miss Merry." Marjorie rubbed her hand over my back, like a teacher erasing a blackboard, and she started writing again.

"*G.*"

"So, that song you heard me humming, it just sort of popped into my head."

"*L.*"

The song. The reason why I'd come up the stairs. Marjorie hummed it again. It sounded even sadder up close.

"*O* and *O.* Did you make it up?"

"Yes and yes and no! It's a real song."

"*M.*"

"Mom and Dad don't listen to it. I know I haven't heard it anywhere. Like I said, and just like the stories, I woke up one morning and it was just sitting there in my head."

"*Y.*"

"It sounds so sad, doesn't it? Like a song about the saddest day ever."

"*S.*"

"But when I hum it, it tickles something behind my throat, and it feels sort of good."

"*V?*"

"Not *V.* Sometimes it's good to be sad, Merry. Don't forget that."

Marjorie didn't repeat the letter I'd missed, but moved on to a new one. The new letter had two slow vertical lines that walked up and then down the length of my back, and one hard diagonal slash to connect them.

"*N.*"

"Yes. It's weird, but I even know the lyrics too."

"*D.* Sing it." I only asked her to sing the words because I knew she wanted me to ask. I didn't really want to hear the words. I was afraid that if she sang it, it'd be about a sister stealing another sister's tongue.

"I don't feel like singing the lyrics. I like humming it."

"*A.*"

"I like keeping the words to myself."

"*Y.*"

"You wouldn't like the lyrics, anyway." She stopped drawing on my back. "So I'll just keep humming it. Maybe, I'll hum it to you in your sleep."

"Marjorie!"

She laughed and tickled my armpits. I didn't laugh; I gave her a quick, high-pitched whine and a snort. "Stop!"

"Stay there. Don't move." She hummed the song as she stood up on the loveseat. I bounced around the cushion as she shifted and adjusted her balance. She swayed over my head like the branches of a willow tree in a storm. I felt the weight of the song; its minor key squeezing the air out of my chest.

Marjorie jumped off, flying above my head. I ducked and rolled back into the loveseat cushions as her shadow passed over me. She landed loudly, and her knees buckled, pitching her almost straight into a window.

Somewhere down below us my father shouted, "What the hell was that?"

Marjorie said, "My dismount needs work. Practice makes perfect, right?" She pinched my belly, and then ran out of the room and into her bedroom with me yelling, "Stop it!" after her.

Marjorie still hummed the song in her room. I sat, listening, and then I hummed along with that simple but heartbreaking melody. I dangled a foot in one of the sunroom's fading sunbeams. I wondered if I would still be able to hum the song when I didn't have a tongue. I decided that I would.

CHAPTER 12

ON OUR TV show, the following is presented as a dramatic reenactment and as the penultimate piece of evidence regarding Marjorie being possessed by an evil spirit. The reenactment is a raw and undeniably effective set piece full of disorienting jump cuts, an ominous if not over-the-top voice-over narrative, and what I have to assume were some low-level CGI special effects along with digitally altered/enhanced sound.

In the scene, the Barrett-family actors lounge in the living room, watching *Finding Bigfoot*. Everyone in the room happily watches some pseudoscientist bellow his Bigfoot call into a night-vision-enhanced forest. Actor-Mom (plain, dash of freckles, very pretty, even for TV) and Actor-Dad (too heavy and too old to be our dad, and his beard was as patchy as a summer-burnt lawn) sit next to each other on the couch, each wearing button-down shirts and wrinkle-free pants. Both Barrett children actors are on the floor, lying on their stomachs, cheeks in fists, feet dangling in the air, heels knocking into each other. This twenty-first-century Rockwell scene of quaint familial tranquility quickly devolves when Actor-Dad asks, "So how did school go today?" The ensuing tornado is not to be contained to the living room, but instead cuts a swath through the house, until everything finally culminates and crashes in Marjorie's bedroom.

It just didn't happen that way. But, I must admit that I was once obsessed with the show *Finding Bigfoot* and would insist that everyone in the family watch the show with me. I'd also have playful arguments all the time with Dad about the existence or nonexistence of Bigfoot. I was the believer and he was not. The unspoken ground rule of our ongoing debate was that neither of us was ever going to change our minds. I was fervent in my belief that the mythical beast was real and I would practically spit on any suggestions to the contrary. While I know he enjoyed the give-and-take, Dad remained coolly rational and scientific in his approach to our arguments. Using the Socratic method of Sasquatch debunking, he'd ask me questions, thinking I'd eventually hit upon the truth. His go-to question—particularly when I'd filibustered my way through previous questions about population density or evolution or ecosystem sustainability—was why had no one ever found the body of a dead Bigfoot? Well, of course it was because they buried their dead and buried them in secret, sacred places. Duh, Dad.

I don't remember us being in the living room that night watching *Finding Bigfoot*, nor do I remember the incident happening there. However, I could be misremembering. Maybe how our TV show presented the living room scene was, save a few dramatic embellishments, how it actually happened. The writers and producers contractually consulted Mom and Dad, and consulted them extensively. Maybe the show relied on Marjorie and whatever it was she told them during their numerous interviews. To my recollection, no one asked me about that night. It's possible that night was such a traumatic experience that I've blocked it, or have somehow conflated the general unreality of our show with what actually happened.

What I remember is us eating dinner at the kitchen table, sitting at our four points on the compass. We were contemplative and quiet; unsure of what was happening, unsure of what to do, even after it ended.

I'll always remember the four of us sitting around the kitchen table, placed like dolls at an imaginary tea party.

THE BARRETT WOMEN WORDLESSLY AGREED that we weren't waiting for Dad and started eating our pasta. Yes, pasta again, for the third night in a row. I'd complained when I'd found Mom boiling water in the big pea-green pot. She'd told me that we could no longer afford to be picky at dinner. I'd walked out of the kitchen, slumped and groaning about how I'd turn into Spaghetti Girl if I ate any more of it. I'd wiggled my arms around bonelessly as a brief demonstration of the not-so-awesome powers of Spaghetti Girl.

Our small kitchen table didn't seem as small because our table setting was so depressingly Spartan. No colander in the middle overflowing with tentacles of extra spaghetti. No glass bowl of red sauce. No cutting board with sliced chunks of garlic bread. No side bowls with sparkling green and red salads. Not that I would've eaten a full salad. My little wooden bowl would've held only little wheels of carefully peeled cucumbers and maybe a few baby carrots.

What was on the table: four plates of spaghetti, serving sizes modest, and four glasses of water. I'd asked for milk, but Mom had said, simply, "Drink water, and quit bellyaching."

Dad sat at the table with his head bowed, eyes closed, and with his hands folded, those thick fingers wound tightly in between each other so that it looked like there were more fingers than there should've been. I counted the knuckles on each of his hands twice to make sure that there weren't extras.

Dad prayed over his food for an uncomfortably long time. He was so focused and earnest that I felt pressured into joining him, even as I worried that I didn't know how to pray or to whom to pray. The other morning, while driving me to school, he'd described praying as a conversation in your head with God. Happy that he was even talking to me as he'd been borderline unresponsive since the night in Marjorie's room, I'd asked who God really was besides some big, bearded old guy up in the clouds. Dad had started by saying God was love, which had sounded nice, but then he'd fumbled around a convoluted explanation involving Jesus and the Holy Spirit. I'd made a joke about my head getting too crowded with all those people to talk to instead of telling him that I didn't want to hear any more about it. Dad had made me feel terribly anxious in a way that I couldn't describe right then, partially because I couldn't be trusted to not tell Mom about his preaching and proselytizing without her permission. Just like I had told on Marjorie. I'd become so very tired of other people's secrets and stories. Dad had laughed at my too-crowded joke, and he'd said to just give it a try sometime, that it'd make me feel better.

I gently placed my fork down and folded my hands like Dad. Before I could say anything to the people in my head, I caught Marjorie watching me from the inside of her hooded sweatshirt. She smirked and shook her head no. I quickly picked my fork back up and imagined Bigfoot crashing through the woods behind our house and into the kitchen, destroying everything.

Mom refused to look at Dad while he prayed. She held one hand to her forehead, shielding her eyes as though there were a glare.

Eventually, he picked up his head and crossed himself; touching his forehead, chest, then each shoulder. He did it so fast, like he'd been practicing all his life. Dad smiled and looked at each of us. He gave me an extra wink. I wasn't good at winking so I blew him a kiss in return.

Marjorie made a retching sound. No one asked if she was okay, which meant something. Then she said, "Sorry. Wrong pipe."

"Please take your hood off at the dinner table."

Marjorie complied. The removal of her hood was a shocking revelation. Her skin was gray, the color of the mushrooms that grew around the snaking tangle of tree roots out back. The circles under her eyes were dark and deep. Her black hair was a dead octopus leaking and sliding off her scalp. Whiteheads dotted her chin and the sides of her nose.

Dad said, "So how was school today?"

"Oh you know, Dad. The usual. I was voted class president, captain of the soccer team, most hottest chick ever—"

Mom cut in with, "Marjorie isn't feeling well. They sent her home because she got sick in the cafeteria."

"What, again? Poor kid. Do you feel good enough to eat? Why are you eating this stuff now? Sarah, don't force her to eat if she's having stomach problems." Dad's hands were folded again, this time in front of his plate.

"I'm not forcing her, *John*. She said she felt better. Right?"

"Hunky and dory."

"You don't look good."

"Thanks, Dad. I feel so pretty."

"You know what I mean. You know you're my beautiful girl." He'd said it like the small print of a warranty or an indemnification clause.

I said, "Hey!"

"You're my beautiful girl too, Merry."

Marjorie groaned. She wrapped a strand of spaghetti around her finger and said, "You're going to make me puke again." Under her nails were black with dirt. Had she been digging in the yard? I imagined her out back, planting growing things.

Dad said, "You look pale. Maybe we should let you sleep in tomorrow."

"I'll be fine. I don't want to miss any more schoolwork. They're threatening to send me to summer school already." Marjorie rested the back of her hand on her forehead. She was in actress mode. I could tell. A hint of a British accent had slipped into her speech.

I practiced eating my pasta while trying not to use my tongue. I was a planner, a considerer of every contingency.

"Don't worry about that. We'll do what we have to do." As if on cue, we all looked down at our feeble plates, our dinner metaphor for doing what we had to do.

Dad then turned to me and said, "Merry! Tell us how your day was. I'd like to hear about one good thing that happened and one thing that made you laugh."

Always pleased to have the family spotlight thrust upon me, I said, "Well," elongating the word by vibrating the tip of my tongue against the back of my front teeth. "We started reading *Charlie and the Chocolate Factory* in class. Ronnie made me laugh when he pretended to be Augustus Gloop drinking from the chocolate river. He got down on his hands and knees and acted like he was licking the rug. He shouted, 'Chocolate, that's good!' " I demonstrated with my impersonation of Ronnie's funny German accent. "Mrs. Hulbig didn't think he was funny, though."

Mom said, "Hmm, interesting. He's probably seen that horrible Johnny Depp version of the movie. That you kids like it and not the original Gene Wilder version is sacrilege."

"Mom, what's your problem?" I said, talking and acting like Depp's version of Wonka: vacant smile, creepy voice full of air and lisp and nothing else.

Dad said, "That's pretty good. I have to admit, you're good at doing voices, Merry."

"I am?"

Both Mom and Marjorie groaned.

"Yes, you've always been great at doing impressions and funny little voices."

I changed my pitch and tone with each word. "I can do voices."

"Just great. She'll be doing voices all night now," Marjorie said.

"I *can* do voices!"

Mom said, "You have no idea what you started, do you?"

I cackled in two or three different styles, then stopped abruptly. "Oh, Mom! I almost forgot. Tomorrow is hat day in school. I need to find a hat! What hat should I wear?"

"I don't know. We'll look for a hat after dinner."

Dad said, "Hey, you can wear my Red Sox hat."

"Gross, no way!" I instinctively covered my head with my hands. Legend foretold of a hat that was older than Marjorie and had never been washed. The once-white sweatband ringing the inside of his hat was black. The red *B* was all grimy-looking and the bill was sweat-stained and misshapen. Dad used to chase us around with the hat, trying to put it on our heads. We'd run away laughing and screaming. The game had usually ended when I'd whine and complain that he was chasing Marjorie more than he was chasing me. It was true, but to be fair, Marjorie was more fun to chase because she was harder to catch. Even though I was fast, I'd give up and stop running, drop to the ground, and roll into a ball. Dad would quickly put the hat on my head, but in two seconds he'd be off again, playfully shouting and chasing after Marjorie. Her taunts were always so clever, and if he caught her, she'd get it worse; he'd rub the hat all over her head and face until her repeated *Dad stop it* sounded angry. Sitting at the kitchen table that night, those hat chases seemed like they'd happened eons ago although the last time we'd done it was only a few months prior at a Labor Day barbecue. During that chase Dad had knocked over a small folding table, spilling paper plates and plastic utensils.

Mom said, "We don't want the school to send her home for lice, John." It was supposed to be a joke but it had an edge to it.

I said, "I want to wear something funny and cool. Marjorie, could I wear your sparkly baseball hat?"

The three of us looked at Marjorie.

Now I remember thinking that her answer could change everything back to the way it was; Dad could find a job and stop praying all the time and Mom could be happy and call Marjorie *shellfish* again and show us funny videos she found on YouTube, and we all could eat more than just spaghetti at dinner and, most important, Marjorie could be normal again. Everything would be okay if Marjorie would only say yes to me wearing the sparkly sequined baseball hat, the one she'd made in art class a few years ago.

The longer we watched Marjorie and waited for a response, the more the temperature in the room dropped and I knew that nothing would ever be the same again.

She stopped twisting her spaghetti around her fingers. She opened her mouth, and vomit slowly oozed out onto her spaghetti plate.

Dad: "Jesus!"

Mom: "Honey, are you okay?" She jumped out of her seat and went over to Marjorie, stood behind her, and held her hair up.

Marjorie didn't react to either parent, and she didn't make any sounds. She wasn't retching or convulsing involuntarily like one normally does when throwing up. It just poured out of her as though her mouth was an opened faucet. The vomit was as green as spring grass, and the masticated pasta looked weirdly dry, with a consistency of mashed-up dog food.

She watched Dad the whole time as the vomit filled her plate, some of it slopping over the edges and onto the table. When she finished she wiped her mouth on her sleeve. "No, Merry. You can't wear my hat." She didn't sound like herself. Her voice was lower, adult, and growly. "You might get something on it. I don't want you to mess it up." She laughed.

Dad: "Marjorie . . ."

Marjorie coughed and vomited more onto her too-full plate. "You can't wear the hat because you're going to die someday." She found a new voice, this one a treacly baby-talk. "I don't want dead things wearing my very special hat."

Mom backed away from Marjorie and bumped

into my chair. I reached out and clung to her hip with my right arm and covered my mouth with my left.

A third new voice; genderless and nasally. "No one here can wear it because you're *all* going to die."

"Marjorie?" Dad stayed in his seat and held out a hand to her. "Marjorie? Look at me. Hold my hand and pray with me. Please. Just try it."

Mom was crying and shaking her head.

Convinced that he was only going to make it all worse, I squeaked out, "Leave her alone," then covered my mouth back up quickly because it wasn't safe to talk.

He said in his most patient voice, which seemed to be not his voice at all, as alien as the voices coming from my sister: "Marjorie is never alone. He is always with her. Let us pray to Him." And I started crying too because I was afraid and confused. I thought that Dad was saying there was someone inside Marjorie and that he wanted to pray to *him*. Dad pushed back his chair and knelt on the floor.

"Okay, Dad." Marjorie slid out of her chair, leaking down toward the floor, and disappeared under the table.

Mom left me and bent down, next to Marjorie's chair. "Sweetie, come out from under there. I'll run you a nice warm bath upstairs, okay? Let's go to bed early. You'll feel better. . . ." She kept cooing promises of hope and healing.

Now I was alone, with my hand still over my mouth. Marjorie slunk and slid on the hardwood somewhere in the depths beneath the table. I could not see her and pulled my dangling feet up onto the chair. My toes curled inside the sneakers.

We waited and watched. Dad suddenly jolted as if given an electric shock and knocked into the table, shaking our plates and forks, and spilling more vomit off of Marjorie's plate, which smelled of acid and dirt.

Marjorie's hand reached up. Her skin was ash gray and her dirty fingernails were as black as fish eyes. Then her muddy voice echoed up from the bottom of a well. "Go ahead, Dad. Take my hand."

He slowly reached out and did as she asked. She pulled his hand beneath the table, to where we couldn't see. Dad was a statue bust, as cold and white as marble. He started a prayer. "In the name of Your son, Jesus Christ, please, Lord, give Marjorie strength. . . ." He paused and seemed unsure of what exactly to say, as though he knew he was an amateur, a poseur. A fraud. " . . . to help her deal with—with the affliction she's struggling with. Cleanse her spirit. Show her the—" Then he screamed in pain.

The table rattled again as he pulled his arm out from under the table. The back of his hand was bleeding, had been slashed open. There were two deep red lines dowsing a path toward his wrist. He clutched the hand to his chest instinctively, then held it out toward Mom, in an expression of childlike fear and incredulity at the unfairness of it all.

Mom: "Did she scratch you? Bite you?"

"Maybe. I—I don't know."

I scooted back in my chair, convinced that Marjorie would come for me next and drag me down beneath the surface and into the shadows, pry my mouth open for its pink wriggling worm.

Marjorie hummed her terrible song and crawled away from the table. Her hood was covering her hair. She stopped humming and spouted gibberish that I tried to spell inside my head, but it was made out of nothing but angry consonants.

My parents both said her name, saying it like her name was a question, and a call, and a plea.

Marjorie slowly crawled away from the light of the kitchen and into the dark of the dining room. "I don't bite or scratch," she said in another voice, a new one, one that didn't sound like anyone who had ever spoken before in the human history of speech. "He scraped the back of his hand on the rusty metal and bolts under the old table." She slipped into more of the consonant-speak, and then added, "We always hurt ourselves, don't we? I'm going to my room. No visitors, please."

Marjorie hummed the song again, changing pitch and timbre so quickly and abruptly it was disorienting and it felt like my ears were popping. She crawled through the dining room, moving like a monitor lizard or something as equally ancient, and into the front foyer and to the stairs.

She said from far away, "I can do voices too, Merry."

CHAPTER 13

ANOTHER SATURDAY MORNING. Everything in the house felt dead, even though I had no idea, at that time, what death felt like.

Mom had gone back to bed after making me a bowl of cereal for breakfast. Rice Krispies. She hadn't put in the usual two spoonfuls of sugar and there wasn't enough milk left to sufficiently soak the mouthy, complaining Krispies. I hadn't dared complain though. Mom had had the look.

I ate until there was only a semi-mushy paste of cereal spackled to the bottom of the plastic bowl. We didn't have any orange juice either so I drank water. I had the TV to myself and watched all the *Finding Bigfoot*s I'd saved to the DVR. Earlier that week my parents had said something about watching everything on the DVR before it had to be disconnected, so I was proud to accomplish that at least.

Around episode four, with the crew of Squatchers somewhere in the woods of Vermont, Dad shuffled down the stairs and into the kitchen. He sighed at the empty milk carton on the table, muttered swears that weren't quite under his breath, and slammed around the kitchen looking for breakfast. He settled on defrosting an English muffin.

When he came into the living room with his peanut butter–slathered muffin, he wordlessly took the remote control from me and flipped over to one of our many sports channels. I hated watching sports, and suggested compromise viewing, a show called *River Monsters*, which featured a charismatic British angler with terrible teeth, who traveled to exotic lakes and rivers to catch giant catfish and these living torpedoes called arapaimas. Dad refused to compromise.

I patiently waited until he was done with his breakfast and then I jumped into his lap, saying, "Dad, play with me. Catch me! You can't catch me!" I bent down and pulled his folded legs out straight and away from the couch. "C'mon! The alligator game." The alligator game: His legs were the jaws of the alligator, and I'd dance in, around, and between them, teasing the gator into snapping its jaws shut on me.

Dad did as he was asked, but it was obvious his heart wasn't in it, that he was still preoccupied. I was manic in my attempt to have fun. If I danced fast enough, if I laughed heartily enough, if I shrieked loud enough when caught, maybe he'd forget about Marjorie for a moment.

His alligator mouth was too sluggish. He missed repeatedly. I pleaded with him to try harder. Then he blamed me for his own lack of motivation and purpose. He said, "Well, you stop being a chicken. You can't dance in and out from out there. You're too far away. You have to come closer to me, stand there longer." When he still couldn't catch me he criticized how I was jumping in his coach voice. He said that I was too flat-footed, too heavy on my feet, that I had to be on the tips of my toes, that I should walk light enough that he couldn't hear my feet on the floor.

I humored him even though I wanted to drop to the floor in a boneless heap and weave myself into the fibers of the throw rug, to disappear under everyone's feet and to be forgotten. I danced on my toes until they cramped while he halfheartedly opened and closed his outstretched legs in weak attempts to catch me. Desperate, I escalated my attack, smacking and pinching his legs. It worked. Dad lunged off the couch with a fierceness and power that was as exhilarating as it was frightening, and he grabbed my arms and pulled me into him. He tickled me and rubbed his coarse beard on my cheeks while I giggled and screamed for him to stop. He stopped too quickly and let me slide off him, thudding to the floor.

"Ow, Dad!"

"Sorry. Look, I'm trying to watch TV. Go upstairs and see what Mommy is doing."

I tried going after his legs again, but he crossed them and said, "Seriously. Stop bugging me."

Fine. I ran up the stairs on my toes as quietly as I could. Thank you, Coach-Dad. I stopped at the top of the stairs and pressed up against the wall opposite the banister. I slowly peeked around the corner and saw Marjorie's door was shut. I did not want her to hear me. I'd been avoiding being alone with her since the sunroom incident.

The hallway was dark and the old, brass-plated, push-button light switch was right next to my face. Nose to nose with my distorted reflection in the brass, I didn't press the little black button, thinking it was best not to change or disturb anything up here. I considered going back downstairs and trying to get Dad to play with me again, or sulking next to him quietly on the couch.

My room was too far away, at the other end of the yawning chasm of hallway. The bathroom door, which was adjacent to Marjorie's room, was also shut, but inside the fan was on, running roughly; revving then slowing like a lawn mower about to run out of gas. Marjorie had been spending more and more time in the bathroom, usually with the fan on, sometimes with the sink running water, much to Dad's consternation. Water wasn't free, you know.

I relaxed. Marjorie wouldn't hear me creeping in the hallway; the fan was too loud. Instead of the long walk and then barricading myself in my room, I bounded across the hall to Mom's and threw open her door.

I said, "Dad said I should see what you're doing," fully knowing that Mom would be mad at Dad for sending me up there to bother her when he should be watching and/or playing with me.

The comforter and sheets had been kicked off the foot of my parents' bed. Mom wasn't in the room. Marjorie was. She sat propped up against the headboard with pillows folded and stuffed behind her back. Her breathing was shallow, but rapid, and she grunted, snarled, sighed; a sputtering engine, the dying fan in our bathroom. Her head was thrown back, chin pointed at the ceiling, as sharp as the tip of an umbrella, eyes closed so tight, like she was hiding them deep inside her head. She had on a too-small black T-shirt, tight enough to outline her rib cage. No pants, no underwear. Her hands were between her long, skinny, pale legs. Both hands, and they gyrated up and down, making wet sounds.

I didn't know what to do. I just stood there and watched. I wanted to yell *What are you doing? I don't know what you're doing!* even though I did know this secret that wasn't a secret. I felt myself flush, turning red on the outside and white on the inside, and then vice versa. I didn't exactly feel sick to my stomach, the feeling was lower, and deeper.

Her hands moved faster and she grew louder, and I didn't want anyone else in the house to hear her, so I quietly said, "Shh," and thought about shutting the door but I couldn't. I was afraid to look at her hands and look between her legs, but I still leaned hard to my right, peering around the hard corner of her knees and thighs.

Marjorie rocked in place, her entire body moved in rhythm with her frantically working hands. She opened her mouth and released a deep sigh.

Politely peering wasn't enough. I tiptoed down to the foot of the bed, and with the new vantage I saw that her hands were red with dark blood, and so was the white sheet beneath, and so was between her legs.

I ran out of the room, stumbling into the hallway, and banged on the bathroom door. "Mom! Mom! Something's wrong with Marjorie! She's bleeding." I tried shouting directly into the wood of the door. I didn't want Dad to hear me.

Mom couldn't hear me over the fan and yelled back, "What? Just give me a sec. I'll be out in a minute."

I turned and Marjorie was in the hallway behind me, perched precariously on her impossibly thin legs, back arched up against the wall, her body a new punctuation mark. One hand still manipulated herself, the other left red smears on the wallpaper. She panted and spoke the same gibberish made of rocks and broken glass that she'd spoken that night in the kitchen. Her eyes opened and then rolled into the back of her head, showing off those horrible bright whites with their convoluted red maps. She laughed, groaned, and said in a small, tight whisper, "Oh my god, oh my god, oh my god . . ." Then something that might've been nonsense or it might've been *I can still hear them*. She stopped talking, and she grunted loudly, like she'd just taken a punch to the gut. Her body shook, and she urinated and defecated right there in the hallway. The smell of shit, blood, and piss was overpowering and I tasted pennies in my mouth. She slid down the wall and sat in her own puddle, rubbing her hands on the floor, herself, and the walls.

I screamed for Mom to please help, to please let me in. I closed my eyes and I hung on the doorknob, turning it with both hands. The bathroom door shook and rattled in its frame. Mom was yelling now too, sensing my panic on the outside.

Dad bellowed our names from down below, those powerless one-word prayers for peace. And he thundered up the stairs, shaking the railing and banisters, sundering the house beneath him, sounding like the end of the world.

PART TWO

CHAPTER 14

THE LAST FINAL GIRL

Yeah, it's just a BLOG! (How retro!) Or
is THE LAST FINAL GIRL the greatest blog
ever!?!? Exploring all things horror and
horrific. Books! Comics! Video games! TV!
Movies! ~~High school!~~ From the gooey gory
midnight show cheese to the highfalutin
art-house highbrow. Beware of spoilers.
I WILL SPOIL YOU!!!!!

BIO: Karen Brissette
Tuesday, November, 15, 20 _ _

The Possession, Fifteen Years Later:
Episode 1 (Part 2)

All right, all right, let's dig into the
first episode, shall we? WE SHALL!!!

First, a quick addendum/important follow-
up point to the previous blog post about
the show's opening. Besides serving as the
patriarchal-breakdown theme of the show
(as I already discussed in GREAT detail),
the show's opening explains (without
having to spell it out for everyone) how
a family would possibly consider allowing
a network to broadcast their living
nightmare: a teenage daughter going through
a particularly nasty, devastating psychotic
break, while believing (or pretending,
yeah?) she was possessed by a demon, and a
stereotypical demon at that. Let me say it
simply: The Barretts were about to default
on their mortgage and lose the house. They
needed cash, and quick! The show's producers
paid them that quick cash for their
televised pounds of flesh.

(aside 1: Sixth Finger Productions was a new
company headed by Randy Francis, who was
a twentysomething venture capitalist [um,
thanks for the money, Dad, gimme more] and
who has since carved out a niche producing
direct-to-video fantasy flicks that rip

off J. K. Rowling, George R. R. Martin, J. R. R. Tolkien, and other fantasy writers with initials in their names. How Sixth Finger heard of the Barretts' story, how they knew to swoop in and offer financial salvation, and exactly where all the money came from before the Discovery Channel became involved is still a bit of a mystery. Father David Wanderly, the priest who befriended John Barrett, is the clear go-between for the Barretts and the production company. However, rumors of Wanderly's involvement with conservative PACs, their monies being rerouted to the production, backroom deals with the archdiocese to keep his parish's church from closing, and rich and powerful and mustache-twisting Opus Dei members ominously being involved are all iffy hearsay at best, as far as little old me can tell. I've found both unauthorized accounts of the show [*To Hell and Back: The Real Story Behind The Possession* and *Possession, Lies, and Videotape: The Dark Angels Behind the Possession*] lacking in the how-the-show-came-to-be department, and frankly, poorly written overall. Yes, I said that.)

Okay. Enough of that. For realsies this time. Let's get to it. To the *it*! To the fictional possession of poor Marjorie Barrett, age fourteen.

After the intro, the bulk of the pilot
is a string of reenactments, and sets of
interviews with the parents and Father
Wanderly. If the intro was the opening
argument about what was at stake for the
soul of family values and patriarchy in
America, the meat of the pilot was the show
laying out their evidence of Marjorie's
possession by an evil spirit, entity, sprite,
demon, impish ne'er-do-well.

The story they present sounds a tad
familiar, yeah? That's because it should.

The Exorcist (the movie directed by William
Friedkin based on the novel by William Peter
Blatty) is a 1970s cultural touchtone and
phenomenon. Admittedly, it has lost some
of its punch, its visceral impact. To wit,
aside 2.

(aside 2: I asked the neighbor's twelve-year-
old kid what his favorite movie was and he
surprised me by saying *The Exorcist*. I asked
him why. He said that, "It was really funny."
I know, the kid is a total psychopath!!!! And
put three locks on my doors now!!!! But you
get my point. Kids these days, ain't a'scared
by that movie no more.)

But, sheeeeet, when that movie originally
came out, it messed people up big-time.

Many a critic/academic/smart lady has written about how *The Exorcist* combined the Hollywood budget and art-house street cred with exploitation, and heavy on the exploitation. I mean, people lined up to see the thing because they'd heard about Regan's potty mouth (literal and figurative!), the crucifix masturbation (fun at parties, not that I've tried it, no), and spinning head (that I've tried!!!). It wasn't the power of Christ that compelled you, but gore, baby, gore! You *Karen wags her finger* shouldn't be surprised that the lukewarm parade of PG-13 possession movies of the 2000s never came close to approaching the critical or popular successes of *The Exorcist*. *The Exorcist* was a wildly popular *event* horror film, and one that, unlike its politically progressive/transgressive, indie counterparts (*Night of the Living Dead*, *Last House on the Left*, *The Texas Chainsaw Massacre*), just happened to be one of the most conservative horror movies ever. Good vs. evil! *Yay, good!* The pure, pristine little white girl saved by white men and religion! *Yay, white men and religion!* All you need is ~~love~~ faith! The triumphant return of the status quo! Family values! Heroic middle-classers battling a foreign boogeyman (the demon Pazuzu was literally a brown-skinned foreigner first glimpsed by Father Merrin in the movie's opening in Iraq)!

Yes, much of *The Possession* follows the urtext of *The Exorcist* and that of other horror films. At times, the reenactment's obviously brazen sameness to classic scenes strikes an innate cultural chord (yeah, I'm making that shit up as I go, sounds good though) within us, and in a weirdly reassuring way authenticating what we're seeing. Other scenes are clever and even subtle enough in their deviations from their antecedents to somehow feel new again. Or their antecedents are obscure enough to feel new, or new enough. Yeah.

Let me break down a bunch of the reenactments:

—Marjorie stands over Merry's bed, hovering over her sister, which clearly recalls the found footage is-it-a-haunted-house-or-demon-possession movie? *Paranormal Activity*. Both camera angles and lighting are similar. Marjorie is dressed just like Katie, wearing boxers and a tight T-shirt. *The Possession* spices up the simple dread of hovering over a sleeping loved one with Marjorie pinching her little sister's nose shut. It adds a layer of sadism that's subtle and hints at possible greater acts of violence.

(aside 3: Yeah, more politics. Sorry. But it's just so there and waggling in our

faces!!!! The reenactment actress playing
Marjorie, Liz Jaffe, was no fourteen years
old. She was twenty-three and looked it.
Marjorie was still a kid. Miss Jaffe was
not. Liz had similar hair color, skin tone,
etc., to Marjorie, but she was obviously
more physically . . . cough . . . mature. She
wore makeup, tight clothing, and in the
masturbation scene, no clothing, but oh,
she had on a few digitally blurred pixels
to protect the poor audience from her
nasty lady parts. So, yeah, "the male gaze"
[please see Laura Mulvey's essay "Visual
Pleasure and Narrative Cinema"] is in full
effect in *The Possession* at both extremes.
The camera ogles a sexualized Liz Jaffe
whenever she's on screen. When the real
Marjorie is eventually on screen [at the end
of the pilot and in the following episodes],
she's ogled in a different though no less
demeaning way. Real Marjorie is an object to
be observed, but never too closely as we the
voyeurs might find she's a real teenage girl
and actually begin to be concerned for her
mental health and general well-being. John
Barrett represented the valiant struggle
of patriarchy in our decaying, secular,
postfeminist society, and Marjorie was the
withering object of the camera's male gaze.)

—Marjorie projectile vomiting all over her
family as they watched *Finding Bigfoot* (psst,

they never found her!) in the living room
was an obvious nod to *The Exorcist*. Maybe
not so obvious, this scene is so over the
top in its gastric viscera, it recalls the
spewing geysers of blood and goo from Sam
Raimi's *Evil Dead* movies (the originals, not
the shitty remakes).

—Marjorie's postpuke, backward crawl out
of the living room, away from the family,
and up the stairs is the film negative of
perhaps the most famous piece of celluloid
to be cut from a film: Regan's contorted
"spiderwalk" down the stairs in *The
Exorcist*. The special effects in both the
show and the movie aren't convincing and
each "walk" scene suffers because of them.

—We get a medley of Marjorie performing
contortions and linguistic horrors in the
hospital and in her psychiatrist's office.
The inner demon getting its groove on for
the benefit of the men (always men) of
reason and science in the white antiseptic
hospital room just might be the second most
stereotypical scene in a possession movie
(with the actual clergy-performed exorcism
as number one). *The Exorcist*, *The Rite*, *The
Possession* (the 2012 movie by Sam Raimi,
featuring a sneaky little Dybbuk hidden
in a Jewish wine cabinet box bought at
a yard sale . . . SOLD!), season two of the

gory and horny TV series *American Horror Story*, and . . . you get the idea. Marjorie's psychiatrist, Dr. Hamilton, refused (of course) to be interviewed for the show. Instead we're treated to creepy witness-protection-type interviews of orderlies, nurses, and office secretaries.

—Marjorie's midnight screamfest, the jangling camera running down the hallway after Merry, and Marjorie's wall climb? See *The Last Exorcism*. But don't see its dumbass ending.

—Dipping briefly into the second episode, there's the basement reenactment. Marjorie surprises her sister, Merry, down in the basement. Her cold clammy hand lands on Merry's shoulder. She whispers more sweet ~~nothings~~ ramblings, clods of dirt spill from her mouth, cue the eyes rolling white, and then she slowly walks after a screaming Merry up the stairs. Marjorie's long hair hangs down over her face for most of the scene so that she resembles Sadako, the angry spirit of *Ringu* (or *The Ring*) and other J-horror films.

—Okay, yeah, the masturbation reenactment scene. *Deep breath* In *The Exorcist*, it represents the ultimate blasphemy and proof positive that the girl is possessed by an evil spirit, right? A cute, innocent little

girl (wearing a prim nightgown, btw) raving
like Tourettic Louis C.K. and jamming Jesus
Christ up her vagina so violently she bleeds
all over the place. Score one for Pazuzu,
and yeah, we're down that it must be the
devil making her do it. So to speak. *The
Possession*'s masturbation scene is both more
problematic and disturbing. It begins with
a camera run from Merry's POV as she opens
her parents' bedroom door. It's dark, but we
can see Liz Jaffe as Marjorie in profile.
She's on the bed wearing only a small black
bra. Digital pixilation boxes obscure her
buttocks and her hands. The camera switches
away from Merry's POV to a straight-on,
close-up, loving view of Marjorie's face.
The camera pulls back and there's a series
of jump cuts that are so fast we feel like
we really *can't* see much of anything in
real time. I've watched this scene with
countless friends and I've asked them what
they saw after viewing it in real time and
no two answers are the same, until I slow
it down. Going frame by frame we see the
following: Marjorie biting her lower lip;
a shadow on the wall of a bedpost, and can
we say phallus?; forearms framing her six-
pack abs and navel; open mouth and tongue
on her teeth; biceps framing her cleavage;
a white inner thigh; blood on white sheets;
a wooden cross hanging on the wall; her
closed eyes, white forehead, and wooden

headboard; a bearded male face covered in
blood (hmm, Satan?); a full shot between her
legs, dark and pixilated so we can't see
her actual fingers in her actual ~~dirty lady
parts~~ vagina; the bedpost again, only its
shadow is larger than it was previously;
her knees together; the wooden cross again,
totally in shadow; her feet with curled toes;
then finally three different shots of blood
on the sheets before the camera returns to
her little sister, Merry, but not her POV.
After the frenetic cuts we see Marjorie
stumbling in the hallway wiping her bloody
fingers (also see the locker room scene in
Carrie) on the walls and we hear her peeing
on the floor, but just in case we don't
get it, Merry says, "You're peeing on the
floor!" (note! Regan peed on the floor in
The Exorcist but it was in a scene separate
from the masturbation scene.) Marjorie says,
"I can still hear them. They've been here
forever!" in a TV-speakers-rattling modulated
voice that crosses the Cookie Monster with
Wicked Witch of the West and the "help
me" man-fly from *The Fly*. The scene ends
awkwardly with the camera POV falling to the
floor and on its side as though, just like
Marjorie, it ~~has blown its wad~~ is spent.
Marjorie is on the floor, her back to us,
buttocks obscured by more pixilation, and
Mom and Dad Barrett rush to the hallway and
huddle around Marjorie's body. The camera

lingers and its male gaze is conflicted, as
it has been during the entire masturbation
reenactment scene. It's both titillated and
horrified by the natural expression of a
teenage girl's body.

Intermission (*Karen drinks more coffee,
must have more COFFEEEEEEEE!!!!*)

Okay. Now, my favorite reenactments and
interviews feature the quieter bits that
deviate from *The Exorcism* game plan but are
no less eerie or disturbing. Let's go rapid
fire on these because I think the quick
accumulation of these nice little moments
generates a cool effect.

—Marjorie's molasses-flood story is legit.
For a riveting account of the 1919 molasses
flood in Boston, check out Stephen Puelo's
Dark Tide. Her growing-things story was
clearly inspired by a short story from
a relatively obscure horror writer. Her
drawing the growing things on Merry's
cardboard house recalls the collected mass
of wooden stick figures in *The Blair Witch
Project*, which is not horror's first found-
footage film, but its most famous. During
Marjorie's midnight freak-out scene, there's
a shot of her bedroom door, which fills the
viewing screen, and then the door subtly
bows outward. The very same shot (in black-

and-white) is in Robert Wise's amazing 1963
film *The Haunting*, which was based on *The
Haunting of Hill House* by Shirley Jackson.
Marjorie's bit about the voices in her head
being so old, ancient, beyond time, and
her consonant-heavy speech sound downright
Lovecraftian. And of course, we find out
later that Marjorie had been exposed to his
works. Chthulu for all my friends! (*Ph'nglui
mglw'nafh* Cthulhu *R'lyeh wgah'nagl* fhtagn!
feel free to check my spelling there!!!)
Her super creepy spiel to Daddy Barrett
about being in heaven and not knowing
if your loved one was real or demon was
gently lifted from Vladimir Nabokov and his
ultimate unreliable narrator novel *Despair*.
The song Marjorie sings and hums in many
of the reenactments (and which the show
uses as a theme quite effectively in their
background soundtrack) is "Gloomy Sunday,"
originally composed by Hungarian pianist
Rezsõ Seress in 1933. It's legendary not just
because Billie Holliday once sang it, but
because it sounded *soooooo* frowny-face sad
it supposedly drove a bunch of unsuspecting
listeners to suicide. How cool is that? (and
yeah, I've listened to it like fifty-five
times in a row now . . . and I'm still here!!!!)

Keeping all that in mind . . . In an interview
toward the end of the pilot, John Barrett
duly informs us that Marjorie claims

she ~~never heard of the Internet or the library~~ doesn't know where she heard the stories or the song, or where she gets her terrible ideas from. He says that Marjorie has consistently told his family, the psychiatrist, Father Wanderly, ~~the mailman~~, and everyone else who ever asked that all that "stuff" just popped into her head, fully formed, like they were always there. She knew that these were other people's stories/ideas, but swears she hadn't learned of them or heard them from outside sources.

So . . . she's precognitive! Or postcognitive! Something-cognitive! Gnostic, a priori horror makes us weep with fear!!!

Again, I think this is another brilliant bit. The show had horror fans hooked at hello because, frankly, most of us are not picky. We're like the family dog that wags its tail at a treat, no matter if it's a crappy store-brand Milk-Bone or a piece of steak. We (yes, I'm still speaking for you, horror hound) don't mind the familiar and recycled as long as we can consume it without gagging. To the general populace, the recycled bits of classic horror might be naggingly familiar in some recess of their pitiful and atrophied culture-lobe of their brains (mmm, braaaaiiiins!!!), but to

them it plays as totally fresh and new, and
frightening.

(aside 4: I've got this whole thing about
how *The Possession* fits perfectly in the
Gothic tradition but I haven't fully worked
it out and I have to save something for
later blog posts, right? Right! But I love
the idea of all these external influences
listed above so obviously affecting the
story and affecting Marjorie herself. If
she was possessed by anything other than
faulty brain chemistry and/or DNA, I like to
imagine her as being possessed by the vast,
awesome and awful monster that is popular
culture. Possessed by the collective of
ideas!)

By the time we finally meet the real
Marjorie (and not her Liz Jaffe reenactment
stand-in) in the final moment of the
pilot, the show has painstakingly built its
thematic foundation through realism, through
the fears of our deteriorating middle-
class and core conservative family values,
and through the recycled cultural lessons
borrowed or reimagined from the classics of
horror literature and film.

When we finally see the surveillance-style
video of *real* Marjorie sitting in a room,

across from an unnamed interviewer, wearing
her soccer team sweatpants and sweatshirt,
flipping her hair away from her face
revealing her tired (haunted?) eyes, we're
afraid for her and we're afraid of her.

When she says, with her voice cracking,
"I'm Marjorie Barrett, and I need help,"
we shudder, and maybe we giggle nervously,
guiltily, but we're hooked. Oh, baby, are we
hooked.

(cue the pilot outro, which is of course in
the same minor key of "Gloomy Sunday")

CHAPTER 15

RACHEL SAYS, "I must say, I'm very impressed by your home, Merry."

"Thank you! It is a nice place to rest my weary bones, isn't it?" My two-bedroom condo is a third-floor unit of a South Boston brownstone. The living room's large bay window overlooks Carson Beach, which really isn't much of a beach. I'm told it was at one time. I spend my sunny mornings in the living room with a coffee, a blueberry muffin, and my tablet, and I watch the joggers running parallel to the water and going nowhere quickly. On rainy days, I watch the encroaching rising waters lash against the helpless seawalls that will no doubt fail one day.

"You're much too young for weary bones." We're standing in my living room with the coffees she bought. She's very thoughtful. Outside it's overcast, and the ocean is sleeping. "That is an amazing view. If you don't mind my asking . . . What was the asking price? I might be in the market for a condo myself. My daughter is out of the house now and I don't need all that space."

I don't mind. So I tell her.

"Wow."

"Yeah, the condo is quite expensive even with our seasonal flooding issues. It costs five hundred a month to rent a parking space in the elevated garage out back. Isn't that ridiculous? But I don't own a car and I rarely leave my perch, so I'm generally dry."

"You don't go out much for fear of being recognized?"

"No one around here knows who I am, or who I was in the context of a fifteen-year-old television show. Maybe that will change when our best-selling book comes out."

"It's possible that it might. I hope you'll be okay with that."

Rachel doesn't have her blue hat with her. I miss it, fiercely, like one might miss a newly casual acquaintance one hoped would become a lifelong friend. I do like that she's wearing a white button-down shirt tucked into her jeans. Her collar practically has the wingspan of an albatross.

I say, "I'll be fine. I have to pay the mortgage somehow, right?"

"Oh, Merry, I'm sad to hear that you don't leave your place often."

I lead her back toward the kitchen and we sit at the granite-topped, L-shaped counter. I say, "There's no reason to be sad. I didn't mean to imply that I'm a shut-in, because I'm not. I have dinner with my aunt twice a month. I go out. I speak to people. I even have a few friends." The last sentence drools with playful sarcasm, and I smile.

"I deserved that." She laughs politely. "I'm glad to hear it, though. You're much too young to be . . . living that way. Right? You should be out and having—fun." Rachel bumbles over her words and pecks at her cardboard coffee cup.

She is much more nervous here in my home than she was at my old house. My not saying anything after her awkward bromide about the exciting life a young, single woman should be living in the big city likely isn't helping her feel at ease, so I say, "I could just sit and marinate in this coffee. You're my hero this morning."

"I'm glad you approve. I just love the hint of nutmeg on a cold morning like this." We hum approvingly as we both take a sip. Rachel switches subjects. "Your high ceilings are dreamy. I love your green kitchen and the yellow in the living room. Unexpected color scheme, but it flows well, especially with the open floor plan."

"Thank you. Each room is a different color. I plan on changing their colors once a year, every February I think. February is such a dreary month otherwise, particularly in Boston."

"How many more rooms are there?"

"Two. My blue bedroom and my red media room."

"Media room?"

"It's the condo's second bedroom that I use as my play area. It's where I keep my TV, tablet docking station, bookcases, movies, video games. All the fun stuff."

She nods, sips her coffee, then says, "Shall we get started?"

"We shall!"

Rachel takes out her phone and turns on her recording app. She places the phone down between us on the counter. There's an almost reverent moment of silence, as though we're both acknowledging the power the device has over our conversation and over us.

"I want to focus on the television show today, focus on what it was like living with the cameras and the production crew. That had to be a strange experience for a child."

"It was. But I think any and all experiences are strange for a child."

"It had to be especially strange for you."

"I guess. I'm not trying to be a smartass, but that's hard for me to say. I haven't lived anyone else's normal experience to compare mine to."

"I have talked to some of the show's producers and former employees of the production company, but I'm still unclear as to how the show came about."

"So am I!" I laugh at my own joke.

"Let's piece it together, then. According to

the timeline I have, the show started filming less than a month after the night you found Marjorie in your parents' room. Can you tell me what happened at home in those weeks in between?"

"Not a lot. I remember Marjorie going away to the hospital for about two weeks, so she could get some rest. That was how Mom put it. It may sound strange, but my world was a scary place, or scarier place, for me with Marjorie gone. In hindsight, it's likely that Mom was suffering from depression. She started smoking in the house instead of going outside. She was drinking a lot, wine mostly, and cried to herself in the kitchen. I remember her sitting there in all that smoke, alternately holding her head up high, defiantly blowing out her smoke, and then crumbling down into herself. I was too afraid to talk to her, to try to comfort her, and she couldn't even look at me if I went into the kitchen to get a drink or a snack. I don't remember Dad being around much while Marjorie was gone, but when he was, he argued with Mom about how long Marjorie would be in the hospital, how they'd pay for any of it, but mostly they argued about letting Father Wanderly try to help them."

"Did they ever talk about remanding Marjorie to the state? Were they worried that the state would step in?"

"I don't remember them talking about that, no. I could be wrong, but I think for the most part, Marjorie behaved like a normal surly teen for her psychiatrist and hospital staff. At least that's what Marjorie told me when I asked her what going to the psychiatrist was like. Anyway, I couldn't take my parents' arguments anymore, and stopped spying on them. After a couple of days without Marjorie, I tried to stay away from my parents altogether. Dad kept trying to bless me and make me pray with him. I ran and hid whenever I felt his big paw landing on my head. When Marjorie finally came back home, it was my turn to leave. They shipped me away to stay with Dad's sister, my Auntie Erin. I stayed with her for a week, maybe more. I did homework, played with her dog Niko, and cried myself to sleep. Erin brought me to school and took me trick-or-treating on Halloween. I went as a zombie soccer player. Because I was so clever, I shouted, 'Goal!' instead of moaning for brains. I remember telling Erin that the candy in her neighborhood was better than mine, but I was just saying it to make her feel good.

"The very day Mom brought me back home, Marjorie was upstairs in her room and Father Wanderly and another priest, a younger guy, Father Gavin, were sitting in the living room. Father Wanderly gave me a crooked smile and the weakest handshake ever. It was like shaking hands with a bird. Father Gavin just waved 'hi' at me, shy, like the boys at school who were afraid of catching cooties from a girl. He was short and pudgy and had too much hair on the back of his neck. Then I remember being rushed into the kitchen and my parents sat me down and told me about how we were going to do a TV show. Dad was excited, manic even, pacing around the room, punctuating his sentences with hallelujahs. Mom tried to be reassuring, but she still couldn't look at me."

"That was it? It all happened that fast?"

"I was only a kid and they didn't tell me much of the nitty-gritty details. I'm sure there are gaps in what I'm not remembering as well. What I remember them telling me was that someone was going to make a TV show about us. That these same people were going to help Marjorie get better and help us, too. Dad said that the TV show was going to be our family's new job, and that we would be paid well for doing our job. Mom said that cameras would be in all the rooms, some people might follow me around and ask questions, and that if I ever got scared by one of them, to tell her right away."

"From what little I know and from what you've told me so far, I'm surprised your mom wasn't more resistant to the idea of doing the television show."

"I think she was very resistant, which is obvious when you watch the show and her interviews, right? As to when or how the final decision to sign the dotted line was made, I have no idea. I was out of that house for more than a week. Maybe Dad wore her down, bullied her into signing the contract. She clearly wasn't as outwardly fervent as Dad with the new old-time religion, but maybe she saw the light. Even knowing better, maybe despite her protests, deep down she believed it would help Marjorie and she was ashamed by that belief. Maybe it was cold and simple pragmatism. Money. We were going broke and the producers swooped in and made her an offer she couldn't refuse, right? I don't know. Your guess about why Mom went along with it all is as good as mine."

"I sincerely doubt that, Merry."

I smile. It's the first time Rachel has pushed back and accused me of not being forthcoming. Good for her.

"I was eight and she was my mom. Her motivations were beyond me, and continue to be. I will say that she never explicitly told me the show would transform us into the town freaks, the laughingstocks of the neighborhood. But only because she never had to say it. It was there, between her lines and in everything she did once the cameras were in our house."

Rachel asks more questions from there and I answer them, or I answer most of them, anyway. Her questions are now about show particulars she probably could've just found out herself. Or maybe she already knows the answers and is testing to see how honest I'm being with her.

I say, "Yes, the lag time between filming and the episode airing was about two weeks. Rachel, let's stretch our legs and finish the tour of the condo. We could go to the roof deck too, if you'd like."

"May I keep taping our conversation?"

"Certainly."

We walk through the kitchen back into the living room, then curl right into the first bedroom, which is shaped like a long rectangle. A print of Andrew Wyeth's *Christina's World* and a small collection of watercolor landscapes and shorelines from local artists dot the walls. My queen-sized bed has a shiny brass frame and is covered with a fluffy white duvet. The bed is underneath a window that overlooks the ocean. The room is quiet and plain, and the walls are a bright sky-blue.

She says, "That is a spectacular view. Your bedroom is quite lovely. I wish my silly daughter would keep her apartment so tidy and—"

"Adult looking?"

"I was going to say *subdued*, but you're more to the point." Rachel walks into the middle of the room, gingerly touches the antique dresser, and does a full turn, spinning like the world's slowest ballerina. "Is this room the same color as your childhood bedroom?"

I resist the urge to say something that would've been totally Marjorie: *Maybe the room was a disastrous and dark blue, the color of a painful bruise, only yesterday.* I say, "I don't know if it's the exact shade or hue. But yes, it's the same. It helps me dream in sky-blue."

"May I quote you directly on that?"

"Of course. I assumed you'd be using many direct quotes. You're not writing fiction with this book, correct?"

We both laugh. I'm nervous, almost dizzy as I walk out of the bedroom, and Rachel silently follows me out and next door to the second bedroom, my media room.

Rachel says, "Now this looks like my daughter's apartment. No offense."

I say, "You're terrible!" and gently swipe her shoulder. "So this is my playroom. What kind of playroom would it be if it wasn't in a state of beautiful chaos?"

The left wall is covered by five black bookcases, each over six feet tall, and the shelves full of books, comics, and movies. On the wall across from the door is the room's only window. No ocean view here, but the brick façade of the neighboring brownstone. On our right is a desk overflowing with more totems of pop culture. Beneath the rubble, somewhere, is my tablet docking station. Next to the desk is a wall-mounted flat screen. In the middle of the room, a lost island in a violent sea, is my lumpy futon couch.

"You weren't kidding when you said the room was red."

"Yeah, it's redder than I thought it was going to be. It looked different on the paint chip. If there was more natural lighting in the room, it would be a softer red I think."

"I must say it warms my writer's heart to see so many hard copies of books filling your shelves."

"I have digital copies of just about everything you see, but I like having the physical artifacts as well. I used to collect vinyl records too, but that became too unwieldy and expensive."

Rachel walks to the bookcases, surveys the spines of books and DVDs. She stops at the fourth of the five cases and says my name like a question.

"Merry?"

I walk around the futon toward the case, and say, "Ah, my horror section."

"I am not familiar with all the titles, but I'd say it's more than a horror section, and that it has a particular focus." Rachel says it like she's angry and disappointed. I can imagine the conversations she has when visiting her daughter's messy apartment. I'm sad for the both of them, and I'm insanely jealous.

"Well, the possession and exorcism stuff is only a subsection of my horror section."

"For the benefit of my recorder, would you mind reading me the titles in this subsection?"

"Be happy to. In no particular order. I've tried to alphabetize on numerous occasions, but I always seem to lose steam. Anyway, in movies: *The Exorcist* and its four sequels and prequels; *The Exorcism of Emily Rose*; *The Last Exorcism*; *The Devil Inside Me*; *The Conjuring*; *Constantine*; *The Rite*; *REC 2*; *The Amityville Horror*, both versions; *Paranormal Activity* and its sequels; *Evil Dead I and II*; *Exorcismo*." I quickly explain how other titles like *Session 9, The Legend of Hell House, Burnt Offerings*, and *The Shining* fit into this subsection as well. For novels, I point out other notable titles besides the obvious one written by William Peter Blatty. Those titles include *Come Closer* by Sara Gran; *Pandemonium* by Daryl Gregory; *Rosemary's Baby* by Ira Levin. For nonfiction I point out *The Exorcist: Studies in the Horror Film*; *American Exorcism: Expelling Demons in the Land of Plenty*; *God Is Not Great: How Religion Poisons Everything*; and even the laughably bad *Pigs in the Parlor: The Practical Guide to Deliverance*.

When I'm done reading titles, Rachel asks, "Forgive the potentially obvious question, but have you actually seen all these movies and read all these books?"

"Yes. Well, yes for this section anyway. I can't say I've read or seen everything in every bookcase."

"I have to admit, Merry, I find it shocking that you would collect all these"—Rachel pauses to wave her hand at the bookcase—"titles."

"Shocking? Really? I don't know, you could say that I have a personal interest in the subject matter." I laugh, then walk over to my desk and sit in the little black chair.

"*Shocking* is an extreme word, but it fits. That you would willingly or obsessively choose to relive, over and over again, the horror of what you went through as a child, is shocking to me."

"I'm not reliving anything. None of these books or movies come close to being like what I lived through."

"Are you searching to find answers to what happened to you and your family?"

"I don't know if I'd put it that way, exactly. But, yeah, I'm always looking for answers in everything I do. Aren't you? Isn't that why you want to write a book about me?"

"That's a good question, Merry. I'm interested in finding the story. An accurate account of what happened."

"Ah, those can be two different things."

Rachel smiles, though she is still clearly unnerved by the bookcase discovery. "Very true. Now, Merry, I know this process can be difficult and will continue to become more so. You have to trust that I am not trying to belittle in any way the nightmarish, traumatic experience you suffered through, okay? And that I will treat it with respect. It's a testament to your character that you've become the responsible and well-adjusted adult that you are."

"You're too kind; my years and years of therapy have helped. And I do trust you. I do. I wouldn't have let you in otherwise."

Rachel carefully considers the bookcases again. "Let me ask you this: Does watching the movies make you feel—I don't know—empowered or comforted in a weird way?"

"In what weird way?"

"It's empowering that you're able to overcome the images on the screen, which are more over-the-top and overtly supernatural than what you actually experienced."

"What does that say about you or anyone else that my sister's nationally televised psychotic break and descent into schizophrenia wasn't horrific enough?"

"That's not what I meant, Merry."

I open my mouth to say something but she holds up a stop hand and keeps talking.

"And it's not your fault. I'm badly stumbling around the point here." She pauses, then adds, "Okay, Merry. Why did you show me your media room? You had to know that on some level I'd be surprised by what I saw."

"Just sharing?" I say it like a question and shrug. We share a smile and a weighty silence. "Okay. I'll admit what you were saying about the books and movies being a comfort, there's some truth there. But it's not about overcoming anything. It's about making what happened to me seem more explicable when compared to the lurid ridiculousness of those stories."

"Are you worried you'll conflate what happened with the fictions you watch and read? You'd said to me on our first day together that your memories were mixed together with what other people told you about what had happened, and you'd included pop culture and media."

"I said that?" I say, and spin around one full revolution in my desk chair.

"Not in those exact words, but essentially, yes."

"Sounds like me," I say. "I'm kidding, I remember telling you that, but I'd meant only the pop-cultural, Internet, and media treatment of the reality show and of what had happened to me and my family. Not the Hollywood movies and books. Let me put it this way: Me and my story might have some fuzzy, blurry parts, but I know my sister wasn't Regan."

"You don't believe your sister was possessed, do you?"

"By a supernatural entity? No, I don't."

"Did you believe it when you were eight years old?"

"The eight-year-old me still believed in Bigfoot. But with Marjorie, I honestly wasn't sure what to believe. I don't think I knew what I wanted to believe, other than I wanted to believe in her. I always did."

Rachel nods, and then slowly turns away from me and back to the bookcases. I wonder how many of the books she's read, which of the movies she's seen. Her fingers drift over the spines.

I think there was too much sugar in my coffee. Or not enough, as I still feel a little light-headed. I stand and say, "Rachel, did I tell you that I just landed my first paying writing gig?"

"No. I had no idea you were a writer. That's fantastic, Merry."

"Thank you, I'm very excited. It's my first paying job that isn't bartending or waitressing. It isn't much, but it's nice to be no longer solely subsisting on residuals from the show, the family trust fund, and, of course, what your publisher is paying me."

"What's the gig?"

"I've been writing a horror blog for a few years now—a quite popular one, if I do say so myself—

and it was just picked up by the horror 'zine *Fangoria*. They'll feature my blog online and I'll write an assignment column for each issue."

"I'm impressed and I'm very happy for you, Merry. Can I read the blog?"

"Please do! It's called *The Last Final Girl*. I write it under a pseudonym, Karen Brissette."

"Why that name?"

"Totally random. Really. Anyway, *Fangoria* has no idea I am who I really am, so they're paying me for my writing merits only. That's important to me. I feel, I don't know, validated. Does that make sense?"

"Yes, yes, it does. You continue to impress me, Merry."

"Aw, shucks." I walk toward the door. "Okay, time for the tour to move again. Would you like to see the roof deck?"

"No thank you, I'm not a huge fan of heights, or exposed heights. I know, I'm a mess."

"Not at all. Let's go back to the kitchen then. Can I get you a drink of water or anything else?"

"Water would be great. And can we get back to talking about what your life was like when they were filming the show?"

"We can."

We walk back to the kitchen and we're back at the counter with our glasses of water. She says, "I'd like to ask you about the basement reenactment from the show. It's quite a harrowing scene with Marjorie eating the dirt and following you up the stairs."

"Yeah. It is. I have to admit, much to my shame, that I exaggerated what happened. Or maybe *embellished* is a better word." I laugh. "It was the first time my parents let me be interviewed in detail by one of the two writers for the show, Ken Fletcher. Ken was such a nice guy. He would play with me downstairs in the living room when there was nothing going on. And there was a lot of nothing going on, at least early on. Anyway, I didn't want to disappoint him, and I remembered how Dad had told me that the new family job was the TV show, so I wanted to do everything I could to help."

"Okay. Let's start with what really happened in the basement, then."

CHAPTER 16

ON THE FIRST day, the crew kicked us out of the house.

It was early, so early it was still dark out when Mom shook me awake. Dad and Marjorie left before us, but I don't remember where they went. We didn't see them again until we came home the next morning. When Mom and I walked out the front door there were already three white vans parked out front and all sorts of people on the lawn. Some of them had clipboards and milled around the yard looking into the windows and taking measurements. Others carried thick black cases and lighting equipment into the house or they brought in electrical cords that had been coiled into tight circles. There was a subgroup of people who weren't carrying anything, and they appeared to be a regular family. They clustered on the lawn, looking up at the house and smiling like they'd just moved in. There was a mom and dad and two sisters. Their clothes were new, unwrinkled, and brightly colored. I waved at the little girl who kind of looked like me, though she was taller. She waved back but then quickly hid behind the older sister, who wore a lot of makeup. The older sister, like the parents, was listening to one of the clipboard-carrying people. The woman with the clipboard gestured at the house while she talked. The family laughed and I didn't like that they were laughing at our house. Once we were in the car, Mom explained that they would be filming what were called "reenactment scenes" and that the other family was a group of actors who were pretending to be us. She kept stopping to ask me if I understood what she said and what was going on. I lied and told her I did. She also told me the actors would only be at our house for one day and night and that we would be the show after the actors left. We spent the day and night at Auntie Erin's house. I remember eating too many hotdogs and watching the movie *Monsters, Inc.* by myself twice and falling asleep on the couch.

On the second day, the crew transformed our house.

Marjorie was in her room, sequestered away like the secret everyone already knew. Mom was in there with her. I hid under the dining room table. We had cleared the table of the folded stacks of clothes a few days before. It'd taken me *forever* to clean my room and put all those stupid clothes away. I'd let everyone in the house know how terrible and unfair that chore was. My parents then had covered the table with the white tablecloth that we had only ever used for holiday dinners. All the prep work had seemed needless to me, especially given my parents' explicit instructions that we were not to act or do anything differently for the cameras.

With the TV people now roaming the house, I pretended the dining room table wasn't the real one but was a ghost table in its white sheet. The crew wouldn't be able to see me under it, which may or may not have been true. But from my ghostly vantage I couldn't see how many people were coming in and out of the house. And I couldn't see who was barking orders, who was laughing that well-deep laugh, and who was banging and drilling the walls and ceilings. So I left the safety of the ghost table and wandered.

Dad was in the kitchen, sitting at the table and talking with two men. I'd later find out that the younger one with the black curly hair was Barry Cotton. He was the show's producer-slash-director. He was nice enough to me, one on one, but I didn't like how he would talk to me like a baby whenever the rest of my family was around. The other man at the kitchen table was Ken Fletcher, the show's main writer. He had freckles, thick beard stubble, and a bright smile. Ken would quickly become my friend.

Crew members mounted small, cyclopic cameras on the dining room, living room, and kitchen ceilings. Horrified that they could be doing the same in my room, I ran upstairs to put a stop to it. There were crew members in the hallway and they mounted more ceiling cameras. They all said, "Hi," to me, with one saying, "Hey there, little lady," as I ignored them and dodged their stepladders. My room's door was still closed. I ran inside and there weren't any crew or cameras, but my cardboard house with its Magic Marker–vine graffiti was back in its old spot. We'd moved it to the basement a few weeks ago because I'd told my parents I didn't want the house anymore, that it took up too much space, but the truth was that I couldn't sleep with it in the room any longer, that I was too afraid of the growing things on the outside and the darkness the house kept on the inside. I yelled through my closed bedroom door, "No cameras in my room and no one is allowed to put stuff in my room!" I hesitantly walked over and kicked the cardboard house, but I jumped backward immediately, afraid it would retaliate. My goal kick dented one of the corners.

I wouldn't be able to drag the house back down to the basement with all those people in the hallway, and I didn't want to stay closed up in my room with the growing-things house. My room was too clean to set up any elaborate security devices. So on the way out I retied my purple robe belt to the corner of the bed and the doorknob. It'd never stopped Marjorie from sneaking in, but maybe it would stop the crew.

On my way back to the first floor I stopped and peeked into the sunroom. One guy who smelled like salad dressing and had a tool belt hanging way too low on his skinny hips nailed up a black drop cloth over the bay window. I stood in the doorway, mouth hanging open and fists planted on my sides. I said, "You're changing our house! It's not a sunroom if there isn't any sun." A woman who adjusted two spotlights, one large and one small, laughed and told me not to worry, that it was only temporary and they'd put everything back the way it was when it was all over. I wanted to ask her what she meant by her *when it was all over*. I told her that I didn't like it. The yellow wallpaper looked old and faded under the harsh spotlights. Another crew member set up some microphones and a camera on a tripod pointed at the loveseat. He wore a black baseball hat that had the show's logo on it. The logo was THE POSSESSION in white, capital block letters, with THE resting on top of POSSESSION so that the letters formed the shape of our house.

I went back downstairs and everyone was so big and loud and busy. I couldn't watch TV and I didn't think I could go back under the dining room table without being seen. I decided I was thirsty and hungry, but I didn't want to go into the kitchen and be cornered by Dad, because he'd make me talk to the producer some more. He'd fire off questions about soccer, asking what my favorite book or movie or song was, and I'd feel pressure to perform, as though it was up to me to prove to the world that Mom and Dad were not at fault here and had managed to raise at least one bright, cheery, normal daughter. So I went down into the basement instead.

Normally, the basement was too dark and scary for me to even contemplate with its dirt floor, the ceiling of exposed wooden beams (those bones of the first floor from which hung more cobwebs than light bulbs), the growly and hissing furnace, and toward the back of the basement on the left side, the bulkhead staircase, which was the creepiest; a literal hole-in-the-wall, a black mouth cut into the foundation that led up to the creaky, rusty bulkhead that opened to the side yard. But since my parents had become flush with TV money, they had gone on a triumphant shopping spree at Sam's Club, buying bulk quantities of all manner of nonperishable food and drink items. Our fully stocked shelves could sustain us through the show, through the end of the coming winter, and maybe through the apocalypse. Of course these shelves and their cornucopia were in the basement.

I reached inside the door with one arm, groped the wall for the light switch, and found it. Already, my basement bravery had leaked away. I left the door open behind me so that the noisy crew could still keep me company. As I tiptoed down, the stairs felt too soft under my shoes. The sounds of the crew didn't follow me down, and instead grew distant. I came to the horrifying realization that if something happened to me in the basement I could yell and scream all I wanted and no one would hear me in the loud, busy world of upstairs. The air was cool and moist and pressed against me. I felt my way along the foundation wall, and the gray, misshapen stones were gritty to the touch. I hated thinking about these old stones and their crumbling mortar holding up everything.

Coming down here by myself had seemed like such a better idea when I was upstairs, but I was too stubborn to leave empty-handed. I quickly scooted past the furnace and hot water heater on my right, washer and dryer and their collection of hoses on my left, past the dark mouth of the bulkhead stairs and to the far foundation wall that held up the back end of the house, and the set of slightly crooked wooden shelves stacked to the ceiling with their cache of goodies: jars, cans, soda and water bottles, and large corrugated cardboard boxes. I wanted to use those boxes when emptied to create a miniature town to replace the white cardboard house in my room.

On the second row of shelves, at my eye level, were plastic-wrapped cases of juice boxes and peanut butter crackers. I had to push, lift, and twist other boxes to get to what I wanted. It was like a life-sized game of Jenga. I almost lost the game as I pulled one corner of a multipack of assorted Cheerios boxes out too far, and everything above it on the shelves shook and settled. I worked a small hole into the plastic wrap, using my teeth like a small, thieving rodent and eventually pried out two juice boxes and a package of crackers. I tried to force the Cheerios back to its spot by ramming my shoulder into the multi-pack, but it wouldn't budge. I kept pushing and grunting and even talking to it, telling the cereal to get back into its stupid place.

"Need some help, monkey?"

I screamed, dropped the crackers, and spun around. Marjorie was there, dressed in jeans and a gray sweatshirt. She was barefoot and her toes wiggled and wormed in the cold dirt.

She smiled and shook her head. "Are you really that afraid of me now?" Her hair was tied back, no loose strands. It felt like I hadn't seen her without her face obscured by her hair or her hood in forever. Her eyes were bright and focused, her neck long, chin sharpened to a point. She looked older; a glimpse of the adult Marjorie I would never see.

I said, "No." I was relieved to no longer be in the basement by myself, and I was happy to see Marjorie dressed and walking about on her own, without Mom or Dad following her around like a pet that wasn't housetrained. But, yes, I was still a little afraid of her.

"Good. You shouldn't be." Marjorie walked to the shelves and lifted up the boxes resting against the wedged multipack of Cheerios. "Here. Go ahead, push it in."

I pushed with all my might and it slid back into place so easily, I lost my balance, stumbled, and bounced my head off the cereal.

"Ow!" I giggled nervously and rubbed my forehead.

Marjorie walked into the far corner, where there was no dangling light bulb, to where our parents stored holiday decorations, summer clothes, boxes of unlabeled miscellany, and old furniture. She said, "Look at all this junk."

I held my ground near the shelves. "Does Mom know you're down here?"

Marjorie picked through some of the open packs and boxes. "Probably not. She fell asleep in my room. Crazy what's going on upstairs, huh?"

I imagined Mom facedown on Marjorie's bed. Maybe there was something terribly wrong with her. I tried not to panic, or at least not let it show in my voice when I said, "Yeah, I don't like it."

"I am sorry about that. Most of this is my fault."

"Did you put my cardboard house back in my room?"

"What do you mean? Hasn't it always been in your room?"

"No, Mom helped me move it down here last week."

"Really. How come?"

"I don't know. I was sick of it, I guess."

"Right." Marjorie made a show of looking around the basement. "It's not down here, is it? No. They must've moved it back."

"They?"

"The TV people. I like calling them that. *The TV People.* And they have TVs for heads and their faces can change when the channels change. Creepy, right?"

"I guess. Why would they put the house back in my room?"

Marjorie looked bored but quickly explained that The TV People had been in our house all day and all night yesterday, with actors pretending to be us, and they were filming what they called the "reenactment scenes." They'd needed the house back in my room so they could film Actor-Merry finding the cardboard house covered in growing things.

I took it all in, not quite sure how she could know all that, and said, "So, it wasn't you, then."

"Nope, dope. I didn't move your house back to your room. I swear." Marjorie crossed her heart and held up her right hand.

I didn't say anything. What she'd said to me about Actor-Merry made sense, but I wasn't sure if she was telling the full truth. It was possible that Marjorie brought the house up herself and The TV People were happy to find it there and use it.

"Merry. You have to trust me. I'm still your big sister. I wouldn't steer you wrong. Right?"

I looked down and nodded. I picked up my dropped crackers, then pried the plastic straw off the side of one of the juice boxes and stabbed its pointed end through the small tin-foil-covered hole.

She said, "I'm going to let you in on a big secret, so that you'll trust me again."

"Is it about Mom or Dad?"

"No. It's about me. It's the biggest secret of all so you can't, you can't, you can't, you *can't* tell Mom or anyone else. Okay?"

I wasn't sure if I wanted to hear such a big secret. It might not fit in my head and then it would spill out everywhere. But at the same time, my skin prickled with wanting to know what it was. "Okay. Tell me."

"I am not possessed by a demon or anything like that."

My face must've performed some impressive contortions because Marjorie doubled over laughing. "What, didn't Dad tell you why this is all happening with the show and the priests? Didn't he tell you that they believe Satan or one of his demon peeps lives deep inside me and makes me do terrible, bad-girl things?" When she said "Satan" she crouched down low, widened her eyes, and spread her arms out wide. It made the word extra scary.

I was embarrassed, and meekly explained that Mom and Dad hadn't mentioned Satan or any demons to me, and they hadn't told me what exactly was wrong with her, only that everyone was just trying to help her get through a rough time.

"Jesus, that's messed up. And I'm the one they sent away for two weeks." Marjorie crossed her arms and walked in a tight circle, as though deciding which one of a million possible directions to go in. "Actually, I am possessed, only

I'm possessed by something so much older and cooler than Satan."

I stood still and stared at her. When she said *I am possessed* I pictured a giant green hand closing over her, hiding her from me forever.

"Ideas. I'm possessed by ideas. Ideas that are as old as humanity, maybe older, right? Maybe those ideas were out there just floating around before us, just waiting to be thought up. Maybe we don't think them, we pluck them out from another dimension, or another mind." Marjorie seemed so pleased with herself, and I wondered if this was something new she just thought up or something she'd told someone before.

I asked, "Is that what the voices in your head tell you?"

"Hey, how do you know about the voices?"

"You've talked about the voices before. Waking up at night, and at the kitchen table."

"Oh right, I guess I have. Hard to keep track of everything, you know. The voices, yeah, I don't know." Marjorie's bright, triumphant tone faded. "I think I'm just imagining them, you know?" She paused, wrapped her arms around her chest, and hesitantly started talking again. "They're not there most of the time but if I start thinking about them or obsessing about them, they happen, almost like I make them happen, like I'm inside my own head only I don't know it's me in there. So I'm trying not to think about them, and now when the voices come back I listen to my iPod on level a billion and drown them out. Seems to work. I can handle them now. No biggie."

"Okay."

"Hey, look, Merry." Marjorie let her arms fall down to her sides, laughed, and shook her head. "Don't you worry about me. I know I've done some weird shit while I've been figuring things out, and the voices are real, but the truth is, I'm fine. And I've been pretending. I've been faking it."

"Faking what?"

"Faking that I've been possessed by something that's making me do *terrible* things."

"Why?"

"What do you mean why? Isn't it obvious yet?" Marjorie looked around the basement and at me like she was genuinely confused, like she didn't know where she was. "Mom and Dad were totally stressed about money and the house, I hated being in stupid high school, and then I started hearing the voices, stress induced probably, yeah, but still it sort of freaked me out. Then I got super pissed when they started sending me to Dr. Hamilton and his fastest prescription pad in the east, when they were the ones who should've been getting help, not me. They're a mess, you've had to notice that they're a total mess, right? And then Dad added to the mess with his new finding God BS, so I decided I'd just keep pushing it, see how far I could go, and I was going to leave you out of it, but I got mad at you for telling Mom about my stories, and by the time that super creepy Father Wanderly got involved, it was easy to keep pushing, keep pretending, keep it all going, and now I don't have to take Dr. Hamilton's pills anymore and we have the show, right? You guys should be *thanking* me. I saved the house. I saved us, all of us, and I'm going to make us famous."

Even as an earnest and gullible eight-year-old and without the gifts and hindrances of hindsight, I saw the gaping holes in her story, and I knew that Marjorie didn't really believe in what she was saying. She was trying to convince herself that she was okay and in control of what was happening to her and to us. In that moment, I was afraid for her instead of being afraid of her. And I wanted to help the house and family too.

I asked, "So, wait, where do your ideas really come from?"

"Everywhere. The Internet, mostly." Marjorie laughed with a hand over her mouth.

"You mean the song and the molasses story—"

"Internet. Internet."

"—the growing things?"

"That one's mine. That one is—real. You still can't ever forget that story, Miss Merry. Hey, isn't this basement just like the basement in the growing-things story? Remember the part where you were in the basement and the growing things came out and up from the dirt, Mom's poisoned and buried body dangling off the vines? So creepy, right? You can almost see it happening right now. You can almost feel the growing things worming up between our toes."

Marjorie bent down and tickled my ankles.

"Stop it!" I slapped her hands away.

"Ow! Merry-slaps are the worst. I have no idea how someone so little can hit so hard."

I laughed, then bared my teeth and raised my free hand, threatening her with more Merry-slaps. Marjorie mock-screamed and I chased her around the basement. I whiffed on trying to slap her butt as she ran by and dashed into and up the bulkhead stairwell. Then the lights went out.

I gasped, losing all my air. Marjorie screamed, but then started laughing. She said, "Come sit with me in here, Merry. I'll hold your hand."

I stood in the middle of the basement. It was dark, but not pitch-black as rectangles of weak light filtered down from the two basement windows. Still, I could see only shadows and outlines, and I couldn't see Marjorie.

I said, "What did you do? Turn the lights back on!"

"That wasn't me. Why do you always blame me for everything? Stay where you are, monkey. I'll come to you."

I heard her bare feet slowly sliding and shuffling on the cement bulkhead stairs and it sounded like she had many more than two feet. Was she walking on all fours down the stairs because it was too dark to see? I didn't want to wait for her or stay where I was. I wanted to sprint back up to the first floor and leave her down here, let her wait, watch, and see if any growing things would finally sprout from the dirt floor. It was her idea anyway.

"Is someone down here?" Dad's voice echoed, followed shortly by heavy pounding on the basement stairs. He and a crew member I didn't know were at the bottom of the stairs and turned the corner before I could announce myself. The crewman had a flashlight.

"Merry, what the hell are you doing? You didn't mess around with the breakers, did you?"

"What? Dad. No. I just came down to get a snack." I held up my spent juice box and unopened pack of crackers. And I also looked to the foundation wall on my right and the bulkhead stairs. Marjorie hadn't come out yet nor had she announced herself.

He said, "Did Mom say you could do that? I guess that's fine, right?"

I wasn't sure if he was asking me if this was fine or the crewman, or if he knew Marjorie was down here and was trying to trick her out. Either way, Dad didn't wait for an answer. He walked past me toward the circuit breaker panel that was on the wall between the bulkhead stairs and the washer/dryer.

"What do you think, turning on our coffee maker from 1975 fried it?" The crewman laughed politely. Dad opened the panel, flipped the breaker, and the lights came back on. Marjorie must've been up at the top of the stairs, pressed right up against the bulkhead doors because I still couldn't see her. She wasn't coming down.

Dad said, "Come on, Merry. You've got your snack. I don't want you playing down here."

"Okay."

Dad put a hand on my back and gently nudged me. His hand was warm and a little sweaty. He and the crewman followed me back up to the first floor. They shut the basement door. I scurried under the dining room table and watched the door. I thought about opening the door for Marjorie, not that it was locked or she needed it opened for her. It just felt like something I should do, but I didn't. When I was munching on my last peanut butter cracker, I heard our front door open slowly, even with all of the commotion and conversations around me. I heard the whisper of the outside coming in, and I heard her quiet but hurried footsteps pattering up the stairs in the front foyer, and again, it sounded like she had more than two feet.

Later, when the crew was done with setup, Barry the director and Dad took me upstairs and told me that the sunroom was now the "confessional room." We would and could go in there by ourselves and talk to the camera about what had happened, or talk about anything that was on our minds. For my first confessional, I went in with the intention of saying only "I want my sunroom back" and then I would fold my arms obstinately and glare at the camera, or maybe I'd scuttle behind the camera and actually tear down the terrible black cloth covering the bay window and explain myself by saying the room couldn't breathe with the window being covered and it could die.

Instead when I went in there and pressed the record button like they'd shown me I thought about Marjorie in the basement and how she had lied about faking everything and saving the house.

I could pretend, I could fake it, I could lie, and help save the house too. So I did.

I told the camera a story about Marjorie sneaking up on me in the basement, her saying weird stuff to me like she had before, her eyes being all white, her eating dirt, making her tongue into a black worm, and how she made the lights go out. I told the camera that Marjorie was being really scary and that something evil was now living inside her.

CHAPTER 17

WE'D BEEN LIVING with the crew for two weeks. It was a Sunday morning, the same day of the show's premiere. Dad woke me up and tried to make me go to church. There were no mounted cameras in any of our bedrooms so he brought Jenn the camerawoman up with him, which totally backfired. I'm sure he was thinking that as the good daughter I wouldn't be able to say no to church with Jenn and her camera watching. I knew that not only could I say no, but that he couldn't get mad and start yelling at me. So I said no, and I told him that church was creepy. I smiled lazily, reached out to hug him around the neck when I said it, and I meant the creepy part as our little joke. When I was in kindergarten I'd gone through a phase where I'd described everything I didn't like as creepy. Mom had been annoyed by it but Dad had loved it and had quizzed me on what was or wasn't creepy: Milk, mud, and airplanes were good; pickles, shoe-laces, and purple were creepy. Dad didn't think my "church is creepy" joke was funny though. He dodged my hug, let out a sigh, and said, "You shouldn't say that, Merry. It isn't right." He did an awkward little dance trying to get around Jenn and then stormed off down the hallway. Jenn followed. I felt bad enough that I tiptoed to the sunroom, peeled back a corner of the drop cloth, and watched him and Jenn drive off to church.

When I got downstairs, Mom was at the table with the writer, Ken Fletcher, and Tony the cam-eraman. Ken had a little black notebook on the table in front of him and he jotted down some notes. He was my parents' age but he looked younger. He wore black Chuck Taylor sneak-ers, jeans, and dark, logo-less T-shirts. He would talk with me whenever he could, and he actu-ally listened to what I had to say. Not like when other crew members would ask how I was doing; they were only asking to be polite, asking for the sake of asking. Tony the cameraman had over-sized earphones looped around his giraffe neck. I didn't like Tony. He wasn't friendly. His beard was too curly and his fingernails were too long and clicky. He was creepy.

The three of them were eating breakfast sand-wiches. Mom had saved one for me. I quickly pulled mine apart and ate just the cheese and egg part. I told Mom that I had a lot of energy and she had to help me get rid of it with a timed obstacle course. Ken laughed, closed his notebook, and wrapped it with a red rubber band. Tony left the kitchen with his camera perched on his shoulder, announcing he was taking a break.

Mom said, "Really, Merry? But you just ate."

I grabbed Mom's arm and pulled her down, her face almost touching mine. "Yes!"

"Merry, stop it. Okay." Mom turned to Ken and said, "We do this sometimes. She has lots of energy."

Ken laughed. It was a loud and bright sound. He said, "I love it."

Mom said, "Okay, listen carefully. Run out to the living room, sit on the couch, then go into the dining room, do two laps around the table, then upstairs to your bedroom, lie down, feet all the way off the floor, then come back down and shake Ken's hand."

I was so pleased that I had to shake hands with Ken. I wanted to show off for him, Mom knew this, and indulged. I said, "Got it. Where's your phone? You have to time me on your phone." I jumped up and down and tugged on Mom's shirtsleeve.

"Relax, I'll just count."

Ken said, "My watch has a second hand, I'll time you. Ready—"

"Wait a minute!" I yelled in a Muppet voice and scrambled out of my chair and into imaginary starter blocks. "Okay."

"Ready. Set." Ken paused long enough for me

to turn, look at him, and give him a scary monster face. "Go!"

I sprinted around the house, following Mom's instructions to the letter. Racing to the finish, I ploughed into the kitchen like a wrecking ball, slamming into Ken. I tried to shake his hand to end it, but he kept moving it away. I yelled, "Hey," with mock outrage, then latched on to his arm, held it still, and finally was able to grab his hand.

Mom said, "Yeah. She's shy."

"Clearly. And strong. Wow." Ken let his arm hang like it was dead.

"What was my time? What was my time?"

"Fifty-two seconds."

"I can beat that."

I ran the course two more times, with my personal best being forty-six seconds. After the third run I told Ken that he should write my obstacle course into the show. Mom's and Ken's smiles dimmed a bit at that, and they both took synchronized sips of their coffees.

Mom said, "Why don't you go outside and burn off the rest of your energy? You probably shouldn't be sprinting around the house with all the expensive equipment we have in here now."

"No." I tried not to sound whiny, but there were way too many *o*'s in my *no*.

Ken said, "I'll go outside with you. Can we kick the soccer ball around?"

"Yeah, okay!"

Mom said, "Ken, you don't have to."

"No, it's okay. I want to get outside. Nice, crisp fall day. And I want to see what kind of soccer player Merry is. I've heard she's real good."

I sprinted out of the kitchen to get a sweatshirt, afraid Mom would change his mind somehow. I heard her say, "She's relentless."

LEAVES COVERED THE BACKYARD, AND the wind had blown a pile into my small, rickety soccer net. Thin white PVC pipes struggled to hold its barely upright shape. The crossbar sagged in the middle. Ken wasn't outside yet so I cleared the goal of as many leaves as I could, and pushed the rest though the square holes in the netting. The leaves were wet and I wiped my hands on my jeans and inspected them for ticks, even though it was too cold for ticks.

I marched around crunching leaves and keeping the soccer ball between my feet while waiting for Ken to come out. I had a white fleece sweatshirt on, with multicolored peace symbols all over it. It was tight and too small, but it was my favorite.

Ken walked out of the back door wearing a thick brown and green sweater and a scarf. He bounded down the small back porch, rubbed his hands together, and said, "Brrr, it's colder than I thought. We'll be warm after I score a bunch of goals on you, though."

I said, "Bring it on, old man!"

We jumped right into a game of one-on-one. It was slow going with all the leaves in the way. It was tough to get solid footing. Ken took it easy on me initially, which made me play harder. I did get the sense Ken used to be very good, but his feet were heavier now and weren't keeping up with the rest of him. He fell a few times and he stepped on my foot once. I didn't let on how much it hurt. As the game went on, he got winded and I had the advantage of knowing how to use the slight downward pitch of the backyard. I won the slightly rigged game five to four with a goal that almost knocked the net down; the ball skimmed off the crossbar and wrapped around the left post.

After the game we passed the ball back and forth. Ken was down toward the bottom of our yard, I was at the top.

"You're a very good player, Merry. I'm impressed."

I said, "Thanks! Your cheeks look like big red apples."

Ken kicked me the ball and then bent over, putting his hands on his knees, breathing heavily. "Well, you kicked my butt, Merry. Your cheeks look like little crabapples."

"Crabapples? What are those?" I laughed. I imagined apples with pincer claws and how difficult it would be to pick them off a tree and bake them in a pie.

"They're little and more purple than red.

Can't really eat them. Believe me, I've tried. We had a crabapple tree in my front yard when I was a kid."

The lazy passing morphed into a playful competition. Our passes became crisper. We both switched legs and stopping techniques. Ken let the ball roll up his foot and into the air, then kicked it with his other foot. I tried to do the same but the ball rolled up my leg and hit me in the chin.

"Ow!"

"You okay?"

"Yeah."

I asked, "Did you know that I have to ask permission to go into the confessional room now?"

"Yes, I heard that."

"It's not fair because everyone else in my family can go in whenever they want."

"Well, you have been going in there a lot, and there's only so much we can show in an hour of TV, which is more like forty-two minutes with all the commercials, and more like thirty-two minutes with the post-commercial scene resets—Whoa!"

I kicked the ball extra hard and a little wide of him. The ball went crashing into the line of tall bushes at the end of our property. I said, "I like to talk. I can't help it!"

Ken had to go in deep to pluck the ball out of the bushes. He walked back up the hill to me with the ball cradled in his right arm. He said,

"That's it. I'm cooked, and I have to do some work."

I wanted to shout *No, stay out here with me*, but I fought the urge. Instead my whole body slumped and went slack.

Ken said, "Come on. I have a great idea. Follow me out front." I grabbed the soccer ball, quickly scrambled up the porch to the back door, tossed the ball into the catchall shoe bin in the mud room, then ran back to Ken. I walked with him around the house, let him lead even though he was taking us the hardest way to go. His scarf got caught as we weaved through and dodged low-hanging tree branches before we finally emerged into the safety of the driveway.

"Where are we going?"

"You'll see."

I ran up beside him and said, "I don't think my parents are going to let me watch the show when it's on tonight."

"You probably shouldn't. It's not a show for kids."

"But I'm *on* it!"

"I know you are, Merry. I know it's frustrating, but I can show you some edited parts, the parts with just you and nothing too scary. Is that okay?"

"What's the big deal? It's supposed to be real, right? Just like *Finding Bigfoot*. It's all about what really happened, and I was there when it happened."

"I don't know quite what to say to that. Yes, you were here when it happened, but you weren't with your sister all the time, you didn't see everything, did you?" He paused and I shrugged. "You should probably talk to your mom and dad about it. It's—It's a scary show. Too intense for you, I think."

We walked across the front lawn to the TV crew's trailer, which was parked half on the street, half on our front yard. Its passenger-side tires had sunk partway into the lawn.

"I've told everyone at school and they're all going to watch it. So I don't know why I can't watch it too."

Ken didn't say anything to that. He knocked on the trailer door, and called out "Everyone decent in there?" Then he whispered down to me, "Tony will change his clothes right in the middle of the trailer."

"Ew, creepy."

"Totally. So, you wait here. I know he's in there. He might be napping."

Ken disappeared inside. I backed away from the trailer and tried to watch his progress through the trailer windows. I couldn't see him. I did watch the trailer tilt and shift as he walked its length. Ken wasn't gone long and came back out carrying a small black nylon bag. He didn't say anything, just dangled it in front of me and then walked to the front steps. I nipped at his heels.

"Here, let's sit. So we're going to call this the

Merry-cam." He opened the bag and took out a small handheld camera.

"Cool!" I took it and turned it carefully over in my hands. Its metal and plastic was cold and beautiful. It was practically all lens with a small pop-out screen tucked to its side.

"It's yours to use however you want. You can film all you like. You can do your own confessionals whenever and wherever you want. I grabbed this for you too." Ken took out a small black notebook wrapped in a red rubber band from his pocket. It looked just like his, but was half the size. "You can use it to write down a short description of the stuff you filmed that you think is important and could be on the show. When you have good stuff or when you fill up the camera's memory, we can download it, go through your notebook, and decide what we should watch and what we should delete." Ken showed me how to turn it on, how to delete the file if I didn't want it, how to zoom, how to turn on a small spotlight, and how to charge the battery.

"Just promise you won't go to Barry with your footage. You have to come to me first. Deal?"

"Deal."

We shook on it. Then he said he had to do some work and headed back to the trailer.

I ran inside and didn't tell Mom about the camera. I wanted to already have used it so it would be harder for her to tell me that I couldn't have it. I wondered if Marjorie had her own camera too, and thought about showing her, but decided against it. She might try to take it away and use it for herself. I went up to the confessional room and turned the camera on. I said: "This is Merry's first video. And I don't need you anymore, confessional room."

Marjorie's bedroom door opened behind me. I turned around and Marjorie was in the hallway, yawning and stretching, hair all over the place, sticking out at odd angles. I pointed the camera at her. "Marjorie. Look what Ken gave to me!"

She groaned, blocked her face with one hand, gave me the middle finger with the other.

ON OUR PREMIERE NIGHT, WE had a full house: Barry, Ken, Tony, Jenn, a handful of other crew I didn't know by name, a tall man in a jacket and tie, and Father Wanderly as well. Everyone milled about the first floor, eating pizza and drinking out of red cups. Mom and Marjorie were the only ones missing. They were upstairs in Marjorie's room, hiding from all of us.

The atmosphere was strange; sort of an almost-party. Crew exchanged fist bumps and handshakes when they thought no one was watching. Dad and Father Wanderly gravely thanked each person for their participation, told them they were all doing God's work, reaffirmed that this process was going to help Marjorie get better. Ken kept to himself, appeared to be very nervous, and looked at me like he was wondering if my parents were really going to let me watch the episode. I walked around with my camera filming it all. I caught a snippet of a conversation going on among the tall man in the jacket and tie, Barry, and Father Wanderly. They used words like *capital*, *contributions*, and *campaign*. When Barry saw me, he waved for me to come over to them, and introduced me by saying, "*This* little star is Merry." He never told me the other man's name, or if he did, I no longer remember it. Barry said, "There would be no show without his help. His generous help." The men all laughed, the one in the tie laughing hardest. I didn't like him. He was too tall and stood like he had metal rods inside his back. His brown jacket had dark patches on the elbows, his hair was a weird color, like an almost brown, not a real brown, his skin looked fake, and everything was too close together on his face. He told me I was a special young lady and that he was excited to meet me. I said, "I know. Thanks." The three men laughed like I'd said the funniest joke in the world and then moved me along. So I went around the party stopping the people that I knew for a brief interview in which I asked them a purposefully silly question. I worked my way back to Father Wanderly eventually. He was standing alone next to the dining room table munching on miniature pretzels.

I asked him, "Would you rather have legs the size of fingers or fingers the size of legs?"

He said, "I can't say I've ever been asked that before. Both options sound dreadful, don't they," and then he waved bye to the camera.

Marjorie and Mom were still upstairs. Marjorie was always in her room with Mom, Dad, or occasionally Father Wanderly and a cameraperson. Since my basement confessional all things Marjorie had been quiet. She ate lunch and dinner with us, went to school some days, and on others she did not. She listened to music a lot. She texted and received texts in random flurries. She occasionally watched TV with us, but mostly she was the ghost of our house, haunting her own bedroom. I began to really believe she was faking and that nothing was wrong with her. Despite my promise to not say anything, I thought about telling Ken what she'd told me. I didn't want to risk doing anything like that right then because I wanted to stay under everyone's radar and somehow manage to watch the show.

Right around my usual bedtime, which was forty-five minutes before the 10:00 P.M. premiere of the pilot episode, Mom came downstairs and announced that it was time for me to go to bed. There would be no arguing. The whole downstairs group waved at me and issued a reverent and relieved chorus of "Good night, Merry."

Dad followed me up the stairs, kissed the top of my head, shoved me into the bathroom, and wished me a quick, "Good night," before heading back down to the party.

In my room, Mom had untied my robe belt

from the doorknob and was already sitting on the edge of my bed and fiddling with the alarm clock radio. She tuned it to a station that advertised playing "bedtime magic." She said, "I'm going to leave the radio on in case things get too loud downstairs."

I didn't argue with her. I would just shut the radio off after she left. Instead, I breathed in her face.

"Yuck, what are you doing?"

"I just brushed my teeth. Smells good, right?"

"Yes, smells wonderful. Get in bed. Are you going to sleep in your clothes again?"

"Yeah, they're comfy." I was wearing a long-sleeved Wonder Woman T-shirt and blue sweatpants. I liked sleeping in my clothes in case I had to run out into the hallway at night.

I put my pocket notebook, my camera, and my glasses on top of my dresser, and I plugged in the power cord like Ken had shown me. The red light meant it was charging. I placed the camera where I could see it from my bed because I wanted to see when the light would turn to green.

I crawled over Mom's lap and under the covers. She playfully smacked my butt.

"Mom!"

"Sorry. It was right there. Hey, did you put that blanket over your house today?"

"Yes," I said, and ducked deeper into the covers. Earlier that afternoon, I'd positioned my camera on the bed and had filmed myself throwing an old, thin, blue baby blanket over the top of my house. It was just big enough to cover the windows in the front.

"We can take the house back downstairs tomorrow if you want." She didn't ask why I'd covered it with a blanket, and she didn't say anything about who or how or why someone had put it back in my room.

"Okay."

The overhead light was still on in my room. Mom brushed my bangs off my forehead, and had trouble holding my stare. She looked older with her puffy, bloodshot eyes. She gave me an unsure, sad smile. I thought about telling her that her teeth looked really yellow, that she was smoking way too much.

I turned over onto my side, away from her, and asked her to rub my back. She rushed through singing a quick song, her go-to song, about falling down an avalanche.

"Are you going back to Marjorie's room or are you going downstairs to watch it?"

"I'm going to go downstairs, have a glass of wine, or four, and I'm going to watch it. I don't want to, but I think I have to."

"I want to watch it."

"I know you do, honey. You're being such a good girl with all of this. I love you and am so proud of you." Mom's voice was quiet, quieter than the radio.

"Is Marjorie going to watch it?"

"No. She's not."

"Does she want to?"

"She hasn't asked."

I was out of questions so I closed my eyes. Mom shut off the light, then stayed and rubbed my back for another minute. When I opened my eyes again she wasn't there anymore and it was a little after one in the morning. I sat up, mad at myself for having missed it all. If nothing else, I'd wanted to try to hear the show, or hear them watching the show.

The charging indicator light on the camera was still red. I didn't care. I got up and brought the camera and notebook back to bed with me, shutting off the radio on the way back. I left my glasses on the dresser. Things were fuzzier around the edges but I could see well enough without them.

I sent my ears out as far as I could but I didn't hear anything happening downstairs. I turned on the camera's LED light and pointed it at the notebook. I reviewed the day's work and decided I could delete the following: my full-sprint tour of the house and backyard; the ten minutes of spy-camming who came in and out of the crew's trailer; the eight minutes of long-distance footage of the Cox kids playing basketball in their driveway; my taping Jenn taping me, with her turning away from the camera first and giving me a raspberry; the footage of Marjorie's closed door.

I put my notebook under my pillow. I popped out the camera's flip screen, deleted some of the files, and played back the most recent footage of the crew party downstairs. I watched the conversation between Barry, Father Wanderly, and the jacket-and-tie man. The mic didn't pick up what they'd said, but they clinked their plastic cups together and passed handshakes all around their little circle. Then I watched everyone saying *Good night, Merry*; their collective call crackling in the camera's small speakers, their faces jumpy and blurry as I walked past them. I kept rewatching and I tried to pick out individual voices to hear who really meant their *Good night*.

I may have fallen asleep while watching the video, because what I remember next is the camera resting on my chest, the flip screen dark but the LED light still on, pointed at my feet. There was a scratching noise coming from my left, from the other side of the room. It wasn't loud, but it was constant, rhythmic.

I sat up, hit record, and aimed the camera out across the room like it was a powerful weapon. Its white light diffused through the room along with the scratching noise, which grew louder. The closet door was shut, the blanket on the cardboard house still there, my piles of books and stuffed animals intact.

I whispered, "Marjorie? Stop it. Who's there?"

The scratching noise stopped. I thought about running from the room, pictured it in my head, but I saw my feet hitting the floor and then thin, skeleton-white hands reaching out from under my bed and pulling me under.

I sat and waited and heard nothing, and the

nothing seemed to last for hours. I waited. My camera bleeped at me, and I yelped. A red number blinked on the flip screen. I didn't have much battery power left.

I watched the blinking red of the screen and then looked over at the blanket-covered house. In the LED white light the blue blanket looked like it was the same white color as the cardboard house, or the same white the house used to be before its growing-things transformation. I stared at or into the blanket, trying to see the blue that I knew was there but wasn't seeing, and then the blanket was sucked inside the house through the shutters of the front window, as though that window was a ravenous black hole. It was pulled in so roughly that the blanket rubbing against the cardboard sounded like the house was being torn open. The chimney piece flew off and landed on the foot of my bed. It all happened so fast, I didn't lose my breath and drop the camera into my lap until after the blanket had disappeared.

I somehow found my voice and said, "I'll scream for Mom. You'll get in big trouble, Marjorie." I pointed the camera back at the house and, feeling more angry than scared, and wanting to ensure Marjorie's torment of me was on video, to have this as a part of the official, permanent record, I added, "This isn't funny."

The shutters had rebounded and again covered up most of the window. There weren't any noises coming from inside the house. From the bed, the LED camera light didn't penetrate the small opening between the shutters. I couldn't see Marjorie.

"I'm videoing this, you know." I waited for a reaction. There wasn't any. So I hit her as hard as I could with, "I know you're faking. You told me you were faking." Letting out her biggest secret while recording, I thought for sure that she'd come out of the house, mad at me, telling me that I was a baby and couldn't take a joke, and that she was doing this just to make the show better, and didn't I want to help? And I would say yes, but I'd also cry and make her feel bad so that she'd stay in my room and sleep in my bed, and then we'd delete what I'd recorded and I would've been happy doing so.

"Marjorie, come on." I hopped off the bed, looking at what was in front of me through the flip screen of the camera, which was much easier for me than seeing the real thing. I tapped the front door with my foot. Still no reaction. I peeled back one of the shutters and slowly traced the house's interior and floor with the camera's headlight. The crayon drawings on the back wall were crudely drawn cave paintings and they hung at skewed angles. My blue blanket was in a lumpy heap on the floor. I whispered my sister's name, and when I did, the blanket started to rise slowly. The rising part was long and thin. It was her arm. It had to have been her arm; she was raising it so that it looked like a snake head, or a vine. I whispered her name again and the rising part stopped. The blanket bubbled with activity underneath it, and then the rising part widened, fattened, to the size of her head, a costumed Halloween ghost without the eyeholes or mouth hole, as she sat there under the blanket with her legs crossed, or maybe she was crouched, balanced on the balls of her feet, her body concealed by the blanket and by the house's window frame.

I told her to get out, to leave my room, to go away.

Those skeleton-white hands I'd previously imagined shooting out from under my bed came out from under the blanket and wrapped around her neck. They pulled the blanket down over her face, skintight, and the blanket formed a shroud with dark valleys for eyes and mouth, her nose flattened against the unyielding cloth. Her mouth moved, and choking growls came out. Those hands squeezed so the blanket pulled tighter and her blanket-covered mouth opened wider, and she shook her head, thrashing it around violently as she gasped and pleaded with someone to stop, or maybe she said she was trying to stop. Her hands were still closed around her own neck, and I'm sure it was some sort of optical illusion or a trick or kink of memory because her neck couldn't have gotten as thin as I remember it getting, and then the rest of her body began to spasm and lash out, knocking into the house, her feet jabbing out from underneath and recoiling like a snake's tongue.

I took another step back and suddenly the

cardboard house exploded and shot out toward me. The roof smashed into my face and knocked me over. I fell backward, landing hard on my butt and with my back pinned up against my bed. I managed to keep hold of the camera, which, along with my arms and hands, was stuck inside the chimney slot of the house. I couldn't see Marjorie over the house she'd dropped on me but I heard her run out of my room and into the hallway.

I punched and kicked the fallen house, the now loose flaps and folds tangled in my arms and legs like thick weeds. The house finally gave in, slumped off, and rolled away toward the closet. I scrambled onto my feet. My blanket was on the ground, in a harmless heap pinned under the collapsed cardboard. Determined to video an escaping Marjorie, I ran out into the hallway.

She wasn't there. The light from my camera failed to reach the end of the hallway and the open mouth of the confessional room. The hallway walls faded and frayed into the dark. I strained to hear movement from Marjorie, from anybody, and all I could hear was my own revved-up breathing.

I walked down the hall to her door, the whole time expecting Marjorie to jump out of a darkened corner, the bathroom doorway, the top of the stairs, or from the confessional room. Her door was closed. I tried pushing it open with my foot but it was latched shut. I turned the knob and threw my body weight into it, and stumbled inside.

Marjorie was in bed, under the covers, lying on her side, her head turned away from me. I kept the camera's light focused on the back of her head. I whispered her name repeatedly as I walked until I was standing right next to her, the light focused into a tight beam on her profile.

Her eyes were closed and she was breathing deeply and looked to be asleep and to have been asleep for quite a while.

"Marjorie?" I poked her shoulder. No response or movement. I watched her on the flip screen: The covers slowly rose and fell with each breath, and her face looked green. I kept the camera light on but paused the recording with a small electronic *blip*.

Marjorie opened an eye and rolled it back toward me. She said, "Did you get it all?" in a low, creaky voice. She calmly repeated herself when I didn't respond initially.

"Yeah."

"Good girl. Show it to your pal Ken tomorrow after school. Go back to bed."

I was suddenly exhausted and could've curled up and gone to sleep right there on her floor. I shuffled out of her room and into the hallway. I looked back and Marjorie was sitting up, muttering to herself, and plugging earbuds into her phone, the music already on and loud, something with heavy, rhythmic synthesizers. Marjorie snuggled back into bed and whispered, "Shut the door, Merry," but I didn't.

Out in the hallway I found Tony the cameraman easing his way up the stairs, night-vision camera perched on his shoulder. He didn't appear to be in any giant rush to get all the way up here.

He sounded annoyed when he said, "What's going on, Merry? Did I miss something?"

I said, "No, nothing."

He asked me something else but I turned and walked across the hall into my parents' bedroom. I shut the door quietly behind me and on Tony who was now at the top of the stairs, filming me. I'd felt the camera pointed at my back. I stood behind the door and listened to him creep a little farther down the hallway and pause at Marjorie's door. Her door creaked and then latched, and Tony walked back downstairs, the wood groaning under his giant, sloppy feet.

I put my camera down on the cluttered nightstand next to Mom's head. I crawled over her and into the bed, easily fitting myself between my parents who slept as far away from each other as they could.

THE NEXT MORNING I WORE my best dress because it was what someone who was on a TV show was supposed to wear. It was dark maroon, squared at the shoulders, and short-sleeved so I wore a white cardigan over it. Mom had bragged about buying it for only ten bucks. She tried to talk me out of wearing the dress to school (it wasn't warm enough, I'd get it dirty at recess or lunch or art class . . .), but I wouldn't budge.

I couldn't wait to ask my friends and classmates if they'd seen me on TV last night. I figured that at least some of my friends might've been able to fool their parents into letting them watch it because they wouldn't have known what it was about or what was on it.

Dad offered to drive me to school, but Mom said she would, and then she was going to run some errands. Plus she wanted him to wake up Marjorie and ask her if she was going to school or Dr. Hamilton today; she had to choose one to go to, she couldn't stay home. A brief, controlled argument ensued. With cameras and crew members watching, my parents had to keep their dramas quick and to the point. I didn't wait for its rushed and hushed conclusion. I sprinted out the door ahead of Mom, who yelled after me to wait for her. I didn't wait. I ran to our car parked in the driveway and started yanking on the locked back door.

"Mom, it's locked, come on!"

As I walked around the car to try the doors on the other side, I noticed there was a small group, maybe five people, holding handwritten signs in the street near our front lawn. Barry was talking to them. I couldn't hear him but he didn't seem happy.

Mom said, "I told you to wait for me." She unlocked the doors. I asked her who those people were. She sighed and said, "I don't know but they better not be here when I get back." I ducked down in my seat as we drove by them, resting my face at the bottom of the window frame so they'd only see the top of my head and my glasses peering out. An old man pointed at us as we drove by and held up his sign, but it was spun around backward and by the time he flipped it around, we were too far away to read it.

At school, when I breathlessly asked my friends if they'd seen the show, most said they weren't allowed to watch because it was an adult show and/or it was on so late. A few said they'd seen commercials and it looked creepy. Samantha asked why I wore a fancy dress to school. Cara said that she saw some of it but didn't see me in the parts that she watched, but then it was too scary to keep watching. Brian said the show was gross. At recess and lunch a pack of fourth and fifth graders, including the neighbor that Marjorie had punched in the face on my behalf a few years ago, made fun of me and Marjorie and called my whole family a bunch of freaks. I immediately told on them. I was more upset that, of my friends, only Cara and Brian had seen it, and they didn't have anything good to say about it. I asked teachers too, and my favorite, Mrs. Newcomb said, politely, that she hadn't seen the show, that, "I don't watch much TV, I'm afraid. I'm just too busy planning for our school day!"

When I got home there were more people

standing out front holding signs. They stood behind yellow police tape. Mom said, "We may have to get used to this for a little while," then went on to say that they were religious fanatics who didn't approve of what we were doing, and there was nothing we could do about them as long as they stayed off our property. Dad had apparently tried to intimidate them away from our house and he even made physical contact with a few of the protesters, grabbing them by the arm and pulling them down the street. Father Wanderly had intervened and calmed Dad down. Father Wanderly was still out there talking to a few of them. Even though it was cold out, his forehead looked sweaty. They waved their signs at us as we pulled into the driveway. Some signs had names and numbers on them, which I found out later were references to Bible verses. Two signs had red block letters. One sign read: JUDGMENT IS COMING. Another: DON'T PROFIT OFF THE DEVIL'S WORK!

Although this new development was interesting, I decided it wasn't my problem and didn't involve me, at least not yet. I ran into the house and changed back into my sweats and Wonder Woman T-shirt. Then Ken and I and my camera went into the crew's trailer. There was a little living room section toward the front with a mini-kitchen and couch, but the rest of it was monitors, equipment, and black chairs with wheels. He hooked up my camera to his laptop, which he'd synced to one of the large wall monitors and we watched the previous night's footage. We heard the scratching noise. We listened to me announce to the cardboard house that I knew she was faking. We saw the blanket disappear. Ken jumped in his chair and grabbed my arm when it happened. We saw the blanket rise inside the house and the skeleton hands wrap around her neck. The hands didn't look as long and as thin as they had when it was really happening. We watched the house fly into the camera. We saw the lens pressed up against a drawing of Marjorie's face, her mouth a big red O while I grunted and struggled to get the house off me. We watched as the camera bobbed down the hall and into Marjorie's room where she appeared to be asleep and I couldn't wake her up.

When it ended Ken said, "Wow. Are you okay, Merry?"

"I'm okay. It didn't look as scary as I remember it."

"I bet. But still, watching it was—That was really scary."

"Is this something you can use?"

"Yes. Most definitely. But, really, are you okay?"

"Yeah. Just a bad day at school." Then I told him about my friends and Mrs. Newcomb not watching or liking the show, and how the older kids made fun of me.

Ken said, "I am sorry, Merry. But as I'm sure your parents have told you, that kind of stuff is probably going to get worse as more episodes air. I think this year at school will be really hard, and it's certainly not fair to you, not at all. What we're doing here will be hard for people to understand."

"I know. I'll be okay. I'm tough."

"Yeah, you are. You're the toughest person I know. Just make sure you talk to your parents or to someone at school, or me if you want, when it gets too hard, okay?"

"I will." I didn't want to talk about school anymore. I asked, "Will you change things?"

"What do you mean?"

I didn't want to come right out and ask if he was going to cut out the part about me saying that Marjorie was faking. "The video I made. Will you change it?"

"You mean will I edit it?"

"Yeah."

"We always do some editing. Sometimes we'll really cut it up and move around the different scenes if we think it'll work better that way. Sometimes we just do small cuts or tweaks, add some sound or music or voice-over narration. But just seeing it once, I don't think we'll change much of what you filmed at all."

I nodded, and was worried that he didn't really pick up on me talking about Marjorie faking everything while we watched it but he surely would later when he showed it to Barry. I didn't want to be there for that so I said, "Okay. Bye," and darted quickly for the door.

"Wait! Don't forget to take your camera

back." Ken held it up and out toward me, and he shrugged, like he knew I wasn't sure I wanted the camera back. Or maybe he wasn't sure he should give the camera back to me.

I actually didn't want it, but I wanted Ken to go on thinking that I was still tough. So I took the camera. I went inside and up to my room. I put it in the top drawer of my dresser, layered some T-shirts on top of it, and decided I wouldn't use it again.

CHAPTER 18

THE MORNING AFTER the second episode aired, I told Mom that I wasn't feeling well and wanted to stay home from school. I told her my stomach hurt and I thought I had a fever when I didn't; I felt fine. She placed the back of her hand on my forehead and that was enough. She didn't question me further or take my temperature. Marjorie stayed home from school too. She hadn't been to school in a week since the first episode aired.

After spending a long, boring morning in my room rereading the old stories Marjorie and I had written in the Richard Scarry book and counting how many cats she'd drawn glasses on and had named Merry (there were fifty-four, I still remember that number), I came downstairs around lunchtime and announced that I was feeling better. I was dressed up as a news reporter: black T-shirt; black tights; a straw fedora; one blue sock and one red sock, both knee-length, the red sock was a regular sock, the blue sock was one of those glove socks that had toes and made my foot look like it was a Muppet foot; a button-up red knit sweater jacket that hung down almost to my knees. The sweater jacket had deep front pockets in which I stashed my reporter's pencil and the black notebook that Ken had given me.

There wasn't any crew on the first floor, but I took notes anyway as I worked my way to the kitchen. Dad was hunched over the sink and washing dishes by hand.

I wrote down: "Dishes. Dirty."

"Hi, sweetie. Feeling better, I take it?"

I asked, "Yes. How come you're not using the dishwasher?"

"There weren't that many dishes to wash."

I pursed my lips and nodded. Onto the next question: "Where's Mom?"

"Out with Marjorie."

I wrote that down, too, and underlined it.

"But she'll be back soon. We have a big meeting in"—he looked at the oven clock—"jeez, less than an hour."

"Can I be there for the meeting? I'm a reporter, see? I'll take notes."

"No. I don't think so. But we may have something to talk to you about afterward."

"What? Tell me!" I had my pencil pressed into the notebook.

"You're too funny. But I can't tell you. Mom

and I and everyone else have to discuss it first. It's nothing bad, though, I promise."

"But I'm a reporter so you have to tell me."

"Sorry to be a tease, but we'll talk after, okay?"

"Ugh. I can't wait until after."

Dad laughed, and despite two thousand volts of frustration tingling and twitching through my body, I laughed too. Everything about him that morning seemed relaxed and brighter than it had in months. He'd always been a moody guy. No one was funnier or more fun to play with than he was when in the right mood and you could feel the barometric pressure drop when he wasn't.

I heard the front door open and hoped that the big meeting was about to happen and that since I was there already they'd let me watch and take notes. But it was only Jenn. She walked into the kitchen without announcing herself. Someone in the trailer must've seen me and Dad together on the surveillance cams, so she was dispatched in case our interaction was video worthy.

"Are you sure I can't be at the big meeting?" I looked at Jenn and the camera when I said it, even though I was talking to Dad.

"Yes, I'm sure. What do you want for lunch, kid?"

I said, "Mac and cheese?" like I was asking if I could get away with something big. Mom would've said no and that I had to stick to the BRAT diet because of my stomach issues (which I seemed to have a lot of at that age) and then made me a plain piece of toast.

"Your stomach doesn't hurt anymore?"

"Nope."

"Did it really hurt at all this morning?"

"A little." I stuck my face into the open notebook.

"Do you think it'll hurt tomorrow morning?"

"I don't think so."

"Okay, good. Maybe I'll have some too. Take down some notes while I make it."

He boiled water and pretended to be a scientific expert on the properties of water boiling, and how long it needed to boil to make the perfect batch of mac and cheese. I wrote it all down and asked him the tough questions. He spoke of the golden ratio of cheese dust to milk and butter, the diameter and girth of the elbow-shaped pasta, the conductive properties and molecular structure of the white froth that bubbled over the pot. He held up the blue-and-yellow box and described the superhuman nutritional benefits of each ingredient. He used a funny scientist's accent. When it was ready we evenly distributed the pasta into two bowls and tested the cheese sauce's tensile strength: which bowl could keep a fork standing vertically the longest. My bowl won. We laughed, ate, and had a good time.

I remember this lunch in great detail because I remember it as being the last time he was happy-Dad with me. That might sound maudlin, sentimental, and hyperbolic, but that doesn't mean it isn't true.

————

MOM TURNED UP THE TV'S volume purposefully loud and took the remote control with her into the kitchen.

I sat in the living room only sort of watching an episode of *Teen Titans*. My parents, Father Wanderly, Barry, and Ken were in the kitchen having their *big meeting*. Because of what Dad had said earlier, I knew I was the subject. After the months of all-things-for-Marjorie, I was pleased that something happening in this house potentially involved me. With Marjorie almost exclusively sucking up all our parental resources, I'd felt like I was getting lost, a loose picture that had fallen out of the family album.

I couldn't hear anything said in the meeting and the one time I tried to sneak across the room and get closer to the kitchen, Dad heard and sternly ordered me back to my spot on the couch.

The meeting lasted forever and I began to hate the *Teen Titans*, particularly Beast Boy and his snaggletooth, but finally, everyone came into the living room. Mom sat next to me on the couch. She still had the remote and shut off the TV, and then she rubbed my back in slow circles, which made me nervous. It was an obvious sign we were to discuss something serious. Barry stood near the front door and spoke quietly into his Bluetooth. Jenn and Tony and their cameras emerged shortly thereafter, each flanking one end of the room. Ken sat in the plush chair by the front windows, lost in his notebook. I waved at him but he didn't see me. Both Ken and Barry stood outside of camera range so they presumably wouldn't be in the shot.

Dad followed Father Wanderly into the room and carried one of the kitchen chairs, which he set directly in front of the TV. Dad sat there and struggled to get comfortable. Father Wanderly had a red leather-bound book tucked under his left arm. He said, "Hello, Merry. I love your red jacket. Looks cozy." He always sounded like his words were full of helium, which rose and dangled above your head. He methodically worked his way around the coffee table to sit on the couch next to me.

I scooted away, closer to Mom, and I stuffed my hands into the jacket pockets. "Hello. It's not cozy. I'm wearing it because I'm a reporter," I said, and looked nervously at Dad. I was afraid that if I didn't address Father Wanderly like he wanted me to he'd get angry.

Dad gave me a reassuring nod and said, "We're going to talk more about what it is Father Wanderly is trying to do to help Marjorie and how he thinks you can help him. Okay?"

I was disappointed at first to hear this was still about Marjorie, but that quickly passed with the realization that these adults, their actions and motives as mysterious as ever, were going to tell me more, and they wanted my help.

Father Wanderly said, "That's right, Merry.

Are you feeling better? I'm told you stayed home from school today."

"I'm better. I think I was just really hungry and that made my stomach hurt."

"I understand." He smiled and showed off his big teeth, which were a dingy shade of gray.

Up this close to him, I could see flurries of dandruff sprinkled on his shoulders. The white collar squeezed his Adam's apple so tightly a small flap of skin folded over it. His face was thick with beard stubble that went higher on his cheeks than it should've, and I thought about making a werewolf joke. His blue eyes were so light I was afraid if I looked too hard and long I could see straight through into the back of his head. He smelled like powder.

"I'm going to take notes, okay?" I took the notebook and pencil out of my pockets.

"Of course." He leaned in closer to me and asked, "Do you know why I'm here?"

I nodded, even though I was still fuzzy on how he was going to help us.

"You know that I'm here to help your sister, and your family, and you."

I nodded again, impatient for him to get to the part where he described how I'd be helping, annoyed that he was talking to me as though I were four, not eight.

"I've watched the video you shot in your room, Merry, and I've watched your interviews, including that—what do you call it, Barry, a *confessional*? I'm not sure I approve of that." Father

Wanderly smiled at Barry, who returned a *Who, me?* shrug. "In one of them you said an evil spirit lived inside Marjorie. Did she tell you that?"

"Yeah, in the basement she said it to me, yeah."

"Well, Merry, my first job here is to figure out if she really has a demon spirit inside her."

"Well . . . it—It's what she told me?" I started looking to Mom and Dad in a panic, thinking that he somehow knew that what I'd told everyone had happened in the basement was a lie.

Father Wanderly said, "Merry, I believe you. And I believe that, unfortunately, your poor sister is possessed. I believe that somehow a demon spirit has gotten inside her and it's what makes her act so strangely, so not like your sister used to be. Yes? My second job, by the Lord's infinite grace, power, and love, is to help her and your family by getting the demon out of Marjorie, so it'll go away and leave her alone forever."

"How?"

"I'll perform the sacramental ritual of exorcism." He patted the leather book that was now resting in his lap.

I was getting more nervous so I drew a chain of circles in my notebook.

Dad said, "Merry, stop doodling and pay attention."

Mom said, "John, she's doing fine." She squeezed my shoulders and it turned one of my circles into a squashed blob.

Ken looked up from his notebook but not at me. Dad crossed his arms over his chest and did that thing where he jutted out his bottom jaw and released air through the side of his mouth.

I asked Father Wanderly, "Are you going to read that to her?" and pointed at his small, red leather-bound book.

"More or less, yes, I will read and pray, which is all a part of performing the rite of exorcism."

"Have you tried it yet?"

"We have not tried it yet. Performing an exorcism is very serious business. The most serious. I first need to get the permission of our local bishop. In order to do so, we must make sure that there is a demon inside Marjorie and that she's not simply—how should I put it?—that she's not just sick."

"Oh. So if she's only sick you can't help her, and we just have to give her medicine, or something and then she'll be better again?"

"Well, our Lord and Savior Jesus Christ can and does always help, but I'm afraid it's not that simple—"

Dad cut in with, "We're all tired, scared, and confused as to why this is happening to Marjorie and to us. But everyone in this house is confident that Marjorie is possessed by a demon. That's how they say it, Merry: possessed. Okay? Otherwise we wouldn't have gone to the . . . to the lengths that we've gone to here. What Father Wanderly is saying is that the church has to be absolutely sure before he can help her and read the special prayers from his book."

"I think you should just read the special prayers

to her now anyway. Just in case." I leaned back into Mom, looked up at her, and said, "Mom?" I didn't say *Do you believe there's an evil spirit inside Marjorie too?* but that was what I meant.

She said, "Remember all of Marjorie's doctor's appointments? We've been trying medicine, and we've been trying everything we can think of, and things with her—things with her are still getting worse. So we're doing what we think is best. Father Wanderly truly wants to help your sister."

No one else said anything right away. Dad leaned back in his chair; the wood creaked and groaned. I wrote the word *chair* down in my notebook and drew a picture of one that had a long back and short legs, and then I quickly drew a ghost that haunted it.

Father Wanderly said, "Merry, this afternoon, Dr. Navidson, who I've been consulting with, is coming over to finish his evaluation—or his, um, checkup—of Marjorie on behalf of the church."

"Who's that? I thought her doctor was Dr. Hamilton. Right, Mom?"

Mom said, "Dr. Hamilton is still her doctor, sweetie. This new doctor is helping out Father Wanderly."

"Why does she need another doctor?"

Father Wanderly said, "Dr. Hamilton is a very good man and doctor, but being an atheist, he does not have the sense of spiritual reality required for Marjorie's case."

"What's an atheist?" I drew another ghost.

Father Wanderly leaned down to get into my field of vision. When I looked up at him he said, "A nonbeliever. Someone who doesn't believe in Jesus or God."

Mom said, "An atheist doesn't believe there are any gods, Merry."

I wasn't sure what I was. I thought about asking if there was a name for that, a name for me. But I just said, "Okay."

Father Wanderly said, "Dr. Navidson is both a man of science and a good Christian. Our Bishop Ford recommended him highly. He has seen all the videos and read your interviews and he's coming over today to talk with Marjorie in person. I'm going to be in the room. Your parents will be there, and I'd like to ask if you would consider joining us as well, because we need your help."

I sat up, scooted toward the edge of the couch, and looked at both of my parents, trying not to seem too excited.

Mom said, "You don't have to if you don't want to."

Dad didn't say anything.

"I want to. I want to help! What do I get to do?" I wondered if I was going to have to dress up in a black shirt with buttons (I didn't like black shirts and I didn't like shirts with buttons) and wear a white collar and say some of the words in the book Father Wanderly had on his lap. I couldn't read the cover. It was in a different language that almost looked like English but wasn't.

Father Wanderly said, "For now, just your being there in the room is the help we need, Merry."

"How will that help anything? I want to do something. I can read stuff. I can use my camera." I tried to get Ken to look at me, but he was hidden behind Tony the cameraman who had left the periphery and now stood only a few feet away from the couch.

Father Wanderly said, "We've all noticed that the spirit inside Marjorie manifests or reacts strongest when you are in the same room as Marjorie, and on more than one occasion, the spirit has taken her to your room, as though seeking you out to be its audience. Please let me be clear, I'm not saying that you are the cause of her affliction or that what she does is in any way your fault, Merry, because it's not. Not at all. But we do think the demonic spirit is attracted to you because it shows itself primarily when you are around. So by being in Marjorie's room today during Dr. Navidson's visit, we'll increase the chances that he'll witness a manifestation event—"

"A what?"

"He'll see something that Marjorie does and will then know that she has a demon inside her. And then he'll be able to report to the bishop that poor Marjorie is truly suffering at the hands of an evil entity."

"Okay." I put my notebook back in my pocket and I leaned against Mom's chest again. I felt cold all of a sudden and thought I might start shaking for the rest of my life.

Mom hugged me and said, "I'm going to be with you and if it gets to be too scary or too much, we can leave whenever you want, I promise."

Dad said in a low voice, "I'll be in there with you too."

I didn't ask for further explanation, but Father Wanderly kept going and said, "If the visit goes like I think it will go, we can petition Bishop Ford for permission to perform the exorcism. I would then prepare myself over the course of the following week: fasting, praying, making confession—not in the room upstairs of course, but in a church—and say a Mass for Marjorie and ask for God's help."

"Then?"

"Then you all will help me perform the rite of exorcism, and we will expel the evil from Marjorie."

"What if it doesn't work?"

"We'll perform the rite again. As many times as is necessary."

"Is that other doctor coming over soon?"

Mom said, "Later tonight. But everyone hold on a second. Merry, sweetie, look at me. It's going to be hard. It's probably going to be . . . scary. We don't really know what she might say or do."

Dad said, "You mean we don't know what the *demon* might say or do, right?"

Mom said, "Yeah. Right. So are you sure about all of this, Merry?"

"I'm sure," I said, but I wasn't sure at all. I didn't know what a rite of exorcism was. I didn't even know how to pray, really, or I didn't know any prayers, anyway. And what if Marjorie did something so bad to me in front of everyone that would make me upset and blurt out that she was faking, that all of it was a fake? But what if she wasn't faking and it was some evil spirit inside her that told me she was faking? I didn't know what to think and just started talking even though Dad and Father Wanderly had already stood up and drifted over toward Barry. "Yeah, I'm sure I can help. I'm not scared. I'm tough. Ken said I was tough when we were playing soccer so I know I can do it."

Ken smiled, closed his notebook, gave me a little wave with his hand, and then left the room and the house. When he opened the front door, the front foyer filled with light.

Father Wanderly said, "You're a very brave, remarkable little girl, Merry. I bet you give all the boys trouble on the playground."

"I don't give anybody trouble."

Mom said, "Why don't you go out back and kick the soccer ball around. I'll come out there with you in a few minutes, okay?"

When I was outside waiting for Mom and kicking the ball as hard as I could into the net, I wasn't thinking about being in Marjorie's room with everyone else including the new doctor.

Instead, I obsessed over Father Wanderly's trouble comment. I imagined being at a playground and handing out little black bags to all the kids, not just the boys. They opened them and found little hard candies inside, each poisoned with trouble.

CHAPTER 19

DR. NAVIDSON CAME to our house shortly after we finished eating dinner.

When the doorbell rang, Mom was upstairs in the confessional room with a glass of wine, Dad was in the kitchen being asked on-camera to talk about what he was thinking and feeling before the arrival of Dr. Navidson, and I was sitting on the living room floor doing my math homework but listening to Dad. Ken and Father Wanderly were in the living room too; Ken lost in his black notebook, Father Wanderly lost in his special red leather book.

I ran to the door and Dad called out from the kitchen, telling me to wait for him. I didn't wait for him. I threw open the door and nearly shouted, "Hello, Dr. Navidson."

He said, "Hello," back and sidestepped around me and into the house, careful not to make any accidental contact. Dad rushed up from behind and practically pushed me away and onto the steps.

Dr. Navidson was shorter than the other men, had light brown hair, and a thick, wooly beard, the kind that had to have taken years to grow. I hadn't seen any foxes in real life but I imagined his beard and hair had the same consistency as a fox. He was younger than I had expected, and wore glasses with thin silver frames that boxed in his nervous eyes. He wore a black sweater and jeans, black shoes that had thick rubber soles, and he carried a laptop that was as thin as my Richard Scarry book.

There wasn't a lot of standing around and chitchat like normally there would be for a new guest in the house. He politely shook hands with my parents and declined Mom's offer of a glass of water while Dad herded him into the living room. He and Father Wanderly greeted by using first names and briefly embracing.

Dad was agitated and paced the living room, running a hand through his hair. "I'm sure Dr. Navidson is a very busy man. We should probably head upstairs as soon as possible."

Father Wanderly put a hand on Dad's shoulder, which stopped the pacing, and said, "Yes, of course, John. I know you're anxious. We're all anxious." Then he insisted that we join hands and pray before going upstairs to Marjorie's room.

I went and stood next to Mom, who put her

hands on my shoulders. I motioned for her to come down to my level so I could whisper into her ear. "I don't know how to pray."

She whispered down to me and breathed on my face. I covered my nose. "It's okay. Just bow your head and think good thoughts for Marjorie and if you want to, ask God for help."

The three men held hands. Dad held out a hand to Mom or me. Mom took it, and then she took my hand. Father Wanderly said a prayer asking for God's love and strength in the face of the evil we might encounter. Dr. Navidson's eyes were closed so tightly, it was as though he was afraid to open them. Father Wanderly said, "Lord, hear our prayer," which was echoed by Dad and Dr. Navidson. Then he started another prayer that began with "Our father, who art in heaven," and everyone joined in, even Mom. I moved my mouth, pretending that I knew the words too.

When we finished, Father Wanderly walked over to me and said, "Do not be afraid, Merry. Anyone who believes in our Lord Jesus Christ has nothing to fear."

Mom bent down and whispered to me again, before Father Wanderly had stopped talking. "Don't worry, I'll be up there with you, and we can leave whenever you want, okay?"

Barry jogged downstairs and asked that we give him one more minute for them to set up the shot and the lighting in the hallway and in Marjorie's room. He clapped his hands together and no one said anything. Dad started pacing again. Mom finished her wine and left the glass on the coffee table.

After getting the okay from Barry, us Barretts led the way upstairs. Dad went first, with Mom and I right behind him. The rest of our wagon train followed: Father Wanderly, Dr. Navidson, and Tony the cameraman. Jenn was already at the top of the stairs, following our expedition's progress.

The second-floor hallway was warm and brightly lit. The ceiling fixtures had been scrubbed clean and the yellowish bulbs replaced with bright white ones. The two spotlights from inside the confessional/sunroom were pointed out into the hallway, flooding the second floor with their wattage. I could feel their heat on the back of my neck.

Marjorie's door was shut, but the doors to the bathroom and the other bedrooms were open. In those other rooms the lights were off, and each doorway was a dark mouth.

Mom and I were jostled by the others jockeying for position in front of Marjorie's door. Dad knocked lightly and said, "Honey? We're here. We just want you to meet with Dr. Navidson and Father Wanderly for a few minutes like we talked about." There was no response from Marjorie. Dad turned the knob and slowly opened the door as he said, "They're going to ask you a few questions."

Dad walked in first, followed by the men. I

was the last one in, shuffling behind Mom. Jenn
stayed in the doorway, effectively blocking off
my promised escape route. I felt tricked and
trapped initially, but decided I'd be able to dash
under and between her legs in an emergency. It
was always smart to have a plan.

Marjorie's desk lamp was the only light on in
the room. Everything looked clean and tidy. Her
posters were gone. Her bureau top was visible
and her closed laptop sat by itself on her desk.
The stuffed animals and knickknacks had been
taken away. The wall she'd kicked and punched
holes into had been replastered but not painted.

Father Wanderly said, "Hello, Marjorie. This
is Dr. Navidson." The two men sat in skeleton-
thin wooden chairs that I'd never seen before.
The chairs flanked her bed. The built-in lights
on the two cameras focused on Marjorie, leaving the two men in shadow. She sat up with her
back against the windowsill, legs hidden under
the blankets. Her earbuds were in and I could
hear faint, tinny music echoing from the bowls
of her ears. She was wearing only a sports bra for
a top. A dusting of acne colored the skin around
her collarbones.

Dr. Navidson said, "Hello, Marjorie. Nice to
finally meet you."

Marjorie didn't acknowledge him.

Dad said, "Wait a minute, wait a minute.
Barry, shouldn't we get a shirt on her?"

Barry had hovered out of camera range to the
back of the room, near her closet. He shook his

head no and made a camera rolling motion with his hand.

Dad threw up his arms. "I'd like to put a shirt on her. She's only fourteen."

Mom said, "Marjorie, do you want to put a shirt on? Are you comfortable being filmed this way?"

Marjorie shrugged and looked bored, as though she were being asked to do some extra homework. "I'm okay, you okay." Her speech was slow. Some of the letters were heavier than others.

Dad said, "Can you take your earphones out at least?"

"I'd rather leave them in. I feel better that way, you know?"

"We just want to talk for a minute and—"

"Dad, I can hear you fine. I can hear everything fine." Marjorie grunted the words not like a demon, but like only surly teens can.

Dad uncrossed his arms and took a quick half step toward Marjorie's dresser, then stopped. What he wanted to do was to stomp over to her dresser, start ripping open random drawers until he found a T-shirt, throw it at her, yell at her until she put it on, and then rip the earphones off her head and chuck them across the room. But he couldn't because of the cameras and his beloved priestly mentor.

That's a lot to read in uncrossed arms and a twitch toward the bureau, I know. Likely it's hindsight, and all that happened after that has entwined with and mutated my memories of that night in Marjorie's room. But it doesn't mean my read of Dad isn't an accurate one.

As Mom withdrew and detached, Dad became both more pious and blindingly angry, and on that night I remember the fury emanating from him in waves, like heat from a space heater. Marjorie knew it too, and she smirked and rolled her eyes at him to make it all worse.

Marjorie finally saw me latched on to Mom's side and she perked up. "Oh, hi there, Miss Merry."

I wasn't sure if I was supposed to answer her, if I was even supposed to talk at all. During the post-big-meeting proposal, the adults hadn't told me anything other than that I was going to be in the room with them. I was mad that they hadn't given me more specific directions. It made me think they didn't really know what they were doing.

I'd been quiet for a long time so I hurried out a quick "Hi?" like it was a question.

Marjorie tied her hair back and then adjusted the straps of her sports bra. She said, "Don't talk to me, Merry. It's not safe. Didn't Father Wanderly tell you that you shouldn't be talking to me?"

I caught Father Wanderly throw a quick look to Barry in the back of the room. Then he looked at me and nodded. "It's okay, Merry. You may answer her if you wish."

I said, "No, he didn't tell me that."

"Oh, man. Mom and Dad, you need to get a better priest."

Dr. Navidson opened his laptop and pecked at the keyboard with exaggerated finger strokes, like he was trying to poke a hole in the machine. He said, "Why is that, Marjorie?"

"Idle and curious chatter with the demon should be avoided at all cost. It's Exorcism 101. I'm surprised you assholes don't know that. No, wait, I'm not surprised."

Dad sucked a breath in through his teeth. Mom squeezed my shoulders. They'd heard her swear plenty of times, especially during the last few months, but in this setting and in this company, they reacted as though she'd just punched each of them in the gut.

Father Wanderly said, "Are we speaking with a demon right now?"

"Yeah, sure. Why not?" Marjorie smiled and winked at me, which seemed like proof that she was faking, or proof that she really did have a demon inside her.

Marjorie said, "Hey, Mom and Dad," and then she paused to blow them a kiss. "Dr. Navidson, and everyone watching at home, did you know that Father Wanderly is breaking, like, one of the most important official rules according to the church?"

Father Wanderly had his legs crossed and his hands folded on top of his leather-bound book. He said, "And what rule is that?"

"No media, right? You're not supposed to

make a spectacle of the sacramental rite of exorcism. Duh. I'll directly quote the Vatican for you." Marjorie cleared her throat and then spoke in a voice that sounded decidedly, if not comically, male. " 'The presence of media representatives during an exorcism is not allowed.' "

Mom said, "Is that true?"

Father Wanderly said, "It is, however—"

Marjorie interrupted. "No, no, no. Let me." She changed her voice again, sounding airy, breezy, words stopping and breaking in an off-putting rhythm, and sounding very much like Father Wanderly. "However, Pope Francis just performed an exorcism in public, right? In front of cameras and everything. You can even watch it on YouTube. It's on there like four different times and one of them has over two hundred thousand views. That new Pope, he's such a rebel!" Marjorie stopped and coughed; it seemed exaggerated. "It hurts to talk like you, Father, so I'm stopping. But lucky for you, I guess, that the no-media rule has already been bent. So why not use me to shoot what's going to be like a recruitment video, right? Some Norwegian dude tried it once already with a documentary featuring a Vatican-approved exorcist. But seriously, who watches Norwegian documentaries, right? Father Wanderly's TV show will be a much bigger hit. It already is. The pilot episode was the Discovery Channel's highest rated debut ever. So I'm told. Already, after two episodes, everyone involved, everyone in this *room* is making fistfuls of money, right? And just imagine all those gawd-fearin' sheep-in-training out there watching our show, itching to come back to the church, soon to be saying their hallelujahs and filling donation baskets."

Mom had moved away from me toward Dad while Marjorie spoke. She put an arm around his midsection. Dad kept his arms crossed and when Marjorie finally finished talking, he started stammering, "Marjorie? What are you—I don't—How does she know all this?"

Father Wanderly said, "Do not be fooled by the lies."

"Lies? What lies? Nielsen ratings don't lie. I can show you the Norwegian documentary. And it would take me two seconds to pull up the clip of Pope Francis and the cute little possessed guy in the wheelchair. Did you know that the chief Vatican exorcist said the reason the guy in the wheelchair was possessed was because of Mexico's abortion laws? Makes sense to me. And now the archdiocese in Madrid wants to hire eight more exorcists. Maybe we can make them bump it up to an even ten after our show, yeah?"

Dr. Navidson was a marble statue lit by the glow of his computer screen. He wasn't typing anymore, and he sat with one hand partially obscuring his face and chin. He asked, "Can you show us on your laptop where you've been getting this information, Marjorie?"

"Laptop? No laptop, necessary. It's all common knowledge. Everybody's talking about it, all my friends at school. You know, that's what we talk about when we're not talking about boys and their penises. No, wait. That's not true. I get this all from the voices in my head, yeah. They're not my friends but they tell me everything. It's cool, but I have to shut them up sometimes, just to get some rest." Marjorie pointed at her earbuds. "Or maybe the voices are useless and just suck and don't really tell me anything but gibberish, stuff that almost sounds like words so I listen. And I think that if I just listen closely enough I'll finally understand what they're saying, and then they'll stop, and then, boom! it's like five hours later and I'm still listening so hard I want to cry, and I've bitten off all my fingernails until my fingers are ragged, raw, bloody, worn-down red crayons, and the voices are still there and I'm ready to stab out my eardrums and then stab everyone else. No, wait, I haven't stabbed anyone yet, so maybe it's all Merry's fault. Yeah, Merry told me and tells me everything about everyone. She's so sneaky! She can't be trusted!"

"No, I didn't! Mom, I didn't."

"Okay, okay, it wasn't Merry. I was born with all of the universe's information hidden in the infinite folds and wrinkles of my gray matter, and the information itself decides when it wants to come out and be known. Isn't that kind of creepy? All that information just there already. How'd it get there in the first place, right?

"Like, I didn't know it until you came in here, but now that I see you and it and everyone else, I suddenly know that the red book in your lap has a Latin title and is called *De Exorcismis et Supplicationibus Quibusdam*. It's a liturgical book—whatever that means—revised and published by the Vatican in 1999.

"Or maybe. Maybe. Maybe I'm just a lost, confused kid, scared of what's happening to me, to my family, to the world, and I hate school and I have no friends, and I spend my days sleeping with my iPod cranked up as loud as it'll go, trying not to go completely crazy, and with all that time alone I'm looking shit up on the Internet, looking up the same stuff over and over, and I memorize it all because I'm wicked smart, because I have to fill my head with something other than the ghosts."

Father Wanderly said, "I suggest that you no longer allow her access to the laptop until after the rite has been performed successfully."

Mom said, "What? No. We—We can't. She's trying to keep up with some of her schoolwork online. She needs it." Mom sounded as slurry and sleepy as Marjorie had when we first came into the room.

Marjorie said, "Dr. Navidson, I'd be really sad and unhealthy without any connection to the outside world, don't you think?"

Dr. Navidson looked at my father and said, "If you haven't been doing so already, her online activities should be monitored."

"You guys are no fun. You can look at my browser history. I haven't scrubbed it. No bad stuff. And sure I downloaded the Tor browser but I haven't used it, not really. Father Wanderly, I'm sure you've heard of or used Tor."

"Oh, I don't think so. I am not very computer savvy."

Marjorie looked down into her lap and started talking fast, so fast that I had a hard time keeping up. "Oh, well, Tor allows you to surf anonymously and go to sites on the Dark Net, which is a fun name for groups of secret sites you can't get to on regular browsers. Journalists and dissidents and hackers use Tor to keep out of the government eye and avoid censorship. Criminals use it too: weapons, drugs, and Father Wanderly's favorite, kiddie porn. It's a diddler's haven!" Marjorie giggled and pulled her bedspread up to her neck.

Dad swore under his breath. Father Wanderly was turned away from me so I couldn't see his face.

Mom crouched down in front of me so that we were face-to-face, nose to nose. "Merry, maybe we should go. Do you want to go?"

I'm sure as an eight-year-old I'd heard the word *porn* and knew it was something bad, or if not bad, per se, then something not for kids, but didn't really know what it meant. I certainly hadn't seen any yet. So I wasn't sure what Marjorie was talking about, but I remember the room feeling like it had just gotten more dangerous. I wanted to stay but didn't say anything to Mom.

Marjorie held out her stop hands and said in

her regular voice, "Stay, Mom and Merry. Stay. I'm sorry, I'm sorry. That was an easy cheap shot. We'll be good from now on, mostly."

Father Wanderly said, "We?" loudly, like he was a courtroom lawyer who had finally broken his witness. He looked over at Dr. Navidson, who just nodded and resumed typing on his laptop.

"Slip of the tongue." Marjorie was twitching now. Her shoulders jerked up and down, legs spasmed beneath the covers.

"What is your name?"

Marjorie laughed for a long time. "I'm sorry, you're being serious. Okay. Marjorie. Or Yidhra. It's an old, old, old family name. No one uses it anymore." She laughed some more. I'd never seen her so manic, so clearly performing, and performing in a way that gained momentum, like an avalanche. It was terrifying.

Father Wanderly asked, "Is your name funny?"

"Maybe. Anyone heard of me? I'm pretty sure Ken has."

Ken wasn't there. I wanted to go get him. I felt a weird pang of jealousy that his name would be brought up by Marjorie.

Father Wanderly said, "We'll be sure to ask Ken."

"*We*"—Marjorie stressed the word, wringing it out like a wet bathing suit—"consulted and have a few questions for you guys. Why is Merry here anyway?"

Dad said, "Because she loves you and wants to help."

"That's sweet. How exactly is she going to help us?" She slipped into a guttural voice, both high-pitched and sonorous, with a lilt of a British accent. It was the voice of Gollum. I thought for sure she'd gone too far, that Mom or Dad would call her on impersonating her favorite character from her favorite series of movies and accuse her of faking everything. But when no one answered right away, she said in her normal voice, "Okay. So Merry's here to be part of the show. The more the merrier! Got it."

Father Wanderly said, "Dr. Navidson, have you seen enough?"

"Wait! Don't rush us. Dr. Navidson, are you a Freudian?"

He ignored her question and closed his laptop.

"We have another question for you, Father. Help us with this one: How come the church recommends that witnesses should be present, like now and during the exorcism, especially if the possessed is a young woman? It actually says that in the *Catholic Encyclopedia*: 'This is specially enjoined, as a measure of precaution, in case the subject is a woman.'"

Father Wanderly said, "I think it's clear we've interacted far too much with the demon spirit already. John, I think you should stay here with me, and help try to settle Marjorie down for the evening. Everyone else should go downstairs."

"He's not answering our question about the witness. Hey, does anyone else think that it's kind of icky? Who is it that needs the protection of witnesses in that scenario?" Marjorie thumped her puffed-out chest and spoke in a man's voice: "The righteous, courageous, humble, holy man who might be tempted by the unclean perversions of a demon-infested slut?" Marjorie then poked fingers into her cheeks, making dimples, and she spoke in a baby-doll voice, "Or the poor, vulnerable, hapless, helpless woman? I'm pretty sure I know the answer, but Dr. Navidson, help us out here. Even if you're not a Freudian."

Both men stood. Father Wanderly made a *please leave the room* gesture at us with his hands. Dr. Navidson walked slowly toward the door. Dad, Mom, and I stayed rooted to our spots.

Marjorie tried one more time, this time in a pleading, near-tears voice that wasn't baby doll, but sounded a lot younger than Marjorie normally sounded. "Father Wanderly, don't leave. I'm sorry. Help me."

"I'm not leaving. I will help you, Marjorie. That is a promise."

"H-have you ever performed an exorcism before?"

"No. But I have been present at many. I've witnessed true horror, and true salvation."

Marjorie scrambled from her sitting position onto all fours and reached out to Father Wanderly. "Tell me. Have you seen a demon before? What did it look like? Could you see it inside the other person, pressing out on the skin from inside their body? Did you see the outline of a claw, a wing, a face, of a monster in skin? Or can a demon be someone who looks just like me, so it looks like a person stuck inside another person? Does the demon inside leave any marks? Are the possessed marked, so you can tell who's possessed and who isn't? Do the marks look like this?" Marjorie sat on her knees and raised her arms so that we could see her midriff. Mom and Dad gasped. I covered my mouth. Red slashes and gouges colored her skin. They crossed and looped and overlapped, like someone was trying to scribble her out, as though she were a mistake.

Marjorie kept talking while the adults scrambled and shouted orders at one another. Someone turned on the overhead light and someone else ran to the bathroom to get a wet washcloth and bandages. I stood there and listened to Marjorie.

"Father Wanderly, have you seen a demon or evil spirit actually leave the body? What did it look like? Could you see anything? Did you see a wisp, like smoke over a campfire? Does the demon get sucked into a void, clutching on to the old, possessed body like a life raft? Or does it go quietly, like a child leaving her parents' home for the final time? What if you didn't see anything? If you couldn't see anything, if the spirit was invisible, then how could you know if the exorcism really, truly worked?"

Mom and Dad gave her a glass of water and asked that she swallow some pills. They said it would help her sleep. Mom mentioned Dr. Hamilton and the phrase "your doctor" to Marjorie repeatedly. They gently attended to her injuries.

Marjorie let them guide her so that she was lying down and back under the covers. She was still talking but she was almost done. You could tell.

"After you performed the exorcism, how did you know that demon wasn't still in there, hiding? How do you know it didn't go in a hibernation state, quieting down to come out later, years and years later when no one would be around to help? Hey, how do you know if the wrong spirit left? What if you expelled the person's real spirit and only the demon's spirit was there to take its place? If I believed in any of that stuff, I'd be afraid that was going to happen to me."

Her eyes closed. She rolled onto her side, away from the room and away from us. Her eyes were closed and she whispered her final questions. "Father Wanderly, how do you know if a person has a spirit inside their body in the first place? Have you ever seen that, at least?"

ALL WAS CHAOS WHEN WE left Marjorie's room.

Dad shouted angrily at Jenn the camera-woman to stand in the hallway and keep an eye on Marjorie for a minute. Jenn yelled down to Barry—he was already downstairs—that she wasn't taking orders from Dad. Mom yelled at Dad to shut up, and quickly led me downstairs. When we got to the foyer, she had her cell phone out and she told Dad and Father Wanderly she was calling the hospital, calling Dr. Hamilton to tell him about the marks. Mom and Dad wrestled over the cell phone. He grabbed her arm and she repeatedly slapped his hand. Father Wanderly attempted unsuccessfully to mediate. Barry and Dr. Navidson then joined in trying to calm everyone down.

I yelled, "Stop it, stop it, stop it!"

They did stop grabbing and talking and arguing momentarily, everyone looking embarrassed. Mom told me to go to the kitchen and she'd be right there. I nodded and backed away slowly, not toward the kitchen, but into the living room, and as I did, I watched and listened for them to start talking again. Dad was first. He said he was sorry for grabbing Mom and he called her sweetie, but then he insisted that they couldn't call Dr. Hamilton about this because he'd put Marjorie away again in the hospital and then she couldn't be saved. He said they'd talked and prayed about this and had decided to believe in Father Wanderly and they had to see this through. Father Wanderly called Mom by her first name repeatedly, and told her that he knew what was happening with Marjorie was a parent's worst nightmare, but that Dad was right about not calling. He told her that after what they'd just witnessed, he was sure that he would be able to get the bishop's permission and perform the exorcism soon.

Mom shook her head the whole time and said, "This is a nightmare, and we'll never wake up from it."

Ken was in the living room waiting for us. I said hi to him and he said, "Hi," back sheepishly. Then he said, "Sorry." I wasn't sure why. I was going to ask him but Barry left Mom and Dad and beelined it over to Ken. He asked Ken if he'd watched everything from the trailer. Ken had. Tony the cameraman, Dad, and Dr. Navidson then swarmed Ken, who looked queasy, like he had my fake stomachache from earlier that morning.

Father Wanderly was still in the front foyer with Mom. I couldn't hear them talking anymore. He shook both of her hands gently and left her in the foyer. As he passed he touched my shoulder and thanked me for my help, that I did great, and that he might need my help again. Then he, too, scuttled off to join the group that had encircled Ken, and he also bombarded him with questions.

Ken held up his hands for quiet. He told the group that he thought the demon name Yidhra was familiar when he first heard it while watching from the trailer but couldn't recall exactly who or what it was, so he had Googled it. Yidhra was a minor demon in the fictional cosmic horror universe of the early-twentieth-century writer H. P. Lovecraft, a universe that featured nameless Elder Gods and tentacled beasties from other dimensions. Ken stressed that Yidhra was completely fictional and not found anywhere in Judeo-Christian or pagan lore. He did say it was interesting that in Lovecraft's stories Yidhra appeared in a seductive female form.

Dr. Navidson said, "Marjorie spoke in a male's

voice when she was presumably under Yidhra's sway."

Father Wanderly said, "The demon is hiding its true identity. It always does until the end."

"Why did she say you would know? Have you been talking to her, telling her about this stuff?" Dad said. He wasn't quite yelling at Ken, but he was loud enough for Father Wanderly to say, "Easy, John."

"What? No, I haven't exchanged more than polite chitchat or hellos and byes with Marjorie since the earliest interviews when we first showed up. And to be clear, I didn't know the demon by name. I had to look it up. I mean, yes, I am a big fan of Lovecraft the writer and all, but Yidhra was such a minor character I didn't remember it."

"So how did she know you were a fan?" Dad sounded like he was picking a fight.

Father Wanderly said, "I'm afraid we know the terrible answer to that."

Ken shrugged, and said, "Look, she probably saw me wearing my Lovecraft/Miskatonic University T-shirt."

Dad said, "Not likely. What fourteen-year-old girl would pick up on that?"

"Lovecraft is a pretty famous writer. She could've made the connection on her own. Or maybe she Googled my T-shirt, found Lovecraft and Yidhra on Wikipedia. Not a huge leap, there, I don't think—"

Barry tapped Ken on the shoulder and shook his head. Ken nodded and stopped talking about

Marjorie and Lovecraft and said, "I'm gonna go back to the trailer, okay, in case anyone needs me."

Father Wanderly, Dad, and Dr. Navidson tightened into their own circle, and they talked fast and over one another so I couldn't really make out who said what. But they were all talking about how Marjorie was in fact possessed by a demon, with the proof being what she was and wasn't capable of doing.

"—fourteen-year-old girl couldn't possibly know all she claimed to know—"

"—to give details advanced seminary students wouldn't give—"

"—the name of the book, in correct Latin—"

"—to refer to Freud and this fictional demon from a long-dead author—"

"—even if she looked it all up on the computer—"

"—no way she could've memorized it all—"

"—she did more than memorize, she synthesized—"

"—never mind anticipate that she'd need to say or use that information during our interview—"

"—right—"

"—a girl like her can't speak as eloquently as she did—"

"—no way—"

"—a girl wouldn't ask the questions she asked—"

Mom yelled at them, "Marjorie has always been an extremely intelligent young woman. Of course she can do all those things you're saying she can't do."

Dad said, "Sarah, we're not saying she's not an intelligent girl. That's not the point. Now's not the time to—"

Mom didn't wait for him to finish. She tugged roughly on my arm and said, "Come on. In the kitchen. With me. Now."

I followed her into the kitchen. I thought Mom was crying but she wasn't. She was seething with anger and muttering under her breath. She slammed cabinet doors and poured herself a big glass of wine and a cup of milk for me. I asked her to warm it up and she put it in the microwave, slamming that door shut too.

We sat at the table with our drinks. I tested the milk with my lips and it was the perfect temperature. I finally asked her, "Who are you mad at?"

"Everything. Everyone. Myself included."

"I'm sorry."

"I'm not mad at you, honey. You're the only person I'm not mad at."

"Marjorie too?"

"I'm not mad at her either. She's sick and she needs help, and I don't think anyone in the other room is really going to help her, but it's my own damn fault that I can't stop it now. I should never have let it happen in the first place. I mean, can you believe this? Any of this? How did we get here? The cameras, writers, producers, protesters, priests. What a mess. I was just so scared that we were losing her and I didn't know what to do anymore—and I wanted to believe. Wanted to believe all of it. I still do."

Mom looked down and saw me staring at her. She said, "Drink your milk."

I wanted to tell her that it was going to be okay, that Marjorie had told me that she was faking so when Father Wanderly performed his exorcism she would fake that it worked too. But I didn't. I can't really explain why. I remember so much of that fall in detail (and I'm in the unique position of having six televised episodes of my family to revisit when I do forget something), and sometimes I feel like I'm still the same eight-year-old little sister who longs for big sis to tell her what to do and how to do it.

I said to Mom, "I believe. You should too, like Dad. Yeah. I think Father Wanderly can help. He can. He'll make her be normal again."

Mom crumbled into chest-heaving sobs. I didn't know what happened so I kept saying *Mom* over and over again, and when I tried to ask her what was wrong and tried to hug her she shook me away. She wouldn't let me pull her hands away from her face, and she told me to get out and go away. When I said, "Why, what did I do?" she told me to leave her alone and go see Daddy and the priest because they had all the answers and to leave her alone, and I still asked her *why-why-why* until she screamed, "Get the fuck away from me!" and threw her wineglass at the wall.

———

LATER THAT NIGHT WE ENACTED a new bedtime policy to help keep Marjorie from hurting
herself any further and to give everyone "peace
of mind." That was the phrase Dad used, and I
tried to make a joke out of it; pantomiming my
presenting him with a literal chunk of my brain.
It didn't go over well.

The new policy: Marjorie was to sleep with
her door open, and Dad was to be in his room
with his door open. Mom was to sleep with me
in my room. I could leave my door open or shut.
It was up to me. Right before he left, I'd heard
Dr. Navidson whisper to Dad about letting me
choose whether or not to leave my door open as
it would empower me, give me a sense of control
over the situation.

Mom had finished a third glass of wine by the
time I was sent to the bathroom to get ready for
bed. When I got to my room she was in my bed
already, still in her clothes but underneath the
covers. Mom told me no stories. She said she was
too tired and that I had to go straight to sleep.
She didn't apologize for swearing at me and
throwing the glass in the kitchen either.

I stood in my doorway, undecided on whether
to leave the door open. I saw it as an important
choice, one not to be taken lightly. I said more
to myself than to Mom, "If I close the door then
we won't be able to hear anything, you know, in
case we need to hear it. But if I leave it open I

think it'll be too bright in here for me to sleep, and too noisy too. But I kinda want to leave it open because everyone else has theirs open. But if I close it"—I opened and closed the door like I was working a bellows—"we might sleep later than everyone else by accident and I'll be late for school. And if I leave it open, I might not fall asleep and be too tired to go to school. If I close it—"

"Merry. Enough. Shut the light off. Get in bed. Now."

I left the door half open, which I figured was a good compromise. I took off my glasses, put them on the bureau all folded up, and I crawled over Mom and into bed. She was on the outside and I was pinned between her and the bedroom wall. Her back was turned to me. I sloppy kissed her ear and said, "Good night, Ear." Mom didn't turn her head and just sent an empty air kiss back to me.

I was wired, twitchy, leaking giggles and random noises. I tried breathing my end-of-the-day sigh, the one that signaled it was truly time for bed. It didn't work. I put my icy-cold feet on the back of Mom's bare calves as a joke. She barely flinched, and told me from some faraway place to go to sleep.

I lay there on my back with my hands folded across my chest, trying to remember and recount everything that had been said in Marjorie's room. I knew that the adults would pick through the video and be able to break down what she'd

said and find the potential meanings and secrets.
I knew that for them, words meant so many different things. I worried that they would figure
out Marjorie didn't have a real demon inside
her, that she was faking, and then they'd cancel the show and our family would be back in
trouble with money again. But then I thought
about her scratch marks and how scary she was,
and I wondered if it was possible for her to be
both possessed by a demon and be faking it too.
And then I worried about getting a demon stuck
inside me, and I worried about it happening to
my parents—what would we do then? I rolled
the word *demon* around in my mouth, squeezing
it with my tongue, tasting it, letting it flick off
the back of my teeth, saying it in my head until
the syllables didn't fit right and it sounded weird
and indecipherable, just like the strange demon
name Marjorie had given them.

I woke up later that night and Mom was snoring deeply. I didn't really have to go pee but I went
to the bathroom anyway. I left the bathroom
door open and my peeing was so loud I giggled
with embarrassment, but I was also laughing at
whoever would be stuck watching and listening
to the tape from the hallway cameras.

I crept out of the bathroom without washing
my hands and stood in the hallway. It was chilly
even though steam whistled in our old radiators
and I could smell the heat, which I'd imagined
was the smell of burning dust. Dad's door was
still open. He slept pushed all the way to the side

of the bed closest to the hallway. His mouth was open and his lips drooped like one of those silly dogs with the saggy skin.

Marjorie's door remained open as well. Getting up to pee when I didn't really need to was how an eight-year-old lied to herself: Of course, I only got up to use the bathroom, not to go see what Marjorie was doing.

I watched my sleeping father as I slunk into her room. Without my glasses, everything was a little bit fuzzy. Like my father, Marjorie was lying on her side, facing the door. But she was wide awake.

"Did you hear me peeing?"

She whispered, "I've been watching Dad all night. I'm worried. I think he might be the one who's possessed. No lie. His face twitches like he's in pain. Hasn't he been acting so strange? So over-the-top religious now, and always so angry? I'm scared. I think he thinks about doing bad things, really bad things, like in the growing-things story I told you."

I shrugged and thought about telling her that Mom had been angry too. "I think he's okay."

"He spent over an hour reading from the Bible. I think he was reading the same passage over and over because he wasn't turning any pages."

"Marjorie—"

"Shh."

I'd forgotten to whisper. "Sorry. Are you still faking?"

"What do you think?"

"Yes."

"Then I am. No worries, monkey."

"Why'd you say all those things? Why'd you scratch yourself like that?"

"I had to do it. To make them all believe."

"Mom doesn't."

"She just says she doesn't. But she does. I can tell. Whenever she looks at me now, it's like she's watching a scary movie."

"Did the scratches hurt?"

She didn't answer my question right away. She said, "Be prepared. It's going to get worse. Mom and Dad are both going to get worse. But this is the only way, now. We have to show them."

"Show them what?"

"The scratches hurt, yeah. But that's nothing. I'll have to do something worse, much worse, eventually. Go back to bed. They'll wake up soon."

I tiptoed out of her bedroom, almost believing that if I was sneaky enough, if I was light enough on my feet, the hallway camera wouldn't see me, or whoever was watching the footage would think I was just coming out of the bathroom again.

Of course, the next morning I got in big trouble. Someone (I've always wondered if it was Ken but I never asked him) must've told Dad about my nighttime wanderings as soon as he got up because he lit into me at breakfast, in the middle of my bowl of chocolate Cheerios, full-on yelling at me for the first time in front of the cameras. It was a serious scolding; he stood so that he towered above the sitting me, his face all red and eyes jumping out of his head. He repeatedly asked if I thought this was some sort of game, if I thought they were all fooling around? I cried and apologized, told him I was worried and only checking to see if Marjorie was okay. Mom didn't say anything and went outside for a smoke while Marjorie's bagel was toasting. He asked why I thought they had made the new bedtime rules. He said that I wasn't dumb and that I was smart enough to figure it out, but in a way that made me feel dumb.

Just in case it wasn't clear, I was forbidden to go to her room or to be with Marjorie if I was by myself until further notice. If I did it again, I wouldn't be able to watch my *Bigfoot* and *River Monsters* shows.

CHAPTER 20

OF COURSE THE show used material from that night in Marjorie's room to fill the third and fourth episodes.

They showed the actual interview with Dr. Navidson in the room from two different angles. They slowed down the film to focus on Marjorie's facial expressions and hand gestures, and at the 12:37 time stamp of the interview, when she first referred to herself as "we," there's a frame (caught from both camera angles) where her irises appeared to be red, as though someone had taken her photo with a flash. The show interviewed two photography experts who analyzed films and arrived at no conclusion as to the source of the red in her eyes. They also slowed down the interview film to point out some odd shadow play that occurred on the wall behind Marjorie, offset to her right, and for the view-

ers, their left. At three different times, there
appeared to be long, tubular-shaped shadows,
waving and writhing in the background. Again,
the photography experts were consulted, and
again, they came to no conclusion although,
without giving their evidence, they immediately
dismissed Photoshop, editing tricks, and other
ways of physically doctoring the film as a possible cause.

Sound and voice experts examined Marjorie's
audio. They dissected the parts where her voice
changed, and examined the speech patterns and
frequency waves, and made readings of her emotional state using Layered Voice Analysis. One
expert claimed that the other voices she spoke
in had totally different voice biometrics (which
reflect both the anatomy of the speaker—the
size and shape of the mouth and throat—and
the behavioral/regional speech patterns/style
of the speaker) and could not have come from
the same person.

They fact-checked everything Marjorie had
said, verifying the sources she quoted, and they
briefly investigated and examined her claims
about the Pope performing an exorcism in
St. Peter's Square. They showed a clip of Pope
Francis laying hands on a man in a wheelchair
who convulsed and slumped as the Pope prayed.
They showed the Vatican's written statement; a
nondenial denial that he'd performed an exorcism in public. They quoted a book Pope Francis
had written when he was an Archbishop titled

On Heaven and Earth, highlighting the second chapter (titled "On the Devil") and its ominous snippets relating to Satan and his terrible influence. They ran a brief third-party interview with the Bishop of Madrid who had indeed petitioned the Vatican to train more of his priests as exorcists.

They outlined a brief biography of the writer H. P. Lovecraft. They detailed an extensive bibliography and the recent renaissance of his ideas and influence on current popular and literary culture, noting the new volume of his work published by the Library of America. They explained his Elder Gods/Cthulhu mythos and where the demon Yidhra fit into it, and attempted to place Yidhra within a wider context in the history of demons/spirits within folklore and religion.

Between the many segments of their dissection of Marjorie's interview, they ran reaction interviews from everyone involved. There were multiple clips of Mom and Dad giving their thoughts and opinions. Dad was always shot in bright light, usually on the back porch, his chest puffed, standing tall, resolute, like he was ready to do whatever it was he was supposed to do. It didn't really look like him, not the him that I remember. His eyes were solar flares, and he smiled too widely, all teeth. And he didn't sound like I remember him sounding. He didn't talk to the camera. He orated. He gave pep talks about how our family would overcome. He proselytized, working in Bible references and "May God bless our family" whenever he could.

The interviews they ran with Mom were shot with her sitting in the kitchen, in dim lighting, almost sepia toned, and with a cigarette trailing smoke in an ashtray more times than not. They painted her as the Doubting Thomas of the family, which she was. But they also made her seem like she was on the verge of an emotional breakdown, which she was, but so was Dad. I'm convinced they employed more than a little creative editing to her interviews. On the show she became the character who was inarticulately denying reality; the reality of our reality show. The off-screen interviewer would ask her to explain the shadows on the film or Marjorie's red eyes (something they didn't do with Dad, or if they did ask him to do so, they didn't run those interviews) or some of the things Marjorie had said and they'd cut to Mom shrugging, stammering, shrinking into her chair, and mumbling, "I don't know" or "not sure."

Dr. Navidson was filmed speaking somewhere in the house, and even I can't tell exactly where he was when he was interviewed since he stood right up against a white wall (Kitchen? Living room? One of the hallways? Stairwell landing? Guest room?) and his head took up the whole screen. He fumbled around and appeared very uncomfortable one-on-one with the camera. He declined to comment on specific details of this case, noting patient-client confidentiality, but admitted that he did recommend to the bishop that Marjorie's was an extraordinary case, one that was beyond science.

They ran a get-to-know-me interview with Father Wanderly, with him sitting in a pew inside his church. He detailed his experience as a Jesuit, his undergraduate and graduate degrees from the College of the Holy Cross, spoke lovingly about his dog, Milo, a cocker spaniel mix that had lived with him at the rectory for sixteen years. The off-screen interviewer asked him if he knew any jokes. Father Wanderly seemed genuinely embarrassed, said that he didn't know many, but did tell one: "Did you hear how the devil is having a terrible time of it with our current economy? The wages of sin have gone up ten percent."

In one of Father Wanderly's reaction interviews (conducted in the foyer, with him standing in front of the stairs, natural light pouring in from one of the windows behind him and to his right) he was much more forthcoming than Dr. Navidson had been in outlining the reasons why he was confident Marjorie was indeed possessed by an evil spirit.

They even ran an interview with one of the protesters out in front of our house, which, shockingly, turned out to be a huge mistake. I'm guessing Barry et al, knew that running the interview with the sign-carrying kook would encourage more protesters, and more protesters would mean more (free!) media coverage. But as sniveling and weasely and so obviously uncaring to our family's well-being as he was, I don't think that he would've purposefully dropped the busload of infamous Baptist hate-group loonies on our doorstep, which is, of course, what happened.

They ran a single reaction interview with me. It was very brief. Ken was off-camera. He asked me questions while I sat on my bed. During taping, which happened after I'd returned home from an especially crappy day at school, we talked for close to an hour. Most of it was about the previous night in Marjorie's room. Some of it was about what it was like living with the cameras, and what it was like just being me in general. They aired only three questions and answers, a snippet used as the closing segment to the fourth episode:

Ken: "Do you love your sister?"

Me: "Oh yes. Very much. She's my best friend. I want to be just like her and I'd do anything for her."

Ken: "When Father Wanderly and Dr. Navidson were asking her questions last night, were you scared?"

Me (after a long pause during which I changed sitting positions on my bed, from legs unfolded to legs crossed, or crisscross applesauce): "Yeah, a little. But I wasn't scared of Marjorie. I was scared of what Father Wanderly says is happening to her."

Ken: "What was the scariest part?"

Me: "Well . . . seeing the scratches all over her. I didn't think she'd do that to herself."

THEY FILLED TWO EPISODES WITH material from and relating to that night because they could. But also because they had to.

Two days after the night in Marjorie's room, Father Wanderly informed us that the bishop heading the northern pastoral region of the Archdiocese of Boston (which was composed of sixty-four parishes in southern Essex County) had given his permission and blessing to perform an exorcism on Marjorie. Father Wanderly, after briefly consulting with Barry, also told us that he would need eight days to be fully prepared. No one questioned this.

For those eight days the world outside our house grew increasingly chaotic. School became intolerable. Kids picked on me more often and more openly. Given the recent bullying laws passed in Massachusetts, which placed considerable legal culpability upon the school if bullying incidents went unreported, faculty and administration were in a tizzy, and Mom was called in routinely for meetings. The adults didn't seem to know what to do but Mom wasn't about to keep me home from school. All I knew was that the kid who called me "Sister Satan" and pinched my arms hard enough to leave bruises three days in a row was suddenly not at school for the next two, and when he returned, he wasn't allowed to go near me.

Marjorie had already stopped going to school altogether but a group of her former classmates set up an Instagram account under her name and posted screencaps from the show—both of her and of the actor playing her. Years later I found out that the screencaps had violent or brutally sexualized captions. There was one picture of Actor-Marjorie masturbating in the hallway with the caption: "Twerk for Satan! Fuck me in the ass, Jesus!" The page's creator and five other students were suspended for a week.

Despite the cold of mid-November, the number of protesters in front of our house swelled so that the road was almost impassable to traffic. Two policemen were assigned detail to keep the protesters from encroaching on the property and from making contact with us or the crew. The police had to replace yellow tape daily and often had to clear people away from the mouth of our driveway whenever a car left or entered.

Mom took a leave of absence from the bank. She didn't tell me, but I overheard her telling Dad that it was the bank's idea. She went grocery shopping in towns that were thirty minutes or more away. She spent her evenings on the phone with her parents (my only living grandparents) who lived in California. They didn't understand what it was we were doing on the show. Mom told me that after everything was done, maybe we'd go for a visit. I said, "Yay! For how long?" She said, "I—I don't know. Maybe for a really long time."

Dad spent most of his mornings at Father Wanderly's parish, attending the two morning masses, and apparently even served as a Eucharistic Minister. He told me it was the best way to start the day. I remember him telling me that "going there fills me with hope, and all the prayers and support from my fellow parishioners are sustaining, like sunshine for a beautiful sunflower." I wanted to tell him that this, all of this, wasn't about him, but I chickened out. He spent most of his afternoons arguing with and attempting to intimidate protesters. He grew scarier by the day.

So while our place or status within the community continued to deteriorate, the goings-on inside our house turned relatively calm. Now that we had a hard date upon which an exorcism would be attempted, Marjorie's bizarre behavior went into a kind of remission. She wouldn't talk much and she still wore her earphones most of the time, and I'd catch her talking to herself and giggling at nothing, but she willingly left her room and came downstairs to eat dinner with us in the kitchen.

For seven days there wasn't anything that happened inside the house that was dramatic or show-worthy. I know this because Barry spent most of that week stomping around, going room to room as though he expected that he himself would find demons defecating in dark corners or

the walls bleeding or something equally enter-
taining. No such luck. He snapped at crew members, especially at Ken, once telling him, "You
have to figure out something. We need *something*
to shoot."

The "something to shoot" turned out to be a
post-dinner family scene. It was the night before
the exorcism was to be performed, and we were
all in the living room watching TV. Dad had
put on a show where a survivalist is dumped in
the middle of the wilderness and eats tree sap,
bugs, and rodents for ten days. In this episode,
the guy was somewhere deep in the Boreal forest. I was watching, but not really watching. I did
cartwheels across the room and front rolls into
the couch, asking Dad to rate them by giving
me a thumbs-up or a thumbs-down. Mom only
halfheartedly asked me to stop, so I didn't. She
wasn't paying much attention anyway, and had
her nose buried in her smartphone.

Marjorie came downstairs and said, "Hi. Is it
okay if I watch TV too?"

We all stuttered and stumbled over one
another saying "yes" and "sure" and "come on
in." Marjorie plopped herself down on the floor
in front of the TV, lying on her stomach, head
propped up in her hands. We all watched her
watching TV. There was an odd feeling in the
room. We were nervous that something would
happen, but at the same time, we were glad she
was there.

Barry and Ken suddenly appeared in the front

foyer. Two cameras, one at each end of the room, were focused on us. Barry announced that he wanted to tape a scene of us together trying to maintain our normal family life. He actually said "normal family life" to us. He whisper-consulted with Ken, read some of Ken's notes, and then gave us some direction.

He said, "Okay, why don't we start with you guys talking a little about what you're watching?"

We all looked around, at a loss as to what to say. Mom said, "This is silly."

Dad flashed angry, and was quick to chide her. "Come on. We can do this. Is acting like a family so hard to do?"

Mom was more than ready to respond in kind. "Right. Kids, gather 'round Daddy so we can all hold hands and sing 'Kumbaya.'"

I quickly back-rolled off the arm of the couch, slapping my feet hard as I landed. I shouted, "Dad! Dad! Rating! You said you'd rate my land-ings." I hoped I'd been loud enough to drown out the start of another fight.

Dad gave me a thumbs-up and said, "Woo," but his enthusiasm for my performance was lacking.

Before they could start back in on each other, I pointed at the TV and said, "Maybe they'll finally find Bigfoot this time."

Marjorie said, "This isn't the Bigfoot show, monkey."

We were pleased and shocked that Marjorie

was casually interacting with us. Barry made that camera-rolling motion with his hands, desperately wanting one of us to respond, to goose the conversation forward.

Dad said, "Right. It's . . . um . . . called *Survivorman*."

I said, "Yeah, I know. But he's way deep in the woods all by himself. That's where Bigfoot lives, so maybe he'll see one."

"Pfft. I don't think so, sweetie." Dad was badly overacting. He had that fake smile on his face, the one that looked painful to wear.

I said, "I bet he heard one but didn't know it was a Bigfoot making that noise because he's not an expert." I punctuated with a one-handed cartwheel.

Dad said, "Of course he's an expert."

"No, he's not a Bigfoot expert." I looked to Barry and then Ken, looking for some sign of approval; that we were doing and talking about the right things in the right ways.

There was a lull, and Barry said, "What do you think, Sarah? Is this guy a Bigfoot expert?"

Mom said, "What? Oh, sorry," then put her phone down on the end table and crossed her arms. "He's not a Bigfoot expert. He's just, um, what, survivorman?"

I said, "Sounds like a superhero name. He needs a cape."

Mom gave me a sad smile, like she'd just remembered that I was there and had been there for a long time. She said, "No capes!" like the character from one of my favorite movies, *The Incredibles*.

At the same time, Marjorie said, "A cape he made out of moss and twigs," but she mumbled. It wasn't a weird, creepy, she's-possessed mumble, but her previously normal, I'm-barely-interested-in-what-you're-talking-about mumble. I heard her and understood her. Mom did too because she laughed.

Marjorie added, "And tight superhero underwear made from squirrel pelts."

Mom said, "It's where he puts his nuts."

I screamed, "Mom!" and everyone but Dad laughed.

The room went quiet again. Barry and Ken whispered to each other some more and consulted the notes again. I leaned on the arm of the couch like it was a pommel horse, and went up and down on my tiptoes. We watched survivorman build a shelter and set deadfall traps for small animals.

I said, "Ew, is he really going to squish animal heads with those rocks? I don't want to see that. Change it."

Marjorie turned, closed one eye, and peered at me through her pinching fingers. "I can squish your head." She pinched her thumb and pointer together and said, "Squish, squish, squish . . ."

I screamed a fake-death moan and fell backward onto the couch, kicking my feet until I rolled over and landed face-up in Dad's lap.

He said, "Come on!" and pushed me off his

lap, onto the couch. "You just hit me in the—" He looked at the cameras and didn't finish his sentence.

Marjorie said, "You hit him in the squirrel pelt." She giggled, and so did I. And so did Mom.

Ken suggested that we put on one of our DVDs, something that we'd all like to watch. Something funny that we could talk about. I shouted, "*Incredibles*," but Marjorie said no. Mom went over to the media cabinet and picked through the small library of films. She suggested other titles and with each title one of us would say no. There was no consensus.

"Forget it, then. John, just find something we all can watch."

I said, "*SpongeBob*."

"No . . ."

Dad changed the channel to hockey and everyone groaned, so he flipped it back to *Survivorman*.

Marjorie started to get up.

Dad asked, "Where are you going?"

"Um, my room? Is that okay?"

"Yeah, sure. Are you—Are you okay?"

Marjorie didn't answer.

I asked, "If she's going to her room can I watch *The Incredibles*? Ken, you can watch it with me."

Barry walked into the room, holding his hands out like a cop directing traffic. "You guys are doing great, here. Marjorie, if you're feeling okay, can you please just give us a few more minutes together, okay? It'd be a huge help."

Her lips moved but no words came out. I had no idea what she would do. So I was most surprised when she silently acquiesced and sat on the floor.

Barry said, "All right." He clapped his hands once. "How about you guys talk a little bit about tomorrow?"

Mom asked, "What do you want us to say?"

"Whatever you want. Are you guys nervous, afraid, excited, relieved? Tomorrow is why we're all doing this, right? Do you guys have anything you want to say to one another or to the cameras, to anybody watching? Just give us something, anything."

Ken gently grabbed Barry's arm, told him to relax, and pulled him back into the foyer.

Mom said, "Okay, okay. Here's what I think: Fuck you, Barry. Did I say that clear enough? Do you need me to repeat it for the mics?" Her face flushed a bright red, lips pulled back over gritted teeth in a snarl's snarl.

Barry said, "No need. I think we got that one, thank you."

Dad sat with his head in his hands, all slumped forward, like someone had pulled his plug. He said, "Tomorrow. Tomorrow is God's day. It always is." When he picked up his head his eyes were closed. He whispered a prayer under his breath.

Mom said, "Well, I sure hope tomorrow is Marjorie's day. God can have the rest of them."

Marjorie stood up, shut the TV off, and walked

over to Mom and sat on her lap. Marjorie was the same height as Mom and fit over her perfectly, like she was drawn on top of Mom with tracing paper. Mom put her arms around Marjorie's waist.

Marjorie said, "I want to tell you guys what it feels like when—when I'm not me. Can I tell you guys about it?"

Mom said, "Yes, of course you can."

Marjorie was quiet and I didn't think she was going to tell us anything, but then she started in. "Last night I got up in the middle of the night to go pee. Then I opened the little window next to the sink because all of a sudden I felt like I was burning up, that I was a thousand degrees, and I crawled up onto the windowsill. It took a really long time to get up there and squeeze my body into the frame. I almost fell out. I tried to scream for help but I couldn't move my mouth and I couldn't breathe and everything in me just started leaking away, running down, like my volume button being turned down slowly. I knew I was dying, that that was what dying felt like, and the worst part was that the terrible horrible dying feeling was going to last forever. I'd never fully run out so the feeling would never stop. And that's it. I crawled out of the window and went back to my room, put on my headphones, and got in bed, but that dying feeling was still with me."

"That sounds just awful, Marjorie," Mom said, her voice stuck in quicksand.

Marjorie said, "Look, I need to ask you guys a favor. Will you be in the room with me tomorrow when it all happens? I want you to be there." She sounded scared and like she might start crying. It was quiet enough in the room that I could hear the hum of the cameras.

Mom said, "Of course we'll be there. Your father and I love you and we'll always be there for you."

Dad mumbled something about God loving her too.

She said, "Thank you. But Merry has to be there too."

Dad said, "I don't know if that's for the best. Your mom and I were talking about sending her to Auntie Erin's for the night, right Sarah?"

That was the first I'd heard of the Auntie Erin plan.

Marjorie said, "No, you can't do that. That won't work. If Merry isn't there—" She paused and repeated herself. "If Merry isn't there, someone will get hurt. Hurt bad. And that person will feel what I felt last night and feel it forever and ever and ever."

"What do you mean?"

"I mean that someone in the room, could be anyone, I don't know who, but I know, I just know the exorcism won't work and then someone will get hurt bad. Unless Merry is there."

Dad stood up and took two steps toward Marjorie so that he loomed over her like a great tree. "Is this the demon talking?"

"No. It's me talking."

"How do you know this will happen?"

"Like I've said before, I just know these things. All these ideas and images I get, they're born in my head."

Dad rubbed hard at his face, like he was trying to take it off. He looked up at the ceiling and said, "I wish Father Wanderly was here. He's told me, repeatedly, that I can't trust what she says because the demon will lie." Then he looked down at Marjorie. "I'm sorry, honey, but I don't know what to believe."

Marjorie said, "Father Wanderly and Barry and the rest of them wanted Merry in the room last time, right? So what's the difference? I'm sure they'll want her in there again, anyway. Makes for good TV, yeah?"

Dad said, "That's not why they wanted Merry there."

Marjorie laughed. "Oh, so they *did* want her there? I was just guessing at that. Why'd they want her there, huh? Just for Merry's love and support, right?" Marjorie struggled out of Mom's hug and off her lap. She walked behind Mom's chair, draped herself in the lacey, white window curtain, then spun around, cocooning herself. It was like the night she was in the blanket in the cardboard house, except I could still see her face's outline, if not her features, through the curtain.

Dad said, "Marjorie, don't do that. Get out of there."

Mom didn't move. She stayed seated and when

she talked, it was like she was talking to the middle of the room. "I know we've already talked with Father Wanderly and Barry about tomorrow, but I really don't care what they say or what they want anymore. I don't want Merry there for the actual exorcism. I don't want her to see what you have to go through. I don't want her to see what you've been made to go through. I don't want her to see you like that, Marjorie. I worry about what this is doing to Merry as much as I worry about what it's doing to you."

Marjorie, still wrapped in the curtain, said, "This is going to help me, Mom, and it will help our family. You'll see. But only if Merry is there. If she isn't, I will not cooperate. I will not go where you'll want me to go and I will not do what you want me to do. I will cover my ears and my eyes when Father Wanderly reads his rite. I will take all my clothes off so you can't film me. If that doesn't work, I'll destroy the cameras. Things will get bad for everyone."

"Marjorie—" Dad was getting louder.

Marjorie leaned up against the wall next to the window. "If you tie me to a bed I will yell and scream and swear and say such blasphemous things over everything Father Wanderly says so the audio footage will be essentially useless. And then someone will get hurt."

Dad started roughly unwrapping Marjorie from the curtain, yelling at the foul demon that was inside her. Mom started yelling too, telling him to stop it, that he was hurting her, and she grabbed his arm and tried to yank him away. He growled at her and ripped his arm out of her grasp. Mom fought harder and hit and scratched at his arms. Barry and Ken went over and tried to break it all up.

I remember it all happening, as cliché as it sounds, in slow motion. My life as a piece of videotape to be slowed down and coolly dissected. Or maybe it's like my memory is a computer with a processing speed too slow for all of the information, and the only way to keep from crashing, to parse any of it, is to artificially slow everything down.

The four yelling adults pushed and pulled one another, and in the middle of it all, the curtain swirled and danced around Marjorie like oxygen-drunk flames. She smiled, showing her teeth through the thin lace curtain before it was pulled away from her face and ripped off the window frame entirely.

She yelled, "Listen to me! I don't know if I can, but I'm trying to save you all too. Merry will help me!"

I'd been saying the whole time that I wanted to be there for the exorcism, but no one was listening to me. I finally reached my breaking point and started crying and screaming for everyone to stop. And then I was just screaming as loudly and as high-pitched as I could, and I couldn't stop.

The adults finally heard me and stopped what they were doing. I was crying so hard I couldn't catch my breath. Mom screamed at me to stop and told me that I was okay, and Dad was crying too and saying he was sorry. Marjorie sat down on the floor, expressionless, picked up a corner of the curtain and put it into her mouth. Barry and Ken retreated off-camera, back into the foyer.

Mom picked me up and rushed me into the bathroom and sat me on the toilet with my head down. She soaked a face cloth in cold water and put it on the back of my neck. Somewhere out in the living room Dad prayed, saying the words so fast and without any pauses for ends of sentences, ends of anything, I couldn't hear any individual words. It all just flowed together with the cold water dripping down the back of my neck.

CHAPTER 21

ON THE MORNING of the exorcism, I stayed home from school. I hadn't known that was going to happen. No one had told me I wasn't going. No one asked if I wanted to stay home. No one woke me up in time to go even if I'd wanted to.

When I woke up it was after nine o'clock. I was nervous at first, like I'd done something wrong. Mom was still asleep in bed next to me. She didn't stir as I quietly crawled out of bed, dressed in sweatpants and a sweat shirt, and sneaked away.

Marjorie was asleep in her room, on her side, facing away from the doorway. I peeked in across the hall and Dad wasn't in his bedroom. I went into the sunroom, peeled back the black cloth covering the windows so I could see out front. His car was gone.

I went downstairs to eat breakfast and found

Ken sitting at the kitchen table by himself with coffee, a laptop, and his notebook.

He said, "Good morning, Merry."

"Hi."

"Need any help? Want me to make you something?"

"No." I acted like I was mad at him though I wasn't really sure why I'd be mad at him. I made cereal, spilling some of the milk in the process, but I cleaned it up myself. I sat across from Ken and crunched away on the fruity O's.

"Staying home from school today?"

"Yes. It's the big day, you know."

"I know it is. You be careful, okay?"

"Will you be here tomorrow? After?"

"I'm not sure. Depends."

"Depends on what?"

"On how today goes. I'm not really sure what the plan is. Barry is meeting with the production company and network reps as we speak. I'm going to guess that we'll be here tomorrow, but you never know. Maybe we'll leave tomorrow but then come back in a few weeks to do some follow-up interviews and stuff."

"But you're the writer, right? You can write yourself into staying a few more days."

Ken said, "I wish writers had that power."

I finished breakfast and poured myself a glass of orange juice. I drank, watching Ken read something on his laptop and make notes. I said, "I'm going outside to play soccer." I didn't ask him if he wanted to come too. He didn't ask if I wanted him to join me.

He packed up his stuff while I tied my sneakers. He said, "It's really cold out. I don't think that sweatshirt will be warm enough."

I shrugged and went outside with my ball anyway.

He was right. It was freezing out. My ball instantly became a hard rock that wasn't fun to kick. Plus, the leaves were damp and frosted, and they stuck to my ball. Mom and Dad still hadn't raked the leaves out back yet. Mom had said they were too busy. Dad had said it looked cinematic and made for dramatic autumn-in-New-England-type shots. We'd all rolled our eyes at him when he said that, even the cameraperson filming us.

I didn't want to go back inside and admit to Ken he was right that it was too cold out. I stayed outside, cutting paths through the leaves until my cheeks were chapped and my toes were wet, unfeeling nubs jammed into my sneakers.

While I was playing soccer in my own self-imposed gulag, there was a chorus of voices, steadily increasing in volume, coming from out front. I was sure it was the protesters, who had become so ubiquitous that they were like wallpaper you didn't notice until you actively decided to stare at it and follow the pattern. I was bored with ice-soccer so I decided to go out front and stare at that wallpaper.

Dad must've just pulled into the driveway, because his car was askew, still running, and his driver's-side door was open. He yelled and pointed at the protesters. Two policemen stood in front of him and appeared to be physically holding Dad back.

Beached in the street in front of our house was an idling, white minibus. A new group of protesters ringed the vehicle. They were off-set and separate from the usual crowd who were clearly unhappy with this new group. The new group's signs were brightly colored in fluorescent yellows and greens, looking, ironically enough, like peace-and-love tie-dye shirts on poster boards. But the text was thick and ugly and black. The signs read: GOD HATES FAGS. YOU'RE GOING TO HELL. GOD HATES FAG CATHOLIC PRIESTS. GOD HATES YOU. GOD HATES MARJORIE BARRETT.

I don't think I knew what the word *fag* meant at the time. I felt queasy because I knew I was seeing something that I wasn't supposed to see.

The new protesters were mostly men, but there were some women, and one little girl close to my age, cheerily holding up the YOU'RE GOING TO HELL sign. I wanted to yell at them, tell them that Marjorie was my sister and that no one hated her. I couldn't understand why anyone would hate her just because, like Mom said, she wasn't well.

I wasn't brave enough to yell at the scary new protesters, and I ran toward the front door.

There was such an explosion of angry shouts

from the crowd, I thought they saw me running for the door and were now coming after me. I stumbled up the brick stairs, twisting and landing butt-first on the stoop. I expected to see the new protesters pouring over the lawn toward me with their signs waving, teeth bared, hands outstretched. But everyone was shouting like crazy because of Dad.

Dad worked his way through the ring of new protesters and tore up all the Marjorie signs he could reach. I cheered him on. "Go, Dad!"

The police jogged into the crowd but were still more than a few steps behind Dad. One protester who'd held his sign behind his back in an attempt to protect it said something to Dad. I couldn't hear him, but I saw his mouth moving and I saw the big *I dare you* smile after.

Dad lost it. He spit in the other man's face and he started yelling, swearing, and throwing wild punches and kicks. The other man didn't fight back at all but instead ducked and covered. The circle of protesters quickly cleared and it seemed like everyone had their smartphones out and pointed at the scene. They laughed, cheered, and egged on the very one-sided fight. The policemen finally caught up to Dad and wrapped themselves around his chest and back. Dad was out of control, yelling and thrashing, smashing the back of his head into the policeman's chest, trying to break free.

I stopped cheering him on and a cry of "Leave my dad alone" died in my throat. I was scared and I wanted the police to hold him, calm him down, to make him stop.

The two policemen held on and eventually brought him to the ground.

I didn't know what to do. There wasn't anything I could do. I opened the front door. Ken ran past me. And I ran past him and up the stairs. Marjorie was awake and sitting on the edge of her bed. I didn't stop at her door; I kept running down the hallway.

Marjorie shouted behind me, "I told you there's something really wrong with Dad. Maybe he's the one who's possessed, yeah?"

I ran to my room and hid under the covers next to Mom, who was still asleep.

MOM HAD TO GO TO the police station to bail out Dad. I'd overheard her shouting on the phone, using that phrase. I knew enough to know she meant something other than Dad was in a sinking boat.

I spent the afternoon watching TV with Ken. My usual shows weren't on, so we were mainly stuck watching cartoons I'd already seen before. We didn't say much to each other. I asked Ken if the new protesters were still out there. He said yes. Actually, he said, "Yes, those awful people are still out there." I dozed off and on, listening for Mom's car, watching the front door. Marjorie was upstairs by herself. I heard her roaming around the second floor, haunting our rooms, opening and shutting doors. I wondered if she'd looked outside, seen the new protesters, and read their signs about her.

Mom and Dad finally got back around 6:00 P.M. Mom had phoned ahead, telling us they'd be home with dinner, so Marjorie and I were sitting at the kitchen table waiting for them when they arrived. As they walked in the door Marjorie whispered to me, telling me again that Dad was the one who was possessed.

My parents weren't speaking to each other. They said quick hellos to us. I tried not to look at them directly, although I was reasonably sure that neither of them knew that I'd seen Dad punching the protester. I also didn't want to look at Dad because I was afraid he'd look different, changed.

Mom carried a large brown bag of Chinese food. They set the table with paper plates and we picked what we wanted to eat out of the white cardboard boxes. Dad said grace. It lasted longer than what had become the usual, and he alternated between near tears and gritted-teeth anger. We politely listened and waited for him to finish. Tony and Jenn and their cameras buzzed into the room like the flies on the wall they'd become.

Marjorie's plate had more color to it than mine but she didn't eat much. I ate a mound of white rice and chicken fingers with lots of duck sauce. I so associate the tangy-sweet taste of duck sauce with that night that as an adult I avoid eating Chinese food. It's funny that I can and have watched all the episodes from our show without ever feeling like I'm reliving the trauma, but duck sauce on white rice will send me over the edge and will instantly bring back all the anxiety and fear of exorcism night.

When we finished eating, Mom asked if we wanted our fortune cookies. I tore into mine, breaking it into glasslike shards. The fortune was some life-affirming aphorism I no longer remember. I do remember the "Learn to speak Chinese" lesson printed on the back of the slip of paper though. *Shui* means water. No one else wanted their cookie so I ate a second one, but I made sure to crumple up the fortune without reading it because Marjorie had told me once that getting two fortunes would bring bad luck.

Dad cleared the table and stacked the white cardboard containers of leftovers in the fridge. With his back to us, he announced that Father Wanderly would be arriving soon to perform the exorcism and that we should get ready. I didn't know what to do to get ready so I went to the small half bath off the kitchen and washed my sticky hands. When I came out, Mom and Dad were sitting at the table with their heads down. I went over to Marjorie and gave her a hug around the neck, from behind, so if she wanted, she could've stood up and carried me around like her backpack.

I whispered directly into her ear, "You'll do great, Marjorie."

She said, "You're going to do great, too, monkey."

Mom got up and said, "Come on, Marjorie. I'll go upstairs and wait with you."

Dad stood too, looking confused, and said, "Oh, okay, yeah, good idea. Merry and I will talk with Father Wanderly when he gets here and then we'll—" He stopped abruptly, and never finished.

I didn't want either of them to leave. I wanted her to stay down in the kitchen with me. I said, "No, let's all stay down here together." I didn't let go of her neck.

Marjorie shook her head no, and her hair feather-dusted my face. She said, "I want to go back to my room. I don't feel very well."

"Can I go upstairs with them too?"

Dad said, "No. You need to stay down here." He sat back down. He put his hands on the table, then on his lap, then back on the table. Those big hands didn't know what to do.

I tightened my grip on Marjorie and said, "I don't want to."

Mom looked directly at Dad and shouted, "Merry can come upstairs with us if she wants!", and Tony the cameraman flinched and bumped a shoulder in the doorway.

"Hey, take it easy. I'm just saying she should stay down here with me. I—I mean *we* didn't get a chance to fully prep her for tonight, right? Like we wanted." He paused and then said, "Look," as though Mom had responded or interrupted him, neither of which happened. "I want to talk to her again about what's going to happen and I want Father Wanderly's help."

She said, "You don't know what's going to happen."

"We need to pray."

"There'll be plenty of that later. She wants to be with her sister, let her be with her sister."

"Right, because them being together has worked out so well before."

"I'll be there too."

"This is fucking crazy. We agreed to have another prep meeting this afternoon—"

"Yeah, well, something else happened this afternoon, didn't it? Maybe we should've had another prep meeting in your goddamned holding cell!"

Dad stood up quickly and sent the kitchen chair crashing to the floor. He looked backward and extended a hand to the chair, like he didn't mean it. He said, "Jenn, Tony, hey, can you leave us alone, please? Seriously, stop taping. Just give us a few seconds."

I couldn't see Marjorie's face. She was still wrapped in my arms. I felt her breathing. It was slow and even. My eyes blurred with tears, and I ducked back down and said, "Stop yelling at each other. I'll just stay, I'll just stay down here," into the back of her head.

Mom shushed me and said, "Oh sure, *now* Mr. Confessional Interview wants to get rid of the cameras."

I didn't know where Ken and Barry were or

if they were watching. I called out silently to Ken in my head, wanting him to show up and calm Dad down, calm everyone down. The two camerapersons didn't respond to Dad and they didn't turn their cameras away either.

Dad said, "Merry and I are staying down here and we're going to pray and talk about how she can protect herself." Dad grew louder, more manic, and in my memory, he grew in size too.

I whispered as lightly as I could, "Go please, Marjorie, just stand up and go. Go away. From them. I'll hang on. Can we go?" I felt so helpless and I wanted to be away from Mom and Dad forever.

She whispered back to me, "Later. I promise."

Mom said, "She and I will talk. And I'll be there to protect Merry."

"Come on, Sarah. Can't you admit just for once that you're in over your head?"

"I'm not the one who suddenly thinks he has the power to magically pray everything better!"

"What can you do to protect Merry? Seriously, tell me. What can you do that you haven't already tried? I mean, aren't you worried about Merry's soul too?"

"I'm worried about everything! I'm worried about what all of this is doing to Merry. And if you're so worried about her soul, tell Father Wanderly to come up with a spell to protect it. Come on, girls. Now."

"This isn't going to work if we don't believe."

"Jesus, John, really? You sound like a Disney movie. Don't worry, I'll believe when I have to."

"Carry me, Marjorie," I said. I was too afraid to let go.

Mom yelled at me. "Merry, will you just get off your sister! You heard her say she wasn't feeling good."

MOM GAVE ME A HURRIED explanation of what to expect, of what might happen. I didn't listen to a word. I paced anxiously around Marjorie's room.

Mom said, "Merry, please. You're making me nuts."

"Sorry." I went over and sat at Marjorie's work desk. I hated her wooden chair. It was so uncomfortable, and it made my legs fall asleep if I sat in it for too long, and then I'd get yelled at for having to stomp out the pins and needles.

Marjorie was in bed, lying on her side, facing her closed door. Mom sat on the bed beside her and stroked her hair.

Mom seemed ready to break down into tears, but said in her calmest voice, "Do you want to talk, Marjorie? Do you want me to put a stop to this? I will. You just tell me. I'll cancel everything."

Marjorie said, "A little late for that now, isn't it, Mom?"

"No. It isn't. I'm—I don't know. It's like a few months ago, when your dad first brought up the idea, I was this totally different person. I had to be, because I don't understand what that other woman was thinking. I don't understand how she could've thought that this was a good idea. And I'm so goddamn mad at her. Why didn't she say no when—"

The doorbell rang. Two-tone. One high note, followed by a lower note.

Mom was still rambling on and Marjorie said, "It's okay, Mom. Stop it. This is what I want now. It's going to help, I promise."

In my memory, heavy and hurried footfalls coming up the stairs immediately followed the ringing of the doorbell, then there were the whispers in the hallway and knocks on Marjorie's bedroom door.

"Hello? May we come in?"

I shouted, "No! Go away!" I wanted everyone to just leave me, Mom, and Marjorie alone. Let us stay in her room like that forever.

"Yes, come in," Mom said.

It was Barry with Jenn and Tony the camerapersons, and a small army of technicians clustered behind them in the hallway. Barry consulted a clipboard he was holding, looked up, and said, "Hi, just a few things. Just wanted to doublecheck that Marjorie was still okay with the exorcism taking place here in her bedroom, like we agreed to earlier?" Marjorie said yes. "Great. You're a trouper, kid." He then clumsily explained that they had some last-minute setup work to do.

Mom swore and said something about them having had all day to do this.

Barry's legion poured into the room with more lighting and sound equipment. One guy had white candles and an ornate brass candelabrum in his arms, another had a large pewter crucifix, and another carried in small statues of the Virgin Mary. Barry shouted at the setup crew that it all had to be ready five minutes ago.

Mom said, "Gee, should we step out for a minute or something?" after one guy almost hit her in the head with a boom mic stand.

"No, you don't have to. But, wait, yeah if you want. That's fine, too. Maybe?"

Marjorie said, "I think I'm going to be sick," and Mom shouted at everyone to get out of the way, to clear a path, and she ushered Marjorie out and to the bathroom.

I followed them out but Mom shut the bathroom door on me. I waited in the hallway outside the door and listened to Marjorie coughing. When it quieted down and I heard the faucet running, I wandered over past Marjorie's busy room and to the railing that overlooked the stairs. I sat on the floor and rested my face between two balusters. I used to do that on Christmas mornings when I was up before everyone else and would just stare down at the bottom of the stairs and the front foyer, which was lit up in the soft white glow of the Christmas tree lights in the living room.

Dad and Father Wanderly were downstairs in the living room. I heard them talking. The front foyer was lit in a harsh white light from someone's camera lamp, or maybe they'd set up a spotlight for a pre-exorcism interview.

Barry led his technicians out of Marjorie's room and they filed downstairs. Barry said, "We're ready for you upstairs, Father."

Mom and Marjorie were still in the bathroom. I stayed sitting and with my head resting against the spindles. Tony the cameraman stood adjacent to me, leaned some of his weight on the railing, and pointed a camera down at the first floor. I told him not to lean on the railing because it could break. Dad always used to say that to me.

Father Wanderly was the first up the stairs. He wore a billowy white tunic over a black robe. He looked so much bigger, so much more substantial than he did in his usual black shirt and black pants. The tunic had lace decoration on the hem down by his ankles and near the collar, but was otherwise plain. His hands were lost inside the tunic's giant sleeves. He wore a long purple stole draped over the back of his neck and it hung down below his knees.

There was another priest, the same one who had come to our house that day I was first introduced to Father Wanderly: Father Gavin, the short, young one with the beady eyes and lots of forehead sweat. He was similarly dressed in a white tunic and purple stole and he carried Father Wanderly's red leather-bound book and this thing called an aspergillum, which is a long wand with a metal ball at the end that held holy water.

Dad came up the stairs next. He walked with his hands folded and his head down. The top of his head, which I normally didn't see from such a favorable vantage, had a new bald spot like a crop circle. With everything else going on, I was still shocked by how much hair he had lost.

Father Wanderly walked right up to me and extended a hand. He said, "Please, stand with me, brave little Meredith." Adults understood the sacred power of names. I had to take his hand and I had to stand with him even though I wanted to stay with my face pressed against the balustrade.

Dad asked what I was doing out here. I shrugged, and told him I was sorry. When I said it, I meant that I was sorry for not choosing to stay with him, even if I would've gone upstairs with Marjorie and Mom if given the same choice all over again. Dad didn't look me in the eyes, but stared at some empty space just over my head. He asked where Mom and Marjorie were. I told him that they were in the bathroom. Dad walked over and knocked on the door. "Marjorie? Sarah? Are you okay? Father Wanderly is here and ready to get started."

Mom: "We'll meet you in Marjorie's room. Give us a few more minutes."

Dad sighed, lifted his arms, and let them fall bonelessly to his sides. He said, "Shouldn't Sarah hear the instructions again, Father? I feel like she's putting this all on me when we both had decided that this was best."

Father Wanderly said, "It'll be all right, John. You are a pillar of strength. You are a fine Christian man."

"No, I'm not. I failed today. I failed tonight. I'm not a good—"

"Nonsense. You stumbled. And you got back up, and you are again standing alongside Christ." He grabbed Dad's hand and mine again. "What I need from you both, and what Marjorie needs from you both, is to believe in the power of God's love."

Dad whispered a thank-you at Father Wanderly. It lacked conviction, though, and sounded like I used to whenever I was reminded or prodded to say please.

The bathroom door opened, and Marjorie peeked around the corner; a hide-and-seek player trying not to get caught. Her face and hair were damp. Mom filled the doorway behind her.

Marjorie asked, "Should I go in the room first?" She held a hand to her stomach. "I feel— funny. There's something not right."

Father Wanderly said, "Sarah, please help Marjorie to her bed. We'll be in right behind you."

Marjorie's bedroom door was closed. The hallway was filled with cameras and priests and people. It was too much for me, so I just stared hard at the door, at the cracks in the wood, and followed them up toward the ceiling and down to the floor until Mom finally passed in front of me like an eclipse and opened the door.

CHAPTER 22

TONY THE CAMERAMAN pushed through the rest of us to walk into Marjorie's room next. Jenn was already inside.

Mom stood in the middle of the room and called out to those of us still in the hallway. "It's freezing in here. Is the window open? You didn't tell me the window was going to be open."

Father Wanderly said they needed it to be "on the cooler side" in the room. He didn't offer any explanation. He dropped my hand and Dad's hand and walked in next. The rest of us followed.

Marjorie's room wasn't her room anymore. Lighting lamps, boom mics, and candle stands lined the perimeter. Her desk had been draped with a white cloth and housed candles and religious idols and statuettes. Crucifixes hung on each wall, with the largest one made from pewter and hanging on the white plaster spot on the wall where Marjorie had punched holes. My eyes were drawn to that crucifix and the deeply etched agony of Jesus' face.

Mom was right. It was freezing in the room. I tucked my chin, hugged my chest, and fought off waves of shivers.

Low murmurs of discussion rumbled through the room. Barry was there—I hadn't seen him come in—and he talked about lighting and angles with Jenn and Tony. Dad hung back toward the door, standing ramrod straight, head bowed, hands folded in front of him, his knuckles gone white. Marjorie sat on the bed—the comforter and sheets were turned down—and stared off to nowhere. Mom stood over her, and she suddenly got louder than everyone else in the room.

"I know we talked about this, but do we really have to tie her down? John?"

Leather straps had been fastened to the posts of Marjorie's bed. They looked like black tongues.

Father Wanderly said, "Yes. As we discussed, the restraints are necessary to keep Marjorie safe. To keep her from accidentally hurting herself or anyone else in the room."

Everyone in the room stood in a half circle and watched Marjorie lie down on the bed. She voluntarily stretched her arms out over her head, toward the bedposts, and said, "Mom, you tie them. Go ahead. Do it." Mom slowly went down to one knee in front of the bed and buckled the straps around Marjorie's wrists and ankles. Mom whispered something to Marjorie that I couldn't hear. Marjorie just watched the ceiling. When she was done, Mom kissed her hand and pressed it to Marjorie's forehead. Marjorie exhaled and it was cold enough that I could see her breath.

Mom was crying. She slowly backed away and stood next to me.

I asked, "Mom, what did you say to her?"

Mom bent down and said, "She'll be all right, Merry."

I nodded my head even though my sister didn't look like she'd be all right. She was dressed in a gray hoodie and black swishy pants, her arms and legs akimbo, strapped to the bed. Her legs and feet twitched, fast, like blinks, and her lips wormed around, making words without making sounds. I tried to read them.

Wind gusts rattled the old, open windows in their frames. Candles burned and wax sizzled. The walls, the statues of Mary on the desk, and Marjorie's face glowed weirdly orange in the candlelight. Everyone in the room settled in and got quiet. I stood between my parents. Each had a hand on one of my shoulders. Their hands were cold and heavy.

Father Wanderly stepped into the middle of the room and said simply, "Let us begin the sacred rite."

He slowly walked to the bed and made the sign of the cross over Marjorie's body; his wavering hand hovered only six inches or so above her, like he was tracing her outline in the air.

Marjorie said, "He's pretending to cut me into four pieces. It hurts. Divide and conquer. He's going to do the same to all of you." She sounded tired, uninterested, like she was in a hurry to get this, whatever this was, over with.

Father Wanderly repeated the sign of the cross over himself, then he did the same to everyone else in the room, including the camerapersons. When he got to me, he bent down and waved his right hand up, down, left, right, in front of my face. I followed his hand with my eyes like it was one of the vision tests I routinely failed without my glasses.

Upon finishing, the other priest gave him the aspergillum and Father Wanderly sprinkled holy water on us all. I ducked and a lone, icy drop spotted the top of my head and it felt like the tip of a finger. He sprinkled Marjorie up and down with the water, waving his wand madly, striking out at an invisible assailant. He doused Marjorie with so much water, sizable wet spots ink-blotted her gray hoodie. Marjorie didn't move or say anything. She only blinked when the drops splashed her face.

Father Wanderly turned to Mom, Dad, and me, and held out his hands, palms turned up. "To all present—"

Marjorie stared at the ceiling, and said, "For all those playing along at home, he's going to kneel next to my bed and recite the Litany of

Saints. This is going to be the really boring part. He has to say the name of, like, every saint ever."

Father Wanderly repeated his instructions. "To all present, please respond with, 'Lord have mercy.'"

Marjorie said, "But later when he invokes the name of a saint you're supposed to say 'pray for us' after each one. Merry, if you don't do this correctly, you're going to get a demon inside you, one that has pointy scales and sharp horns, and then you'll be in hell, like me."

Mom and Dad breathed out fast, air hissing through their clenched teeth.

Marjorie said, "In my hell, my parents are teakettles." She giggled, but it was forced. I could tell. She was scared. I don't know if she was afraid because she didn't know what was going to happen or if she was afraid of what she'd already decided would happen. Even now, I'm not sure. I think it was a little of both.

Father Wanderly said, "Barretts, you must ignore what she says. Remind yourself that it isn't the real Marjorie saying such awful things."

"It's me. It has always been me."

Father Wanderly knelt by Marjorie's bed, and his purple stole and tunic pooled around his knees, giving the illusion that he was disappearing, melting into his vestments. He opened his red leather-bound book and he said, "Lord have mercy."

Dad and Father Gavin were the only ones in

the room who gave the response. "Lord have mercy."

Father Wanderly: "Christ have mercy."

I tried to respond like I was supposed to, but I did so incorrectly. I said "Lord" when I was supposed to say "Christ." It happened again with the next response when I got it totally wrong when they said "Christ, graciously hear us."

Mom squeezed my shoulder. She wasn't participating. She whispered in my ear that I could just respond in my head if I wanted to.

I shook my head no because if I didn't do my part this wouldn't work and we'd all be stuck in Marjorie's hell forever. Marjorie had told me she was faking and doing it all on purpose and I believed her, but just in case she wasn't faking, just in case there really was a demon inside her, I was going to do what Father Wanderly said. Even if I didn't believe in him or his God, I wanted to believe that what he was going to say would make her better, would turn her back into who she used to be.

Ultimately, it didn't matter what I believed because Marjorie wanted me to be there for a reason. I didn't know what that reason was, and until I did, until I knew what I had to do, I would do what was expected; I'd play the part of the scared little sister that she and everyone else wanted me to play.

"Have mercy on us."

Marjorie said, "And here comes the litany."

Father Wanderly: "Holy Mary, pray for us."

Father Gavin echoed with, "Pray for us." Father Wanderly waited until the rest of us said the same. Mom whispered it too.

Marjorie said, "He'll say fifty saints' names. Try counting along, Merry."

Father Wanderly read the litany. I was supposed to say "Pray for us" after each name, and I did, but I also couldn't help but counting the saints. I used my fingers to help, curling each one into a balled fist, then starting over again with an open hand. She had the correct number.

Father Wanderly said, "From all evil, deliver us, O Lord," and he waited.

Marjorie said, "Now the response is, 'Deliver us, O Lord.' Come on, now, try and keep up. Didn't anyone else do their reading homework?"

"From all sin—"

"Deliver us, O Lord."

Father Wanderly continued to pray, like he was reading a grocery list, and we responded in kind. Marjorie started talking over Father Wanderly. He tried to project his voice louder, but she matched him in frequency and decibel. Their voices were synchronized sound waves and Father Gavin and my parents were off in their response timing, as though they couldn't distinguish between who was saying what. I focused on Marjorie. I watched her speak and in my memory, she was as clear to me as if she were speaking inside my head.

She said, "He'll ask to deliver us from an unprovided death and deliver us from earthquakes and storms and plague and famine and war. Those prayers have never worked, have never stopped those things from happening. They won't now and they never will. And I don't see what any of these prayers have to do with helping me. These prayers are designed for you, Merry. To make you think his God controls all things, especially you."

At some point the response changed to "We beg you to hear us." Dad was nearly shouting.

Father Wanderly stood up shakily, and he was breathing heavily, frozen breath billowing from his mouth like he was a smokestack. The younger Father Gavin rushed to his side.

Father Wanderly said, "I'm all right. Just my trick knee acting up." He gathered himself and recited the Lord's Prayer and read Psalm 54: "Turn back the evil upon my foes; in your faithfulness destroy them."

Upon finishing the psalm, he launched straight into a solo prayer that for the first time directly addressed the evil spirit inside Marjorie. The prayer seemed to go on forever and no one else spoke, including Marjorie. In it he referred to a God who was merciful and forgiving, and he said something about an apostate tyrant, a noonday devil destroying God's vineyard. At the end of the prayer, he finally said Marjorie's name, and he called her a servant of God.

Everyone said, "Amen."

The younger priest handed Father Wanderly a white cloth. He wiped his face with it.

Marjorie suddenly became animated, like a switch had been flipped. She squirmed and pulled on her restraints. Her lips were blue and her teeth chattered.

Father Wanderly addressed the demon directly. "I command you, unclean spirit—"

Marjorie said, "Wait. Please, wait. It's me. I thought I could take the cold, but I can't. I'm freezing. Please, Father. I'm doing the best I can, but I'm soaked with holy water and I'm right next to the window, the freezing cold air is blowing directly on me. My demonly powers don't keep me warm, you know. I'm joking. Seriously though, can someone just shut the windows or pull up the blanket?"

Mom stepped forward and Dad grabbed her arm. "No. Not unless Father Wanderly says it's okay."

"Let go of me."

Marjorie spoke at the same time, "Dad, please. I'm so cold."

Father Wanderly stopped reading. He said, "Family members cannot come into contact with her now that we've started the rite, particularly when I'm directly addressing the demon. It's not safe. Her pleading could be a trick."

Marjorie said, "Yes, I've made my lips turn blue, willed goose bumps to appear on my skin, and I'm fake shivering. Just like all those women the church had drowned and burned as witches were trying to trick the faithful with their screams."

Mom said, "I'm pulling up the blanket."

Father Wanderly said, "Please," and held up a hand to stop her. "Let us do it. We'll pull up the blanket, okay?" He asked the younger priest if he would pull up the blanket.

Father Gavin stepped forward as Mom retreated back to me. I was freezing too. I wanted a blanket but I wouldn't ask for one. He hesitated at the foot of the bed. "Should I pull up everything, or just the comforter?"

Father Wanderly didn't really answer him. He just said, "Quickly, now, please."

Father Gavin wrestled with the turned-down sheets, leaving them behind and crumpled at the foot of the bed, finally choosing to pull the puffy white comforter slowly over Marjorie. He was quite nervous and avoided any contact—both eye and physical—with her.

She watched him; watched him hard enough to burn a hole into him. She said, "Please tuck it up as close to my chin as possible, and get as much of my arms under it as you can. Thank you so much." Father Gavin did as he was asked, and carefully molded the thick blanket around as much of her outstretched arms as he could without covering her face. "That's so much better." Marjorie shivered, and her body shook under the sheet. Father Gavin skittered away from the bed, a rabbit sprinting through an open field.

Father Wanderly started in again, commanding the unclean spirit to name itself and obey him.

Marjorie said, "Really? We need to go through this again? Fine. I know what you want me to be: I can be Azazel, the serpent, the fallen demon."

Father Wanderly soldiered on. He put his hands on Marjorie's forehead and prayed for her healing.

Marjorie said, "I'm exaggerating my cosmic standing a little bit. How about if I'm just plain old Azazel, as described in the Hebrew Bible? I'm only the scapegoat, the outcast sent into the desert." Marjorie had recovered. Her voice was hers again; calm, matter-of-fact, tinged with that unmistakable undercurrent of teen dismissal and disdain.

Father Wanderly read the first of three gospel lessons.

"Maybe we should spice it up, and because Ken is such a big fan of H. P. Lovecraft, I can be Azathoth: the demon sultan, the nucleus of infinity. No one dares speak my name out loud and I feast in the impenetrably dark chambers beyond time and space. Rawr!" She thrashed and wiggled about in her restraints, and the carefully tucked comforter slid down, away from her arms and away from her chin and pooled around her midsection. "I am the dead dreamer, older than sin, older than humanity. I am the shadow below everything. I am the beautiful thing that awaits us all.

"Hey, Merry, that reminds me. I miss your books. You don't bring me your books anymore. I miss writing and making up stories for you. Do you miss my stories?"

I wanted to answer her, though I knew I wasn't supposed to interact with her in any way. She looked over at me and her face flashed disappointment when I didn't say anything. So I nodded my head, just slightly, so only she could see it.

Father Wanderly did not engage her in discussion but continued to read his gospels. He droned on without any change in pitch or timbre. I couldn't tell if he was listening to her or not. His head and neck glistened with sweat.

"I'm cold again. Can you pull up the blanket again? Sorry, I'll try not to move around so much."

Father Gavin didn't wait for permission. He swooped in and pulled up the comforter, this time wrapping and tucking the corners under her arms and shoulders.

Fingers snapped somewhere behind me, and then Jenn the camerawoman crept up in front of Mom, Dad, and me, toward the headboard for a hard close-up.

Father Wanderly crossed himself and made the sign of the cross over Marjorie again, slow and deliberate. He picked up one corner of his purple stole and draped it across Marjorie's neck. She strained to look down at it. He placed his other hand on her forehead and gently pushed her head back into the pillow.

Marjorie smiled and said, "Your hand is warm. Make sure you say the rest in accents filled with confidence and faith, like it says in your book."

Father Wanderly nearly shouted his prayers, and Dad eagerly shouted back the responses. I didn't turn around but he must've been on his knees because he was shouting in my ears. I covered them with hands and fingers that hurt they were so cold. I wanted to leave that room, that house, and I had a brief runaway fantasy where I ran away to California, which I'd never been to, to where all the Bigfoots were, and I'd disappear into the woods and live alone, become a rumor, an occasional blurred sighting.

Father Wanderly filled himself up and shouted, "Let us pray." Then, shaking, voice breaking, he asked that he would be "granted help against the unclean spirit now tormenting this creature of God's." He traced the sign of the cross on her brow three times.

Marjorie said, "I'm not a creature. I'm—I'm Marjorie, a fourteen-year-old girl, scared of everything, who doesn't know why she hears voices that tell her confusing things. And I try to be good and I try. Try not to listen to them." She paused in places where there weren't supposed to be pauses and she stumbled over the words like she'd forgotten her lines she hadn't spent enough time memorizing. Marjorie was suddenly unconvincing. Unlike when Father Wanderly and Dr. Navidson had previously interviewed her, it didn't feel like she was in danger, and it didn't feel like she was a danger to us.

An emboldened Father Wanderly said that Marjorie was "caught up in the fearsome threats of man's ancient enemy, sworn foe of our race, who befuddles and stupefies the human mind, throws it into terror, overwhelms it with fear and panic."

Marjorie asked, "Are you scared and confused like I am?" Her voice was as small as I'd ever heard it. "I think everyone is secretly like me."

Father Wanderly asked that this servant be protected in mind and body. He folded down the blanket and traced the cross on Marjorie's chest, over her heart.

"What are you doing? Why is he touching me there?" Marjorie twitched and arched her back against the restraints, trying to avoid the priest's touch. The rest of the blanket slumped off the side of the bed.

Jenn retreated a few steps back from the headboard, toward the newly plastered wall with its heavy pewter crucifix. Jesus peeked out over her shoulder and she kept her camera pointed at Marjorie like it was a gun.

Father Wanderly traced the sign of the cross above her heart twice more, and said, "Keep watch over the innermost recesses of her heart; rule over her emotions; strengthen her will. Let vanish from her soul the temptings of the mighty adversary."

Marjorie turned and looked at Mom, with a look that said: You're letting him do *that* to me? Mom couldn't return the look.

Father Wanderly paused to drink from a bottle of water he'd placed on Marjorie's desk.

Marjorie said, "This isn't working," and she sounded so far away, so lost inside herself. "You know, I thought I'd play along and that it couldn't hurt, but you're making everything worse." Her voice broke and she started shivering again.

I looked down at my feet, feeling guilty, but I wasn't sure about what. I guess I had to blame myself to have something to hold on to.

Mom must've felt the same way. She said, "I'm sorry, honey. This is all my fault."

Dad whispered a prayer.

Father Wanderly drank deeply from the water bottle. When he put the bottle back down, the middle desk drawer sprang open. Still covered by the white cloth, that desk's ghostly tongue protruded out into the room toward Father Wanderly, and then slammed itself shut.

Marjorie yelled, "What was that? That's not me! That's not me! I didn't do that! What's happening?" She tried to sit up and she spun her head wildly left, right, then left again, looking accusatorily at everyone.

The wind gusted outside, whistling through the window frame, fluttering the curtains and the candle flames. The desk drawer continued opening and closing as regularly as the ticks of a metronome.

Father Wanderly shouted, "He now flails you with His divine scourges!"

"What do you mean? I didn't do anything. Don't blame me for that. Mom, Dad, help me! I don't know what's happening!"

Mom and Dad were shouting now too. Dad shouted Jesus Christ's name; Mom shouted Marjorie's name. Mom pulled me over to her, held me in front of her like I was a shield.

Father Wanderly: "He in whose sight you and your legions once cried out: 'What have we to do with you, Jesus, Son of the Most High God? Have you come to torture us before the time?' "

There was a loud banging sound from underneath Marjorie's bed, like something was trying to ram up through the floor.

Marjorie screamed and my parents went quiet. She said, "Who's doing this? Stop it! What I'm doing and saying isn't enough for you? Everything I've done isn't enough for you? I'm scared and I'm cold and I want to stop. Stop it! Stop it! Stop it!"

Father Wanderly continued. "Now He is driving you back into the everlasting fire."

Father Gavin quickly scurried to the bed and bent down at Father Wanderly's feet to gather the comforter.

Marjorie cried hysterically, her chest heaving. "I'm so cold. Please stop banging. Please, Father. I'm so cold. Can we stop? Take a break? I'll stop too. Make them stop. Make them stop . . ."

Father Gavin quickly readjusted the comforter and pulled it up to her chin again.

Father Wanderly: "Begone, now! Begone, seducer! Your place is in solitude. . . ."

Marjorie shot her head forward and clamped her teeth onto Father Gavin's meaty and hairy wrist.

He let out such a high-pitched scream it made my knees wobble. He tried to extract himself by lifting his arm over his head, but he only got it halfway up. Marjorie still held on with her teeth. The large sleeves of his tunic slid down past his elbow. Blood leaked from the sides of her mouth and ran down his arm. Father Gavin screamed for God to help him. Dad rushed past me and, along with Father Wanderly, stepped in and tried to separate Marjorie and the younger priest, and separate them they did, but slowly. Dad pulled Marjorie back and her mouthful of flesh was still tethered to Father Gavin's arm by a thin rope of skin that stretched out like taffy. Father Wanderly pushed the younger priest off the bed and that spaghetti strand tore down the entire length of his forearm, all the way to his elbow.

Dad and Father Wanderly fell on top of Father Gavin, who thrashed around on the floor as though he were having a seizure. Father Wanderly was knocked backward and he rolled into my ankles. He held his left shoulder with a shaky right hand and his eyes were closed against the pain.

Dad worked to pin down the younger priest so Jenn—she'd abandoned her camera—could wrap the man's bleeding arm in his billowy tunic sleeve. The sleeve quickly turned a dark red, almost purple. And I know it's probably a faulty or cross-wired memory, but Dad was wild-eyed, his teeth bared; he wore the same expression he had before he assaulted the protester.

Marjorie slid as close as she could to the edge of her bed. Her mouth was red and full. She breathed in quickly through her nose, and I knew she was going to spit so I turned away. I didn't want to see what came out. I heard a wet splat hit the hardwood floor, though, and my stomach flipped. When I looked up again, Marjorie sat up and hopped out of bed like the restraints were loose, weren't tied, weren't ever there.

She ran over to her desk and flipped up the end of the white sacramental cloth, which sent statues of Mary and a candelabra and its burning candles crashing to the floor. She yanked opened the stubbornly sentient desk drawer and sent it crashing to the floor, spilling the contents everywhere. She reached down and picked up something black and metallic that sort of looked like an opened-up stapler, but I didn't get a great look at it. She held it over her head, waved it around, and screamed, "See? See? It was *this*! The drawer wasn't me," and then threw it at the window behind her. "Why would you do this to me? Did you put it there, Merry? Did they make you put it there when I wasn't looking?" She wiped the back of her sleeve over her bloody mouth.

I screamed, "No! I didn't do anything! I—" But I stopped and covered my own mouth. I saw the blood on her face and on her sweatshirt and I was afraid, so afraid that she would make good on her old promise to rip out my tongue. There, in that freezing meat locker of a room with its coppery, sweet smell of candle wax and blood, and with screams, groans, and breathless prayers echoing off the walls, all I could think was that my tongue and I were next, and that everyone was wrong about everything.

Mom was behind me, on the floor weeping, her knuckles white from her hands being clenched together so tightly. She said, "Marjorie, you promised. You promised no one would get hurt if Merry was here."

The door opened behind us and an EMT rushed into the room and tended to Father Gavin.

Marjorie said, "No I didn't. That's not what I said. Check the tape." Her voice sounded funny, like all her teeth had gone all loose and wiggly so the words slipped and fell out between them.

Dad leapt past the EMT, Jenn, and Father Wanderly as they slowly helped Father Gavin shuffle away from Marjorie and to the side of the room. Dad wrapped his arms around Marjorie's waist. Marjorie pulled the desk drawer off the floor and hit him in the head with it. Dad let go and fell away.

Marjorie looked at me and said, "I said someone would get hurt bad if Merry wasn't here. But I never said what would happen if she *was* here. In fact, I thought I already told you all that everyone was going to die."

I yelled, "Stop it, you faker! You told me you were faking! You liar! I hate you! I hate you so much! I wish you were dead."

I turned to run and bumped into Barry. He

didn't try to stop me. I pushed him out of the way, opened the door, and ran out. The heat in the hallway was dizzying and my glasses fogged up instantly so I couldn't see where I was going. I took them off and stuffed them into my pocket. Behind me, in Marjorie's room, there was more yelling and there were loud thumps and crashes like everything inside was imploding, falling apart.

Marjorie yelled after me, "Merry?" and it sounded like she was in the hallway right behind me.

I didn't turn around. I took a hard right and ran down the stairs. I ran too fast, trying to jump two stairs at a time and I tripped and twisted my ankle on the second landing and stumbled down to the next, crashing onto my hands and knees. I scrambled back onto my feet and limped down the last section of stairs to the front foyer.

Ken was there with Tony the cameraman. Tony's camera was perched on his shoulder like a black bird and he dropped down to one knee so that he was down at my height and the lens pointed in my face. Ken wouldn't look at me, so I wouldn't look at him. I had a staring contest with the camera instead. I breathed through my nose and I didn't blink.

Ken said, "Jesus . . ."

Tony slowly panned the camera up above my head. I turned around. Marjorie was on the staircase, just a few steps below the second floor, leaning on the banister railing.

She'd untied her hair and let it dangle in front of her face. She bobbed her head back and forth, swinging her dark hair like a clock's pendulum. I could see her eyes. I remember seeing her eyes and seeing what they saw.

Mom and Dad yelled for Marjorie. They had to be out in the hallway, maybe a few steps behind her. Marjorie didn't react to them. She calmly said to me, "Stay there, Merry. We're almost done."

Marjorie yelled, "Wait for me!" and jumped and pushed up and off the railing with her hands, as though she were playing leapfrog. Her hair bounced away from her face. Her mouth was open, so were her eyes, and I remember her there, over and beyond the railing, hanging in the air, in empty space, time frozen like a snapshot.

She was *there* and she's been there in my mind ever since. *There* is in the air, past the railing, and above the foyer.

I turned around and covered my eyes with my cold hands. I was afraid to watch her fall, and I was afraid if I watched she wouldn't fall, that she actually wasn't falling.

I screamed and screamed and screamed until I finally heard her land behind me.

PART THREE

CHAPTER 23

THE LAST FINAL GIRL

Yeah, it's just a BLOG! (How retro!) Or is THE LAST FINAL GIRL the greatest blog ever!?!? Exploring all things horror and horrific. Books! Comics! Video games! TV! Movies! ~~High school!~~ From the gooey gory midnight show cheese to the highfalutin art-house highbrow. Beware of spoilers. I WILL SPOIL YOU!!!!!

BIO: Karen Brissette
Friday, November, 18, 20 _ _

The Possession, Fifteen Years Later:
Final Episode

I know, I know, you were worried after
watching the "clip show" episodes four
and five that *The Possession* was running
out of steam. Hey, I don't blame you and I
don't judge you. I mean, we can only watch
and break down the same interview so many
times. And the Norwegian exorcisms and
the-Pope-performing-street-exorcism clips get
old. We get it: the Pope swings a big cross,
yeah?

But if we haven't learned anything else,
we've learned this: Trust the awesomeness
and audacity of a show that works in found
footage shot by the eight-year-old sister!

Instead of the usual opening credits,
the final episode opens with the camera's
POV run through the house that starts in
the basement. It's a brilliant choice to
forgo the show's usual over-the-top hype
and hysteria. The tour of the house is
incredibly effective and creepy. There is
no voice-over, no narrative, no soundtrack.
We only occasionally hear the footsteps of
the cameraperson and whispers of prayer and
conversation elsewhere in the house. We know
the lingering shots of dark, empty rooms
will eventually dissolve or descend into the

chaos of the exorcism, and we can't bear
the tension and we can't wait for it to be
broken.

After a slow pan of the basement, we walk
up the stairs, the camera goes dark before
we get to the door, and then we're in the
living room. Wait, what? Yeah, they're
fucking with us. But we love it. You can't
get to the living room from the basement.
Can you? Isn't the basement door in the
dining room? And the dining room is just
off the . . . Hmm. Let's stop and think about
it. (*Karen stops and scratches her head
thoughtfully. *scritch scratch scritch*)

There are very few transitional scene-
setting sequences in *The Possession*. Unlike
run-of-the-mill TV cop shows (the forever-
running *Law and Order* was the most notorious
in continuously implementing the walk-
and-talk scene), where people walk to and
from crime scenes, into apartment rooms
and hallways, buildings, parks, boxing
gyms (always a boxing gym somewhere in a
cop show), and the like, and while ~~walkin'~~
~~struttin'~~ ambulating, the characters have
important, quasi-ludicrous, we'd-never-
talk-about-this-shit-out-in-the-public
conversations relating to the plot. Those
cop shows decided it would be too boring to
have their cops standing around the same

place (or sitting in their car) yakking, so
we got a tour of their interior and exterior
locations instead.

Contrast to how we've been presented the
Barrett House: The only hallway in the
Barrett House we've ever seen is the
upstairs hallway and that hallway seems
to have more doors than bedrooms that
we've been in. I mean, there's Sarah and
John's room, Marjorie's, and Merry's, but
isn't there a door between the parents'
bedroom and the sunroom? Or is it on the
other side, adjacent to the sunroom and
the hallway banister? Does that go to some
attic we haven't seen? How about the first
floor? Sure we've seen the living room and
the front foyer, but where is the kitchen
exactly from there? And isn't there a dining
room mashed in there somewhere? Is there a
separate dining room or is that a section
of the living room area, to the right of
the TV, or is that just more living room?
There's a half-bathroom down there somewhere
too, we think. Wait, where's the basement
door again? Kitchen? We the viewers aren't
sure. We've never seen it. In fact, the only
door that has ever really been the subject
of their camera's deep, intense focus is the
door to Marjorie's bedroom, and there, it's
an overexposure; the camera has been too
focused, too close, so her door fills the

screen and shows nothing else but door. A
closed door.

The Possession simply doesn't show you open
doors; those entrances and exits. We only
get to see closed-off rooms. It's like we're
watching actors in a series of Sartre's *No
Exit* being performed over and over again
in the compartmentalized spaces inside the
house. The Barrett family is in the house,
but at the same time, they're nowhere.
We're not allowed to see or dwell on the
connections between one room and another
inside the house, so there's never any hope
of an escape for Marjorie or the Barrett
family. And we the viewers watch from this
eerily liminal vantage point. I mean, we're
there with them but not really there. We
watch from the spaces between their spaces,
and that's always where the monster dwells.
Dwells, I say!!!

SCARRRRYYYY! I mean, damn, so here we are in
the opening minutes of the final episode and
we discover that we actually know jack and
shit about the house's layout and ARRGGGH,
OUR HEADSSSS ARE EXPLODINGGGGG!

Anyway, it was during the final episode's
whacked-out tour of the house that it hit
me like a ton of Emily Brontë novels. *The
Possession* fits neatly into the Gothic

tradition, starting with the Barrett House
itself. The house is a maze, a labyrinth. We
can't know its map because it doesn't have
one. The Barrett House (not the real one,
but the one as presented in the TV show; I
want to make this distinction as clear as
possible) is as mysterious and foreboding
as the castles of *The Castle of Otranto* and
Wuthering Heights. The Barrett House is
as dark and as confusing as *The Shining*'s
Overlook Hotel (check out the Escher-
esque map of the hotel in the insanely
fun *Room 237*), or Shirley Jackson's Hill
House, or the ever-expanding house of Mark
Danielewski's *House of Leaves*. The Barrett
House is an important character of *The
Possession* and it tells us secrets as well,
if we pay attention. For example, the house
tour ends with a rough jump cut from the
kitchen to the sunroom. We know the sunroom
was converted to be the confessional
room. In case we forgot, the camera crawls
along the black-cloth-covered windows, the
confessional camera perched on its tripod,
and lighting lamps. We hear prayers and
responses echoing from what we presume to
be Marjorie's bedroom, and the camera then
pans across the sunroom and focuses on the
weathered (can I say *wuthered* without you
all smashing your computer screams over my
pun? can I please?) yellow wallpaper. The
lens goes out of focus purposefully, so that

the yellow wallpaper fuzzes outward like
an exploding sun. Marjorie screams, the
camera sharply refocuses, and *The Possession*
title credits bleed out of the yellow
paper. Charlotte Perkins Gilman's "The
Yellow Wallpaper" is one of the greatest
feminist gothic/horror short stories ever
written. In the story . . . wait for it . . .
an oppressed young woman goes cray-cray
nuts! Or does she??? After having a kid,
her husband relocates her to a creeptastic
mansion for the summer. Her misogynistic
and controlling husband/physician John (yes,
John!) prescribes his "rest cure" for her
"nervous condition" and "slight hysterical
tendency." She is forbidden to work,
forbidden to do anything really, even think
for herself (the dude doesn't even want
her writing in her journal because she's
too fragile and pretty to be, you know,
thinking for herself). She's confined to an
old creeptastic nursery that's plastered
with funky yellow wallpaper. The young
woman slowly goes insane, thinking that she
sees a woman on all fours creeping in the
background of the wallpaper, and eventually
decides she's got to set ms. creepy-crawly
free. At the end of the story the young
woman endlessly circles the room, tearing
off strips of wallpaper and crawling over
the (dead? god, I hope he's dead) body of
her husband.

Is the Barrett House telling us that our own
diabolically challenged and/or mentally-ill
Marjorie is the young woman trapped in the
room with the wallpaper, or the metaphorical
oppressed woman in the yellow wallpaper who
yearns to be free? You decide!

After the opening, we're in the quiet living
room. Another brilliant decision made
by the show's producers was to forgo the
show's narrator for the episode's entirety
and let the action and audio unfold before
us without introduction or interpretation.
Cinema verité, reality-show style! In the
living room, and all holding hands and
quietly praying are John Barrett, Father
Wanderly, and young Father Gavin.

(aside 1: Father Gavin is making his first
appearance on the screen, and they might
as well have given him the tunic equivalent
of a *Star Trek* red shirt to wear. It's so
obvious that he's only there to be ~~the~~
~~sacrificial lamb~~ going down, and going down
hard.)

The scene fades to black and flashbacks to
earlier. We know it's earlier because they
tell us in big, white letters. The letters
fade into bright sunshine and we see John
wading into a sea of protesters gathered out
in front of the Barrett House. The extra-

special-douche-bag-Baptist-protesters-who-
shall-not-be-named are holding up signs. Most
of the signs are blurred out, but the ones
we can read are "God Hates Marjorie" signs.
John tears down those signs and punches one
of the blurred-out faces of the protesters.
John is taken to the ground by the police.
While we root for him, his flipped switch
(into manic violence setting) is more than
a little scary, and we see this, his fall
from grace, in slow motion. Next, we cut to
a scene in the kitchen. The Barrett family
quietly finishing a meal of Chinese food.
Mmmm . . . Chinese food . . . John says quietly,
"I want to talk to her again about what's
going to happen and I want Father Wanderly's
help." Sarah explodes, yelling, "Merry can
come upstairs with us if she wants!" The
scene jumps to John standing in front of the
camera, begging the cameraperson to stop
taping for a few seconds. The scene cuts
abruptly to a black screen, then comes back
to the kitchen, and John saying, "This isn't
going to work if we don't believe."

(aside 2: Now, I'm no editing expert [well,
if you insist on referring to me as "Karen
the expert of all things relating to horror
and pop culture" I won't stop you. I won't
even disagree with you!], but it's clear
this kitchen scene is a shitty clip job, and
that whatever conversation John and Sarah

actually had was smashed to bits and the
pieces moved around.)

We get some interviews with the players, but
nothing new or memorable being said. Sarah's
interview is only worthy of note because
she's so worn down. The circles under her
eyes look like purple tea bags.

We're eventually brought into Marjorie's
empty bedroom and shown how creepy they've
made it look with the white cloth on the
desk, statues, candelabras, a giant pewter
cross, and straps on the bed. We get a
shot of a crew member holding a digital
thermometer. He holds it to the camera: 59
in big green letters. He tells us that the
temperature has dropped ten degrees since
they've been in the room. The crewman looks
nervous and we're supposed to believe that
evil has cranked up the AC.

Okay, kids. After all the blog posts and
tens of thousands of words of Karen's
wisdom, we're finally here: Marjorie enters
the bedroom to begin the rite of exorcism.
Continuing with the smartly subdued theme of
this final episode, *The Possession* doesn't
endlessly tease us with false entrances or
reenactments of reenactments, and they don't
dress it up with church choruses chorusing
or violins screeching minor chords. Marjorie

simply walks into her bedroom and leads
in the oddly weddinglike procession of her
family and the two priests.

Though I'm tempted, I'm not going to give
a frame-by-frame breakdown of the entire
exorcism rite, which times out at thirty-two
minutes and sixteen seconds of footage. I
mean, I could write a book on those thirty-
two-plus minutes, but I won't, at least not
here. I'll just hit some of the highlights
that you craven blog readers may or may not
have missed. I've watched this episode going
on forty times, so, yeah, I've got the deets
down.

—After a brief argument with Father
Wanderly, Mom Barrett ties her daughter down
to the bed as everyone else in the room
watches. Can you say awkward? Uncomfortable?
So fucked up on so many levels? BUT WAIT A
GODDAMN MINUTE!!! Rewatch the scene closely.
Go ahead, I'll wait. (*Karen taps her feet*)
Back, yeah? RIGHT! We only see Mom Barrett's
back as she supposedly places Marjorie's
wrists and ankles in the happy-fun-time-
what's-the-safety-word restraints. I mean,
holy jeebus, it's an old and obvious stage-
magician technique. Keep your back to the
audience/camera and us saps and suckers
will believe Marjorie is tied down solely
by the context of the scene. It (almost)

works because it's so bald-faced in its
obviousness. We see close-ups of just about
everything else in the room at some point
during the exorcism scene, but the camera
never zooms in on Marjorie's bound wrists
or feet. A full twenty-seven minutes passes
before a bloody Marjorie gets up off her bed
with the restraints magically melted away. By
then, the chomp-a-priest scene has our heads
spinning (see what I did there?) so we're
panicked and thinking *Oh yeah, right, Mom
tied her down a long time ago and OMG, THE
DEVIL SET HER FREEEEEEE!!!!!* And I bet some
of us watching even falsely remember seeing
Sarah tying Marjorie's wrists down. I know I
did at first. The clever show monkeys let us
fill in those details because they knew if
we were distracted enough by all the other
craziness, we would. ~~It would've worked too
if it wasn't for those meddling kids.~~ Ah,
but we're too smart for them. Maybe. Anyway,
what we might've subconsciously or initially
suspected on the first viewing is all there
on the video: Sarah Barrett never tied down
her daughter. She only pretended to, and
Marjorie played along.

Agreed? Good. Now, why would Sarah Barrett
do that? And what does it mean?

Maybe the Barretts refused to actually
strap their splayed-out fourteen-year-old

daughter to the bed, and her fake-tying was
an improvisation spurred on by necessity.
Maybe the show's special effects budget had
runneth over and/or they were concerned
the restraints would look obviously untied
or broken. Possible, especially given the
shabbiness of the other special effects used
in the room (which I'll get to a bit later).
Or, maybe Sarah did it all on her own and
went rogue! To be honest, though, I really
don't care about the practical whys and hows
of the nonrestraints. I'm more interested
in what it says about Sarah as a character.
If we stay on board with the premise that
what happens on the show is fiction, then
we can analyze the fake-tying-down in the
context of Sarah's character development.
And it's a big development. Sarah only
pretending to tie down her daughter so that
Marjorie can escape later is a Big Fucking
Deal. The show went to great lengths over
the previous five episodes to build Sarah as
the passively sarcastic nonbeliever, one who
ultimately deferred to the will and judgment
of her husband, drank wine, and moped around
the house. Whether the writers intended
it or not, the fake-tying scene is Sarah's
melancholy moment of redemption. Melancholy,
because we know it's too late for her to
truly help her mentally ill daughter. Tired
of being told what to do by the cabal of men
in her home, Sarah finally rebels and aids

her daughter's eventual escape, even if it
is only a brief and terrible escape.

—While we cheer Sarah's growth of a
backbone, we face-palm as Marjorie's
knowledge of the rite is *again* presented
to us as proof positive of her possession.
This is one of the most misogynistic aspects
of the show: not only is it impossible for
a silly *girl* to know what the patriarchy
knows (i.e., Christian verse and scripture,
canonical works of literature; everything
written by and for men, of course), we're
supposed to actively fear that she has
acquired that knowledge. That obnoxiously
Christian theme of forbidden knowledge hits
us over the head as heavily as a cudgel.
Yes, I said a cudgel. Marjorie even seems
almost bored with her recitation of ~~tired shit written by men~~ the lines.

—The misogyny is so obvious and pervasive
that it's almost ho-hum by this point. So
let's go goth again! (*Karen dresses in
black, puts on old Morrissey CDs*)

Like many of the greatest characters of
gothic literature, Marjorie is a doomed
protagonist, one who mirrors the themes of
the ~~story~~ show. Is Marjorie going *mad* (in
the parlance of the gothic!) or are there
supernatural forces at play? Marjorie is a

liminal being. She's presented as both human and animalistic demon, as both hero and villain. The danger she presents (the taboo, forbidden knowledge she attained somehow, her becoming what we fear before our eyes) is both threatening and seductive.

The protagonist having to deal with a *wicked father* is also a trope of gothic literature and film. Yeah, I know, I blabbed on and on about how the show tries to make John Barrett the hero of its God-n-family-values psychodrama, but that doesn't mean they succeeded. From episode one, John's unyielding mania shines through the cracks, and only worsens. Like Jack Nicholson's not-exactly-nuanced portrayal of *The Shining*'s Jack Torrance, John Barrett is as crazy as a bedbug (I love that saying) from scene one. He just needed a catalyst to get his full-crazy on. And no, you can't call this hindsight. John Barrett infamously poisoning himself and his family (with only the youngest, Meredith, surviving) one month after the final episode aired will be forever intertwined with the show's narrative.

(aside 3: Despite my light/jokey tone throughout this deconstruction of *The Possession*, I have a very difficult time separating a campy reality show from the real-life horrors the Barrett family experienced. Together they make for a compelling and important story, one that I admittedly get lost in, one I'm clearly still trying to wrap my head around. And, no, I don't care to comment on the irony/ spookiness/synchronicity/coincidence of the father killing his wife in the "Growing Things" story Marjorie repeatedly told Merry, paralleling their real father poisoning his family.)

Other jackasses have tried to argue that it's John Barrett, not Marjorie Barrett, who becomes *The Possession*'s true tragic figure, and that the show is really about his descent into madness, his being *possessed* by the ugliness of hatred and zealotry. His daughter's illness, his family's dysfunction, his unemployed status, and his beloved Catholic church abandoning him post-exorcism, are the aforementioned catalysts to his own psychotic break (see the *Howard Journal of Criminal Justice* and their breakdown of the four types of men who kill their families), and blah, blah, blah. Fuck that bullshit. *The Possession* tried to position John Barrett to be its hero and failed miserably, and his cruel and cowardly poisoning of himself and his family further discredits the show's reprehensible social and political agenda.

Marjorie is our doomed hero. John Barrett
was and is the wicked father, the wickedest
of fathers. The show did succeed in one
aspect: John was indeed a symbol of decaying
patriarchy.

—*The Possession* deciding to shoot the
exorcism rite in real time (or at least shot
in a way to give the appearance of it being
shot in real time) was the right decision,
even if it meant some of the special or
practical effects they employed weren't all
that special.

It's so cold in the bedroom during the
exorcism that we can see everyone's smokestack breath. *Scary, cold, eeeevil!!!* It's all
very dramatic and reminiscent of Friedkin's
The Exorcist. We get three "live" shots of a
plummeting thermometer, with the temperature
dropping as low as thirty-nine degrees in
the room. They hit us over the heads with
the freakin' thermometer. They don't come
right out and explicitly lie to our faces,
but the implication is that the room is
freaky cold solely because of the presence
of the demon. They certainly don't tell us,
*hey, it's November in northern Massachusetts,
so we turned off the heat and opened the
window because people breathing frozen
breaths inside a house looks creepy*. Check
the video. The window behind Marjorie's bed

is covered by the curtains so we can't see
if it's open or not. But in two shots (one
when Sarah pretends to tie down Marjorie's
feet, the other when Marjorie sits upright
in the bed) the curtains blow and billow
into the room. Curtains don't billow into
a room without wind or, granted, without
Satan! (*Satan's Window Treatments is the
name of my punk band*) Wind is the much more
likely culprit. So, yeah, the window is open,
folks, and that's why it's cold.

The self-opening and self-closing desk
drawer. Horror stories and movies (and
funhouses for that matter) have long
employed the inanimate becoming animate as
a go-to scare tactic. There's no denying
the power of that particular flavor of
the uncanny, or *Das Unheimliche* in Freud's
German (oooh, look at Karen showing off . . .
thumps chest). There's a scene in Sam
Raimi's *Evil Dead 2*, the brilliant sequel
to the ultimate cabin-in-the-woods movie,
where a roomful of inanimate objects comes
to life and laughs at the bloodied and
beaten hero, Ash; the deer head, the turtle-
shell lamp, desk drawers, bookcases, each is
given its own unique voice and laugh. It's
a hilarious spoof scene, shot in a weird
kind of frenetic stop motion, which imparts
a twitchy/strobelike appearance, so it looks
like a cartoon or a comic book, nothing to

be afraid of, right? But the scene quickly
becomes deeply unsettling as the laughter
swells, becomes manic, our own smile starts
to fade and the scene starts to feel like it
has been running a long time, yeah, and we'd
like it to end now please and thanks, stop
the scene before it gets worse before we
see and hear something we can't unsee. . . .
And so along with Ash (who's bellowing like
a full-blown maniac by this point), we feel
ourselves being pushed toward the edge of
madness. In *The Possession*, the animated
desk drawer isn't played for laughs, but the
drawer does push Marjorie over the edge:
her repeated denials—she wasn't the one
moving the drawer, she wasn't in control—
her asking for someone to stop it, and
then her agitated state ultimately explodes
into her attack on Father Gavin. Unlike the
phantom restraints on the bed, which we
never really get a good look at, the camera
repeatedly focuses on the desk drawer. Its
movement is mechanical, like a player piano,
or the funhouse coffin lid that opens and
closes by itself. I've timed six different
drawer opening and closing intervals that
are fully caught on screen and their times
are identical. Either the evil, furniture-
moving entity is OCD, or there is a
mechanism hidden inside the drawer. Yeah, I
think there's a' somethin' inside the drawer.
We never get to see inside the drawer, of

course. Even when Marjorie rips out the desk drawer and sends it crashing to the floor, we're never shown what was or wasn't inside. The camera focuses on the people tending to the injured and bleeding Father Gavin. That means what it means.

And speaking of the bleeding Father Gavin . . . Marjorie's attack scene is set up in much the same way John Carpenter staged his famous jump-scare blood-test scene in *The Thing*. In that movie, Carpenter shows us MacReady (Kurt Russell), from the same vantage point, dipping the hot needle into petri dishes filled with his crew's blood samples. The needle hisses quietly in sample after sample. Even though we know something bad is going to happen eventually, we've been subconsciously trained to believe that the repeated shot of Russell dipping the hot needle into the blood is a "safe" shot. We're continually shown those same *safe* shots until by process of literal elimination we're down to two blood samples, down to two men, one of whom *has* to be the monster. MacReady distractedly argues with the man he thinks is the monster as he puts the hot needle into the blood sample from the other guy, and whammo, the infected/thing blood jumps away from the hot needle and we jump out of our goddamn skin. In *The Possession*'s exorcism scene, Father Gavin covers Marjorie

with a comforter three times (hmm, a
trinity?). Each time, we're shown the same
camera angle. It's a perspective from the
middle of the room so both he and Marjorie
are in profile. It's a wider shot so we can
see the length of her body on the bed, but
Marjorie's head and Father Gavin's body
are left of center, subtly telling us that
there really isn't anything to see here. His
covering Marjorie with the comforter is thus
established as a *safe* shot for us to see.
The second time he pulls up the comforter
reinforces this, so much so that our focus
remains with the voice of Father Wanderly,
standing in the right foreground reading
from his red leather-bound book. When Father
Gavin goes to pull up the comforter the
third time, we notice him, but he's become
part of the background, part of the rhythm
of the overall scene. All of our focus is
on what Father Wanderly and Marjorie are
saying to each other, so when Marjorie
strikes like a cobra and clamps down on
Father Gavin's wrist, it's totally unexpected
and horrifying. Father Gavin's screams are
so loud and high-registered, they turn to
static in the speakers, and underneath it
all is a mix of shouts and stamping of feet
on the hardwood floors. The video image is
pixilated/blurred out around Marjorie's face
and Father Gavin's arm. What's happening is
apparently too gory and awful for them to

broadcast. We can see red in the pixels and
the damage we imagine is likely worse than
what they could've shown us. When Marjorie
finally pulls away, a blurred-out section of
Father Gavin's forearm sickeningly elongates
and stretches.

(aside 4: My favorite aunt loves horror
movies like me [hi, auntie!!!] and often
proudly talks about how she's seen the movie
JAWS like fifty times. But when it comes to
the scene at the end of the movie, where
Quint gets bitten in half, she can't watch.
She changes the channel or leaves the room
or covers her eyes. She was in fifth grade
when she first saw the movie. Watching
that beloved whiskey-soaked rascal Quint
screaming and spitting blood into the camera
and then his lower half disappearing into
the gaping mouth of the shark scarred her
for life. She insists that she will never
watch the Quint death scene again even
though she knows that it probably looks
totally fake and the adult her might scoff
and chide her younger self for being so
silly, so easily scared. But there's another
part of her that knows she can't ever watch
it again because maybe watching it again
would make her feel just as frightened, as
sick, and as lost as she did when she first
watched it. *What if seeing that scene now as
an adult would be somehow worse?* That's how I

feel about the Father Gavin attack. I've seen
thousands of scenes that were more gory and
disturbing (on a visceral level) than what's
in *The Possession*, but that attack scene,
man . . . when his pixilated skin stretches
out away from his arm and Marjorie is still
clearly attached to the other end . . . I can't
deal with it. But I forced myself to rewatch
the Father Gavin scene for the first time
in over a decade right before I sat down
to write this blog post. It was as horrible
as I remembered it. Maybe worse. Definitely
worse. Rewatching it made me want to give
up on finishing this series of blog posts,
made me want to give up doing anything other
than burrowing into my couch with a bottle
of wine, a can of honey-roasted peanuts, and
further numb myself in the glow of classic
Simpsons episodes. You have no idea what I
put myself through for you!!!!!!)

The Father Gavin attack scene is a worthy
penultimate act for what I would argue is
one of the most disturbing endings of a
television show, before or since.

—Of course we have to end with the end; end
with a discussion of the floating elephant
in the room.

Moments after the attack on Father Gavin
the major players are either writhing on

the floor or screaming for help, screaming
at one another, desk drawer crashing to
the ground; everything is set into chaotic
motion with Marjorie in the middle of it all.
The audio only gains a focus when Meredith
(off-camera) clearly shouts, "I hate you!
I hate you so much! I wish you were dead."
Then the scene jump cuts.

We cut to the empty front foyer. It's a
wide-angle still shot, framed in such a way
that we know this is the same camera that
took us on the fragmented tour of the house
to open the show. Everything is quiet and
still and we focus on the front staircase;
the stairwell walls and vertical risers are
white, the horizontal treads are black. We're
allowed this artificial beat in the action,
a chance given to us to catch our breaths,
if only for the moment.

Then we hear, in the distance, the same
screams and shouts we'd heard previously.
It's an oddly voyeuristic vantage point
without us actually being . . . well . . .
voyeurs. We understand we're in a Rashomon
moment, reliving Father Gavin's attack
and Marjorie's escape from the POV of the
empty foyer. The muffled screams and thumps
base-drumming through the ceiling are
disorienting because without the visual of
the room, we're not sure who is screaming

what, and this version of the audio doesn't
gibe exactly with what we remember hearing.
Finally, Meredith screams that she hates her
sister, that she wishes she were dead. The
camera remains focused on the stairwell.
We're so afraid of what we're going to see,
we can barely watch.

Suddenly Meredith enters from the top right-
hand corner of the scene. She comes crashing
down the stairs; a wobbling wrecking ball.
There are three sets of stairs and two
landings between the second floor and the
foyer. Meredith's feet tangle and she trips
on the middle set of stairs, and she crashes
hard onto her knees on the landing. She gets
up and limps down the last set of stairs.
Meredith rubs her right knee. We don't know
this yet, but this foreshadows her sister
Marjorie's injuries to come: broken right
ankle and a concussion.

Meredith sees the camera and stares into it.
The camera stares back, filling its frame
with her face, which is smeared with tears.
Her hair is tangled and greasy. She's not
wearing her glasses. It's the only time in
the show that we see her without her glasses
and she looks like someone else to us. She
could be Marjorie's misunderstood spirit;
broken, mistakenly exorcised/expelled, and
doomed. Meredith could be our own collective

subconscious silently judging us, chiding
us for our shameless complicity, for our
doing nothing but watching the terrible and
systematic torture of a mentally ill teenage
girl under the guise of entertainment.
Meredith doesn't blink and neither do we.

The camera pans, putting Meredith in the
lower left corner of our TV screen. Above
her, up on the third set of stairs and
leaning on the railing is Marjorie. The
story started with the sisters and will end
with the sisters.

The audio cuts out. It's been removed. We
don't know why and we don't know what to do
with the silence.

Meredith turns around. We only see the back
of her head. Marjorie's long, dark hair
falls over the railing. There's no sound
and we can't see any faces. Meredith could
be Marjorie and Marjorie could be Meredith.
We only know who is who by context. Six
excruciating seconds pass before Meredith
turns around again to face the camera.
During those six seconds we sweat and we
cringe and we understand that the entire
series has built to this moment. And with
all the implications of what has already
happened and what is about to happen, we

know the terrible truth that this is their story. It's their story.

As Meredith turns around to face the camera, Marjorie jumps up over the railing. Their movements are choreographed, linked, one cannot move without the other. Meredith covers her eyes with her hands even though it's far too late for her and for us all to see no evil. As those little hands cover her eyes, Marjorie is still rising above the railing and her hair parts, opening like wings, but we still can't see her face.

Meredith screams. We don't hear her but her screams shake the camera so that the edges and details of our viewing window blur and start to dim. And Marjorie is still there, over the railing, hanging in the air for an impossible moment, before she starts to fall, and the screen goes black.

The *levitation* scene (complete with *The Sopranos*-type fade to black) has been argued over by fans more rabid and critics more discerning than little old me, but I'll add my two cents (well, more like three cents). Scores of film editors have weighed in on the supposed levitation, and for every editor who claims adamantly that the film hasn't been cut or tampered with to

give that briefest illusion that Marjorie
is indeed floating in the air above the
foyer, there's one who swears up and down
that there are clear signs of special
effects and editing. Oscar-winning film
editor Ian Rogers claims *The Possession*
used a sophisticated split-screen/split-film
technique to create the levitation shot, a
shot that he re-created in his crowdfunded
short film *Every House Is Haunted* with mixed
(to be kind) results.

Karen's semiprofessional take: The only
part of the shot that's doctored is the
obvious shaky-cam bit when Meredith screams.
Everything else, film-wise, is legit. That's
not to say that I think Marjorie is floating
any more than I believe that YouTube street
magicians or yoga masters can levitate. So
I'm saying the film hasn't been doctored
and Marjorie ain't floatin'. I'll give you
three simple reasons why. *One*: Between the
lighting, the blurred/shaken camera, and
Marjorie's baggy sweatshirt, it is simply
not clear on the video when Marjorie's hands
are no longer in contact with the railing.
Remember, she puts her hands on the railing
and pushes up and off. I can't pinpoint the
exact moment her hands leave the railing,
but they are there for quite a while. It's
more than probable that when you think
she's floating, her hands are still anchored

to the railing. *Two*: The camera angle. We
simply can't tell the precise moment when
she starts to fall because we're looking up
at her. Her seemingly hanging in the air is
an optical illusion of angle. She's falling,
only it doesn't seem like she's falling
right away because she's falling *on top of*
us. *Three*: Because you never see her land,
it's easier to believe that she's floating.
It's how you remember it. How you choose
to remember it. Ultimately, you think she's
floating because you want to believe it.
Admit it. You believe, despite yourself, and
even if it is only for that moment, that
Marjorie is possessed by some supernatural
entity. You believe because it's easier
than dealing with the idea that you just
willingly watched a sick, troubled teenage
girl purposefully choose to jump from a
ledge.

Karen takes a deep breath

All right, kids. Thanks for playing along.
I gotta tell ya, it's been a grueling
experience. I've been writing and thinking
about nothing else besides *The Possession*
for a week straight. I drank all the coffee
(seriously, I'm out, can someone pick me up
some?), ate all the chips and salsa, and
yeah, I ate all the bags of peanut M&M's.
I mean all of them. There aren't any left

in _ _ _ _ _ _ _ _ _ (geographic region
redacted). I read all the books and articles
and blogs. I watched and rewatched all the
movies, and of course, all the episodes. I'm
cooked.

Maybe I'll add a summation essay or
aftermath rumination tomorrow, or maybe I
won't. Maybe I won't be able to stop myself
and I'll just start watching the series from
the beginning. Again.

CHAPTER 24

I'VE BEEN AVOIDING Rachel and our final interview session, last-minute canceling on her twice already. It's now early December and I finally promised to meet her at a local coffee shop in South Boston the day before she is to fly out. Rachel is due to travel to Amsterdam for another nonfiction project she just sold to her publisher. Over the phone she admitted to me that our collaboration has unexpectedly made her fall in love with writing nonfiction. The interview and research process has been fulfilling in a way that her fiction hasn't been, at least not lately.

It's midafternoon on a brisk and rainy Tuesday. I walk the five blocks from my apartment and I listen to the raindrops pounding on the umbrella canvas. I'm wearing a black sweater, black jeans, black boots, and my favorite jacket; a garishly red overcoat that isn't warm enough.

The coffee shop is on the first floor of a refurbished brownstone. Rachel is already inside and sitting at a table for two. She smiles and waves, not upset that I'm late, but relieved that I actually showed up. I feel guilty for making her feel that way, but she has to know that what we're going to talk about today is something that I don't want to talk about and have never really talked about with anyone else. I've had to build up to this moment. I've been building up to it for fifteen years.

It's steamy warm inside and there are no other customers in the shop. After I hang my coat on a wobbly, skeletal rack by the bay window, we exchange a quick hug and she squeezes my hands and my heart melts. I've always missed Mom but I really miss her right now. I can't help but wonder what she would've looked like as a graceful and middle-aged woman. Would she have grown her hair out long? Would she have tried to keep the gray out, or show it off? Would she have been supportive of my new writing gig? Would she have been worried that I might not have a sustainable career? Would she have been afraid to wade into the big city by herself, or would she have reveled in the trip? Would she have ordered the decaf because caffeine this late in the day would keep her up at night? Or would she have said "What the hell" and ordered a double shot of espresso?

We walk side by side to the glass counter. The hardwood floor creaks under our footsteps.

Stilled black ceiling fans hang above our heads like sleeping bats. The barista is a man around my age. His white sleeves are rolled up, exposing the intricate tattoos he's clearly proud of. He makes sure his hands are always moving, always doing something, even if it's only pushing the bangs away from his sweaty forehead. He smells of clove cigarettes and something citrusy, and he disappears out back after he fills our orders.

Back at the small table, Rachel and I chitchat about how nasty it is outside but how warm it is in the coffee shop. We talk about her upcoming trip. I tell her that I'm jealous even though I'm not. I also tell her that I've been busy with my blog and other writing assignments for *Fangoria*.

"I've read your blog, Merry."

I keep my coffee cup in my hands and held close to my body. "Oh yeah? What do you think?"

Rachel puts down her coffee cup, folds her hands on the table, and then on her lap. "I've read the series of essays on the show three times, now. It's very well written and a compelling criticism and deconstruction, Merry."

"Thank you."

She stirs her coffee with a black swizzle stick, alternating clockwise and counterclockwise. "How did you find the—the distance, to write about the show as if you actually weren't a part of it? Aren't you afraid of that distance closing in on you?"

"The distance is easier than you think, and

I'm always afraid. But I think it's good to be afraid. It means that I'm alive."

"Do you plan on revealing that you are Karen Brissette?"

"No, not ever. And I hope that you won't reveal it either."

Rachel nods, but a nod isn't a promise. "Are you Karen Brissette? What I mean by that is, do you, Merry Barrett, believe everything written under Karen's byline, or is Karen more like some character you've created?"

"Karen is just a pen name, nothing more. I have no interest in writing fiction. Yes, I believe in everything I wrote, otherwise I wouldn't have written it."

"How many times have you watched *The Possession*?"

"More times than I care to admit."

"Are you going to blog about what happened after the show?"

"No. I'm sure my editor and readers would prefer I stick to writing about fiction."

We pause and both look out the bay window and watch the unrelenting rain fall. I can tell my blog has upset her in a way she's having trouble articulating. She also doesn't know how to ask me what she wants to ask next. I don't blame her at all. I decide to help her because now that I'm here, I know it's time to talk about what happened after the show.

I say, "Tell me everything you know about the

weeks between the filming of the final episode and the poisoning. And I'll do my best to fill in what I can."

Rachel says, "Oh. Well . . ." and then rummages around in her bag and pulls out a manila folder, fat with paper, and a notebook. The notebook is a cheap spiral notebook you could buy in a pharmacy for a buck. I love this small bit of utter unpretentiousness and I miss my mother all over again.

She says, "Are you sure, you just want me to tell you what I have?"

"Yes. It'll be easier this way, I think."

"Well, all right. I haven't yet double-checked the exact timeline of everything here but I know that Marjorie's fall resulted in a slew of injuries, including a concussion and a fractured right ankle."

"Yes, but it could've been worse. She was in a walking boot only three weeks later. Sorry, I won't interrupt again until you're through."

Rachel scribbles notes into the notebook. "No, no, please do. Okay. I also know that her jumping off the stairs was reported as a suicide attempt to the police and that she was hospitalized, kept in protective care for two weeks, and then released to your parents under the stipulation that she'd have homecare visits from a new, state-assigned psychiatrist twice a week. Does that sound right to you?"

"It does, but I have to be honest. What I

remember of the weeks between the filming of the final episode and, you know, the day of the poisoning, is kind of foggy, and um, loose."

"Loose?"

"Loose. It's all there, I believe, but difficult to gather and keep together. Like trying to scoop up and hold a thousand pennies in my hands at once." I pause, and laugh at myself. "Yuck. I don't think my attempted metaphor is making sense."

"No, it does, Merry. It does."

"Yay, me," I say, and give myself polite applause.

Rachel scans her notebook. She asks, "Do you remember if Ken or Barry returned to your home after the exorcism? According to my sources they did not perform any follow-up or post-exorcism interviews, as they'd originally planned. Barry claims they stayed away not because of the public backlash and controversy surrounding the aired finale, but because your father had apparently threatened to sue the show and the archdiocese for medical damages and emotional trauma."

"Dad didn't really discuss his legal plans with me back then, but I wasn't surprised to learn later that he threatened to sue. Anyway, no, no one from the show ever came back to the house. At least not when I was there. I'm sure they were freaked out by what happened, and I think they anticipated that Dad would be pissed, would blame them for how it all ended in the foyer, so they packed up all their cameras and stuff and got the hell out as quickly as possible. That same night, I think. They made sure Marjorie's room was spotless, too. After they were gone I remember searching for the leg and wrist restraints and whatever it was she pulled out of the desk drawer, but I never found anything.

"I do remember news vans and trucks, and reporters and cameras replacing the protesters out front, but my parents never let any of them get near the house."

"Have you heard from, talked to, or seen Ken since the show?"

"No. I haven't. Those early days after the show I wrote him some letters, but I never ended up mailing them. They were silly, little kid stuff. I'd draw some pictures of soccer balls, the back-yard full of leaves, then I'd ask him what he was doing, if he was writing for a new show and if he was, would he name someone after me. I asked him if he wanted to know what I was doing, if he was wondering if I was okay, you know, totally passive-aggressive, angry, sad, confused-kid stuff. I missed him terribly when the show ended. I missed having all those other people around, even the ones I didn't like all that much. It felt like we were alone all over again. And it didn't feel . . . safe."

Rachel launches right into her next bit of info. "Two days after the final episode aired the Department of Children and Families filed a 'Care and Protection case' or 51A, as they call it, on behalf of Marjorie. The report was 'screened out,' meaning her case was dropped because the claims against your parents were not considered abuse or neglect under the law. The filing of the 51A was later leaked to the public after Marjorie's and your parents' deaths." Rachel stops and looks at me.

I say, "It's okay. Keep going."

"I know that you were pulled out of school and that your parents hired a private tutor."

"Yeah, Stephen Graham Jones. Funny that I remember his full name like that, but that's how he was introduced to me. He wouldn't let me call him *mister* like my regular teachers, and I liked saying his whole name out loud, whenever I could. It became a little OCD tic of mine. I'd say, 'Good-bye, Stephen Graham Jones,' or, 'I don't know what an obtuse triangle is, Stephen Graham Jones.' "

Rachel laughs. "His name does roll off the tongue, doesn't it?"

"It does! He was this short, skinny grad student with huge eyes and terribly crooked teeth. Wow, I haven't thought about him in a long time. I only remember meeting with him a handful of times. I remember that for a tutor, he wasn't very good at math. I have no idea where my parents found him." We both smile and drink amiable sips of our coffee. "What else do you have?"

Rachel turns some pages in her notebook. "I have the Neilsen ratings for each episode. The final episode pulled a stunning twenty share."

"Maybe I'll go back and mention that in my blog."

She says, "I have a printout of the antipsychotics prescribed to Marjorie, which include Clozaril and Fanapt. When I had a friend who knows what she's looking for dig through the police report, however, those drugs didn't come up in the toxicology screening."

"I have no idea if Marjorie was taking her meds. I think Mom was taking her own stuff. Scratch that. I *know* Mom was taking her own stuff. So, she really wasn't all there. And Dad, he still wanted to cure Marjorie with prayers, of course. He'd started spending a lot of time down in the basement by himself.

"Maybe on the days the visiting psychiatrist was there Marjorie took her meds, but the other days, who knows. Those days when it was just us, everyone just sort of floated around the house, and only occasionally would we bump into each other. I spent a lot of time outside by myself. Dinner was takeout or delivery most nights."

Rachel nods. "Included in the police report is a printout of emails that your father and the pastor of that Baptist church from Kansas exchanged for a period of one month."

"He was the same protester Dad punched out, right?"

"That's correct, and that same guy was arrested three years ago on—"

I interrupt her. "Do you have those emails with you? Can I see them?"

Rachel looks at me. She's been looking at me the whole time, yes, but now she's looking at me like I'm an object to be carefully observed, or maybe she's worried that if she takes her eyes off of me I'll disappear.

She doesn't think I should read the emails. I won't push her if she resists. But she doesn't. She slides the folder with the printouts across the table to me.

The first emails from the church leader feature the same hate-filled slogans that graced their protest signs. Dad's initial responses are typed in all caps, full of profanity and physical threats. But as the emails continue there's a subtle and slow shift toward a dialogue. Dad tries arguing theology and scripture with the other man, which becomes Dad blaming Father Wanderly (who had "forsaken" him) and the Catholic church for failing and abandoning him and his family, which becomes Dad also blaming the television show producers who duped him into believing what he was doing was for the best, which became Dad lashing out at his former employers, politicians, the economy, modern society, and American culture, which eventually became Dad asking for help and for advice from this other frothing lunatic of a man who never once offered a single word of love or comfort or support and only said that God was unhappy with Dad, unhappy with the whole family. Sent three days before the poisoning, the pastor's last email ended with: "John, you know what you have to do."

I say, "My God."

I give her back the printouts and my hands are shaking. Rachel reaches across the table to hold my hands, but I pull away and hide them under the table.

She says, "Sorry. Should we stop? Do you need a break? Should we go somewhere else to talk?"

"No, it's okay. Thank you. Nothing personal, but I just want to get this part of it over with."

The barista makes a brief reappearance behind the counter as if he can sense some emotional storm that calls for a soothing seven-dollar scone and equally overpriced latte. He asks if we would like anything else. We tell him no thank you, but then I ask him if he can turn down the heat. He shrugs, and while backing away from us he says, "I can't control the heat in this crazy place. I wish I could, believe me."

After he leaves I say, "So, they never found where Dad got the potassium cyanide from, right? They thought it was from some jeweler who was a member of that Baptist church or something?"

Rachel says, "Jewelers use potassium cyanide for gilding and buffing. I did talk to a detective who worked on this case, and she said they first tried every jewelry shop and jewelers' supply house in New England, and when those inquiries turned up empty, they tried chemical suppliers and sales reps from all across the country. Nothing. There were tons of online places he could've ordered it from, but they didn't find anything relating to cyanide on the family PC's hard drive. They never found any suspicious charges to his credit cards or PayPal account. All they found were the emails to the church leader. One of the higher-ranking members of the church was Paul Quentin, who ran a jewelry store in Penobscot, Kansas. But they couldn't find any evidence that Quentin supplied your father, or anyone else, with potassium cyanide. The detective told me it was surprisingly easy to get that stuff back then, so it could've come from anywhere. But to this day she thinks the pastor in Kansas had it sent to your father somehow."

My head starts to fill with fuzz, like my brain was a radio and the dial was just spun to a dead station. I ask, "Can you tell me what the report says about fingerprints?"

Rachel looks at me quizzically. "Fingerprints?"

I wave my hand around like I'm impatiently shooing away a fly. "Can I just read the report? Do you have time for that?"

Rachel says, "I—I think so. It's rather long." She passes the thick manila envelope across the table.

I don't want to read the report right now. I don't know why I asked to do so. Maybe I just wanted to see what her reaction would be. Sitting here in the coffee shop with her outlining her research findings, I'm getting the sense that she's hiding something from me. I don't know how that would be possible.

She wasn't there when it happened. And I was.

I push the report back across the table to her and I say, "I remember my last day with my family. I remember our last day together. I do," as though I'm trying to convince myself that I'm telling the truth. "I'm going to tell you about it as quickly as I can."

CHAPTER 25

IT WAS SATURDAY afternoon. Six days until Christmas. I'd been promised that we were going to put up a Christmas tree, a real one, on that day. But Mom hadn't gotten out of bed until super late and announced that we would get a tree on Sunday instead.

I was mad, so mad I went and hid in my bedroom. I decided I wasn't going to talk to anyone the rest of the day. I made signs instead. If Mom or Dad asked me something, I'd just hold up my sign with a simple message-answer. The signs were nothing fancy; I used lined notebook paper and a blue pen.

I made the following signs: NO. GOOD. WHAT'S FOR DINNER? YES. I DON'T KNOW. READ IT. MILK. WATER. COOKIE? I'M FINE. WHEN ARE WE GETTING A TREE? I'LL TALK THEN. WHERE? CAN I GO OUTSIDE? PLAY

SOCCER. I ALREADY READ. NOTHING. TV? TOO EARLY. IN MY ROOM. NO BATH. NO SHOWER. I'M NOT TIRED. I CAN HEAR YOU. PLEASE DON'T YELL. BIGFOOT IS STANDING OUTSIDE THE WINDOW!

I lay on my bed, practice-answering imaginary questions with my signs, shuffling through my pile of papers looking for the intended responses. While I attempted to construct what I thought would be a logical, easy-to-remember card-cataloguing system, I heard an approaching clunking, and another piece of paper, this one folded in half, slid under my door and into my room. It was a note from Marjorie.

> *Come into my room, now. I need to show you something. This is <u>SO</u> important! Like, life and death important, Miss Merry.*

Since returning home from the hospital, Marjorie had kept to herself and generally stayed out of trouble. She hadn't liked trying to get around in her walking boot much, and going up and down the stairs was especially difficult, so Dad had put a new TV in her room. He'd hung it on the freshly plastered wall adjacent to her bed. Her TV stayed on almost constantly; a drone of voices at low volume echoed in the hallway until it was time for lights-out and Dad would go into her room and shut the TV off himself. Late at night there'd been occasional bouts of her talking or even whispering loudly to herself, her words and sentences always just out of reach. I don't remember if Mom or Dad went into her room to try to comfort her or quiet her down, or if they stayed in their room, content to pretend what we were hearing was Marjorie's television. Either way, the nocturnal outbursts were mild compared to what they used to be and they didn't last very long. The next morning Marjorie would be as quiet as a painting all over again.

I read Marjorie's note three times. Despite everything that I'd gone through, that our whole family had gone through, I felt that old excitement, that familiar flutter in my stomach: Marjorie wanted to spend time with *me*. I don't think I can ever fully explain the power she had over the eight-year-old me or the power she still has over me.

I folded up the note and stuck it underneath my mattress. I ripped one more piece of paper out of the notebook and quickly made another sign: MORE STORIES?

Her bedroom door was open and I peeked in. The TV was off and her computer was on, but she wasn't at her desk or on her bed. Marjorie popped out from behind the door, said, "Quick!" and then grabbed my arm, pulled me in, and shut the door behind me.

I nearly jumped out of my sneakers and yelped like a puppy accidentally getting her paw stepped on, but I didn't drop my signs.

"Shh. Sorry, sorry, didn't mean to scare you. Is Dad home? Did he see you come in?" Marjorie loomed over me and I wondered if she'd gotten taller and I'd gotten shorter somehow. She wore purple pajama pants and a black hooded sweatshirt. She had on one fuzzy blue bunny slipper, the one with the floppy ears that threatened to trip her at any moment.

I didn't know where Dad was. I assumed he was down in the basement doing whatever it was he did when he was down there. I hadn't been in the basement since the last time with Marjorie.

I held up my I DON'T KNOW sign.

"Not talking?"

Pleased and vindicated that my Marjorie understood me right away, I shuffled through the deck, and then held up YES.

Marjorie smiled. "That's fine, monkey. We can work with this, I think, yeah. Hey, do you remember my story about the growing things? Do you remember the two sisters in the cabin, and the father who killed their mother and buried her in the basement?"

I held up YES, and nodded my head hard enough that it could've fallen off.

"I told you that story as a warning. Okay? Something that could actually happen."

I looked for an appropriate sign to use, but didn't have one. I sighed. I wanted to say "I know. You've told me that a thousand times." I thought about showing her my BIGFOOT IS STANDING OUTSIDE THE WINDOW! sign to try to make her laugh, but it didn't feel like the right time.

"I'm not fooling around now. I need you to

read some more stories. I need you to think really hard about them. And I need you to understand." Marjorie looked all around the room as though making sure that no one else was watching us. "They're not good stories, but they're important stories, and I promise, they're true stories. All of them are true. They actually happened, okay?"

She led me to her desk and the computer. She called up the browser, went into her bookmarks folder, and clicked on one of the links. At the top of the webpage, white capital letters BBC were block-outlined in red.

Marjorie said, "Here. Read this story."

It was about a man who, after being laid off by his longtime employer, shot his wife and his two kids. Then he burned himself up along with their house.

I held up my MORE STORIES? sign because I knew that was what she wanted.

"Yes. There are more. So many more. Read this one."

This was about another man. His wife had just divorced him. He had been in contact with a protest group called Fathers 4 Justice. On Father's Day, he connected a hose to his Land Rover's tailpipe and ran it through the back window. He parked in the middle of an empty field and he and his two children died because of carbon monoxide poisoning.

"Read."

I read about another man who'd poisoned himself and his children after his wife had left him. And then I read about another man who'd jumped off a bridge with his kids in his arms. And then I read about another man who drove into a lake with his kids locked in his car and strapped into their car seats.

There were more and more and more. Marjorie clicked to a new link whenever I looked away from the screen and up at her. There were so many I stopped reading and just pretended to read. I didn't have to read everything though; the stories were there in the bold headlines and pictures of the fathers and their wives and their smiling children (always smiling) and their houses and apartments and cars and backyards strung with yellow police tape. And I remember thinking that all these stories started off sounding like the old fairy tales Mom and Dad used to tell me, and instead of witches putting kids in ovens and evil queens conjuring poisoned apples, the fathers and husbands were the monsters doing the unspeakable things to their families, and these stories all ended without anyone saving anybody. No one was saved. I couldn't believe there were so many stories like that and that people would choose to read them.

I turned away from the computer. It was too much, way too much. I crumpled up the MORE STORIES? sign and dropped it to the floor. I flipped over my I'M FINE sign and wrote WHY?

She spun me around and put her hands on the arms of the desk chair, caging me in. Her face was only inches from mine, and it looked as big as the moon. She calmly launched into a long, rambling spiel, the gist of which was about how she'd read these stories after finding something called the *Howard Journal of Criminal Justice*. After conducting a decade-long study, the journal had outlined the types of men most likely to murder their families. These men all blamed the breakdown of their once-ideal family on something outside their control, something outside themselves. Some blamed their family's problems on their lack of economic success and/or his not being the breadwinner for the family (I remember when she said "breadwinner" that I pictured Dad winning a giant loaf of bread in some sort of carnival-like contest). Many fathers blamed their wives for pitting their own children against them. Some men believed the entire family itself was to blame because they didn't act the right way; they weren't following his traditional religious values and customs. And there were the men who thought that they were actually saving or protecting the family from some outside threat or force.

Marjorie stopped and backed away from the chair.

I held up my new WHY? sign again.

She said, "Don't you get it? Everything I've said and you've read, they describe what's going on with Dad. He's going to do something like that to us, to all of us."

I carefully picked through my signs and held up NO.

Marjorie said, "I know you love him and I love him too, I do. And I know it's hard to believe, but there's something wrong with him. He's sick. It's so obvious. Haven't you figured it out yet? He's why I put us through everything, Merry. I knew he was getting sick, so at first I faked that I was sick so that someone would figure out that Dad was the one who needed help."

Marjorie knelt down in front of my chair and the hard plastic boot on her right foot clunked on the floor. She folded her hands over one of my knees and rested her chin there so I had to look down at her. I shook my head and held up my NO sign. She told me that all of her sessions with Dr. Hamilton were really about Dad and what she thought he was going to do to all of us. I tried holding up my NO sign again but I accidentally held up the GOOD sign. She told me that she tried telling Mom but Mom wouldn't listen to any of it, so Marjorie pretended to be beyond sick, to be possessed in order to make Mom finally listen and pay attention. I held up more signs, random signs, anything to get her to stop talking. Marjorie told me that when the unexpected opportunity of the TV show happened, she thought for sure that everyone would see who was really sick and who needed to be saved, only it didn't work that way. During the exorcism, she was so frightened and confused by what they did and tried to do to her, she wanted out, wanted literally to jump out of the family and out of the whole situation. So she jumped.

She continued to talk and I was crying, and I tried to cover my face with my signs. I was so tired of her filling my head with her stories, filling my head with her ghosts. I found a pen in her desk drawer and tried to write "I don't believe you," before she took the pen out of my hand.

Marjorie said, "Merry. Stop. Listen. Forget everything else I just said. I have proof about Dad. I'll take you down to the basement later if you want, so you can see for yourself." She stopped talking, pulled my hands away from the signs and held them, trapped them in hers.

She said, "He's created this big, weird shrine down there with drop cloths hanging on either side of the big metal cross that the show let him keep. Remember that ugly thing? He's got other pictures down there too, leaning against the foundation walls, and I guess they're religious, or you know, show some scenes from the Bible, but they're awful, terrible, scary-looking scenes, with some bearded guys in robes holding knives and sheep bleating and screaming, and, I don't know, just weird stuff like that. He set up a little altar too, using an old wooden bench. Listen. I found a small glass jar with a metal cap sitting on top of the bench. Right out in the open and everything." Marjorie paused, looked around again, and dropped her voice into a whisper. "That small glass jar, it's full to the top with a—a white substance or powder. And it's . . . What's the word? Granular. So, you know, it looks like a cross between sugar and flour. You know what sugar and flour look like, right?"

I nodded.

Marjorie stood up and turned my chair around slowly so I was again facing the computer. A picture of someone else's dead father was still there, and he leered at me. Marjorie clicked onto the search engine, typed in the phrase "potassium cyanide," clicked *images*, and then the screen was full of pictures of jars and bags of white powder. She said, "This is the stuff. He's got this stuff downstairs. It's poison, Merry. He's going to poison us all. And soon."

I sat and stared at the screen. I didn't know what to think anymore. So I let Marjorie think for me.

Marjorie talked so fast I could barely keep up with her. She whispered in my ear, filling me up with more stories. These were about Mom and Dad, stuff from before I was born, or when I was so little I couldn't possibly remember. Some of the stories were nice. Some weren't so nice. They were the early stories of our family. There were stories about our parents taking us to playgrounds and letting us sit in their laps on the swings and slides, about us all walking to the dairy farm to see the cows and goats. There were graphically detailed stories about them loudly fucking each other in their bedroom, and late at night on the living room couch and on the floor in front of the TV. There was a story about them drunkenly slapping each other in the face after a date-night gone bad, with Mom kicking out a window in the back door as the final blow, and how the following week they went away for two days of marriage counseling. There were stories about simple day-to-day stuff like Dad giving us horsey rides and being made to sing us songs at night before we went to sleep. There was a story about the time that Dad yanked Marjorie away from my crib because she was writing on my face with a marker and he accidentally pulled her arm out of her socket, and there was the time Mom started screaming wildly at two-year-old me because I wouldn't uncover my ears for the eardrops I needed. Even though I didn't remember any of it, I felt like I did. It felt like I was there and could see everything.

Marjorie told her stories until the sun went down and her bedroom turned purple. Finally, she stopped and put a pen in my hand and flipped over one of my signs.

She said, "Mom is getting sick too. You know she is. She's breaking down and can't handle it. I've seen her down in the basement with him, praying, saying, and doing weird things. We have to do something before it's too late. We have to help them, have to save them. We'll do it by saving ourselves first. If we don't do anything, Dad will bury us all in the basement."

I wrote WHAT DO WE DO?

Marjorie told me what we were going to do. And I made some new signs.

————

I WALKED INTO THE KITCHEN with my WHAT'S FOR DINNER? sign held up in front of my chest.

Mom sat by herself at the kitchen table. She smoked a cigarette and flipped through an entertainment magazine.

She said, "What's this?"

I pointed at the sign.

"Are you not talking because we didn't get the tree?"

Sign: YES.

"What do you want for dinner then? Do you have that written down on a sign?"

My next sign: SPAGHETTI.

"We can do that."

Sign: OKAY.

"Do I get a kiss?"

Sign: OKAY.

I WENT BACK UPSTAIRS. I still hadn't seen Dad and assumed he was in the basement. I waited with Marjorie in her room. She let me keep one of her pens and a pocket-sized pad of paper, one with a glittery yellow cover, so I could write new signs more quickly. She also turned on her TV and let me watch *SpongeBob*. It was an episode that featured a pirate ghost that was big and green and kind of scary.

Partway through the show Marjorie dropped to all fours and stuck her arms under her bed.

Her walking boot crashed heavily into the floor twice. She emerged with the glass jar of white powder that she'd told me about.

Sign: IS THAT IT?

"Yes."

Sign: YOU SAID IT WAS FULL? The jar was taller and skinnier than I imagined, and it was only maybe a quarter full.

Marjorie smiled. "Nothing gets by you at all, does it, Merry? It was full. I dumped most of it out."

I LET MARJORIE WALK DOWN the stairs first. Her boot sounded like a bowling ball rolling down the stairs.

When we reached the foyer, Marjorie surprised me by putting the jar into my hands. This wasn't part of the plan. I shook my head no and tried to give it back to her.

She whispered, "This will only work if you do it. You heard me walking down the stairs, yeah? I'm just realizing now that she'll hear me clomping around the kitchen if I do it. Don't worry. I'll distract her for you. It'll be easy."

Marjorie put two hands in the middle of my back and pushed me away and into the living room. She limped into the dining room. The dining room table was covered in clean clothes as usual.

Marjorie called out, "Hey, Mom? Can you help me find my purple PJ top? I can't find it and

I want to wear it tonight. It gets so cold in my room."

Mom walked out of the kitchen and said, "Wait, hold on a second. Don't just go picking through all the piles. I killed myself folding everything!"

I wasn't going to do it. I wasn't going to do anything. I was just going to stand there in the living room with the cold, glass jar in my hand and wait for someone to take it away from me. I swear, I don't remember walking from the living room and into the kitchen and then next to the stove. But there I was.

I don't remember if I'd taken off the silver lid, or if Marjorie had done so for me. The blue gas flame of the burner was low. The sauce bubbled slowly. Mom and Marjorie bickered in the dining room. I poured white powder into the saucepan and quickly stirred until it disappeared into the red, until it looked as though I hadn't added anything.

I did it because I believed in Marjorie and I believed that her plan would work, that it would help everyone.

I tiptoed out of the kitchen and I heard Mom say to Marjorie in an exasperated voice, "Find it yourself, then."

MOM SAID, "NO SAUCE, RIGHT, sweetie?"

I held up my YES sign. I used a fork to mix the butter into my plain pasta.

Dad asked what all my signs were about.

I held up my hastily scribbled CHEESE sign.

Mom told him that I'd decided to stop talking for the day. She didn't tell him why.

Dad passed me the Parmesan cheese.

I don't remember where in the house Dad came from. What I mean is, I don't remember where he was before we were all in the kitchen eating dinner. I only remember him being there at the kitchen table like he'd always been sitting there, like a gargoyle. He was hunched and his unkempt beard jutted out in random places, and his eyes darted around the room like he was always looking for an emergency exit. Dad prayed silently to himself as Mom served herself a bowl of pasta and covered it with red sauce. The saucepan was avocado green and dinged up. It'd been used a lot. Dad served himself when Mom was finished.

Marjorie was the last to come to the table. She had been in the downstairs bathroom for a long time. She tickled my neck with freshly wet hands as she scooted by me and sat down. Using her fork instead of the wooden serving ladle, Marjorie speared a staggering amount of spaghetti onto her plate. It all clumped and stuck together like a ball of tangled yarn.

Mom said, "Wow, someone's hungry."

"I could eat the world. Merry, pass the sauce, please," Marjorie said, and winked at me. Her eyes were red, as if she'd been crying.

I didn't know what to do or what her asking

for the sauce meant. And when I looked around the table I thought Mom and Dad were staring at me extra hard, like they knew I'd done something wrong. The empty glass jar Marjorie had given me was still in my sweatshirt pocket. My skin tingled with fear as I thought Marjorie had told them what I did to the sauce, had told them our plan, and had told them it was all my idea and my fault.

I held up my NO sign.

Dad said, "I got it." He reached his big paw across the table and passed the saucepan to Marjorie. She said, "Thank you, Father," in her faux-British accent and poured the rest of the sauce onto her pasta. She twirled her fork in the middle of the red mess and shoved the glob into her mouth. She chewed, swallowed, and watched me watching her.

The moment I saw the sauce pass between her lips, I was as angry as I'd ever been in my life. Marjorie had fooled me again. I'd believed her. Tears filled my eyes so I kept my head down near my plate. She had lied to me, made it all up: her theory about Dad, the family stories, and our plan. Our plan: Have Mom cook us spaghetti and we'd spike the sauce. I famously didn't like sauce, and Marjorie would say her stomach hurt so she'd have her pasta plain just like me. We'd put enough of the powder in the sauce to just "knock out" (Marjorie's phrase) our parents or make them sick enough so that we could then run away, escape the house. We'd bring the poison jar to the police as proof of what Dad had planned to do to us and then we'd be safe. Dad would get taken away, yes, but he'd also get the help he needed and maybe someday he'd be well enough to come back home to us, just like how every time Marjorie was sent away, she came back to us. This made sense to the eight-year-old me. People went away and they came back and would continue to come back because they had always done so previously.

So it was clear that Marjorie had tricked me into pouring a mix of sugar and flour into the sauce. I was the dummy again. Right? I mean, why else would she eat the sauce too?

I held up my WHY? sign to her.

Marjorie said, "This is the best sauce ever. You should have some, monkey." She was laughing at me behind her big, red smile. I hated her so much right then. I whispered it as I chewed on my plain pasta so no one else could hear me. But I did. I whispered, "I hate you. I wish you were dead."

Marjorie said, "You eat pizza with sauce. You love pizza! I don't understand why you don't eat it with your spaghetti. It's crazy. Right, Dad?"

Dad said, "Whatever. I've long given up trying to figure anyone out."

Mom said, "Leave her alone. She'll eat sauce when she wants to."

My sister and my parents talking about my not eating red sauce were their last words. No explanations or realizations or regrets or pleas for forgiveness. No good-byes.

And it happened quickly. I still can't believe it happened so quickly. The high-pitched *scritch* of forks rubbing against the ceramic dishes stopped. Breaths became heavy and as loud and as infrequent as whale spouts. Chairs groaned, slid back. Hands dropped forks and squished into their plates. Glasses knocked over. My stack of signs slid to the floor. Elbows banged on the table. Legs kicked out. Eyes fluttered and closed. Heads dropped. Bodies slouched and sank.

I stood up and backed away from the table slowly, initially afraid that a sudden movement from me would make the scene implode further, with the table and chairs and everyone sliding and sinking into the basement. Mom's and Dad's heads lay on the table as though they were schoolchildren napping on their desks. I tried poking Mom in the shoulder and her arm dropped below the table. I jumped back, banging into the counter and rack of dishes behind me and no one reacted, no one moved. I screamed as loudly as I could and paced the room.

Marjorie's head was tilted back, face pointed at the ceiling. Her hair had fallen out of her ponytail and hung down behind her, a half-drawn curtain. Red saliva bubbled out of her mouth and dripped down the length of her long, white neck. Her eyes were half open. I stood next to her on my tiptoes and craned my face over hers.

I said her name three times. I didn't use my signs. I asked her what we were supposed to do now. Her eyes were dark and reflected the light above her. Her skin had turned to clay.

I asked her how long it would take for the powder to wear off. I asked her how long it would take them to wake up.

I told her that this was a bad idea, that she didn't have to eat the sauce like they did. I told her I needed her and I didn't think I could go to the police by myself because I didn't know where they were.

I put the empty glass jar in Marjorie's hand, wrapped her fingers around it, tried to make her hold it like she was supposed to. But it kept falling out, so I took it back.

I sat in my chair and waited. None of them was breathing. I stood up, covered my eyes and told Mom and Dad that I was sorry I played such a mean prank on them, and that it was all Marjorie's fault. I started crying.

I went down into the basement. I was terrified but I had to see what was down there, see if anything that Marjorie had told me was true. I ran down the basement stairs. I wanted extra light with me, so I carried two jumbo flashlights, and the beams danced and bounced off the stone foundation walls.

There was no shrine with tapestries and pictures and altars. There was none of that. Up against the back wall of the basement, next to the shelves of food there was the giant pewter cross that had briefly hung on the wall in Marjorie's room. A dirty rag covered Jesus' head. His body was tarnished and smeared with dirt.

I sat on the basement floor and I waited for Marjorie's growing things to come bursting out of the ground, wrap me in their green tentacles, and pull me underneath the house, or pull me apart, piece by piece, bit by bit until every part of me had been torn away.

Everything gets foggy after the basement.

CHAPTER 26

"WHAT I REMEMBER is going to the second floor and leaving everyone's bedroom door open in case they wanted to come upstairs. I left my door open so they could find me. I had my Richard Scarry book and the empty poison jar with me. I was in my bedroom three days later when Auntie Erin came over to the house and found me. Found us."

Rachel says, "Merry—" and holds up her hand to stop me. But I'm not done talking. Not yet.

"But apparently, that last part didn't happen. I know I sort of insinuated before that I hadn't read the police report. But I've read the police report. So I know that Marjorie's psychiatrist came by for her appointment, found cars in the driveway, a locked house, and called the police after no one answered the door or the phone. I know the police broke in and found me in the kitchen with my family. I know that I was underneath the kitchen table. I know I was sitting in the filth and foul of three-day-old bodies and I know I was sitting down at the foot of my mother, leaning up against her legs, sitting there with her thumb in my mouth."

I finally stop talking, for what feels like the first time in days, and take a deep, greedy breath. I'm not crying, but I am trembling all over. My hands wiggle in my lap like dying fish. I'm cold and reach for my jacket. I say, "Is it me or is it now totally freezing in here?"

Rachel stands up and slides her chair over next to me so that she can put an arm around my shoulder and hug me. I lean into her. She's warm and comfortable. I close my eyes and we sit like that until Rachel lets me go. She wipes her eyes with a napkin from the table.

I say, "That memory of Auntie Erin coming into my bedroom, saving me, carrying me downstairs to her car, it has faded a little, but it's still there. Only it's been reassigned, or shuffled off to be part of another more appropriate memory of the years spent living with my amazing aunt. Maybe it's not the same as actually remembering, but what the police report describes as having happened in terrible detail, I can see it now, and I can almost feel it."

Rachel says, "I wish I knew what to say, Merry."

"I've never told anyone what I've admitted to you. The police, psychologists, my aunt; no one.

I imagine there'll be a giant shit storm when it comes out in the book. But I think I'm ready for it. I'm ready to live with the truth, anyway."

Rachel writes something down in her notebook and lets loose a long sigh. She says, "Wow, Merry. You break my heart and I—I don't know what to do now."

"What do you mean?"

Rachel slips into her coat and says, "It has gotten cold in here, hasn't it?" She opens and closes her notebook twice. "What is the truth, Merry? And please, I don't mean that to sound accusatory or in any way callous to the horror you lived through, that you live with. It's just given what I knew, or what I thought I knew going into this, and what I've read and researched and now heard from you, I'm not at all sure what really happened."

I say, "There are days it all seems like something that happened to someone else, and in a way, that's a truth. I haven't been that little Miss Merry in a very long time. There are days when I want to believe it was all some horror movie that I've watched repeatedly, and in that horror movie, a demon inside Marjorie magically made the poison appear under the bed and it was the demon that tricked an innocent child into killing her family. There are days when I want to believe that Dad only got the potassium cyanide because he was desperate to polish up that ugly pewter cross in the basement. There are days when I like to think that Marjorie was right and that she truly believed in the plan she pitched me but mistakenly thought the supposedly smaller amount of poison in the jar wouldn't be enough to kill them.

"Most days, I really don't know what to think or believe. All that I do know with one hundred percent certainty is that Marjorie and perhaps my father were very sick, our entire family was put under impossible stresses and strains, we were all manipulated, and we were all irrational, maybe even willingly so. And when I was eight years old, I was manipulated into poisoning my sister and my parents."

We sit in silence. A young, giggling couple bursts into the coffee shop, slamming the front door open. The bell rings angrily. They both make loud *brr-we're-freezing* noises as they walk toward the counter. The barista reappears. He rubs his hands and arms furiously, trying to keep them warm. He sees me watching, winks, and says, "Heat's off, but it wasn't me."

Rachel starts in with questions about the police report, about there being some inconsistencies regarding my story and some of the gathered evidence, including the glass jar. She says that most of the prints on the jar were smudged and unreadable and the only partial they could lift belonged to my father.

"Yes, I'd read that about the prints, but I don't know what else to tell you about the jar. I told you everything I know and everything I remember. Anything else would be speculation or two-bit

detective work on my part. I've given you everything that I have to give regarding my story. The
rest is really up to you. You wanted my story.
Now you have it, and I trust you with it." I stand
up slowly and say, "I'm sorry, I didn't mean to
sound snippy. I really do mean it when I say that
I trust you with this story. If anyone is going to
write it, I'm so very glad it's you, Rachel."

Rachel smiles, stands, and says, "Merry—"

I interrupt. "I'm exhausted and suddenly not
feeling that great. I think I need to go home and
lie down now. Okay?"

"Yes, of course! You need to take care of yourself, Merry."

We share a long hug. We declare ourselves
friends. Rachel offers to give me a ride home.
I politely refuse and tighten the belt of my red
coat.

Rachel puts on her gloves and wraps a scarf
around her neck. She promises to check in with
me after she gets back from Amsterdam. She says
that we should have dinner or lunch together
sometime and not talk at all about the book. I tell
her that I would like that very much, but I doubt
the just-for-fun lunch/dinner will happen. She'll
be too busy writing our book and busy with
interviews and assignments for her new one. And
despite how friendly and motherly she's being,
the way she looks at me now, it's different.

Behind the counter, the barista is on the phone
with someone and grumbling about the heat not
working. I turn and walk toward the front door

thinking that it must not have shut all the way after the couple entered because of how cold it is in the coffee shop now.

Rachel calls out to me, "Merry! Don't forget your umbrella." Rachel hands it to me and it's still wet. I thank her. After an awkward silence, and after Rachel and I say our good-byes again, it's cold enough that my breath is a visible mist.

ACKNOWLEDGMENTS

FIRST AND FOREMOST, thanks to Lisa, Cole, Emma, and the rest of my family who love, support, and put up with me. My wife, Lisa, went above and beyond this time around being a beta reader and her input was invaluable. Thanks to my sister Erin and brother-in-law Steve, who let me fictionalize their house.

Huge thanks to this novel's other beta reader, the talented John Mantooth. I think it was Louis Maistros who once said, "Being asked to read another writer's rough draft is the literary equivalent of being asked to help a friend move a couch to a new place." He's so right, and I so appreciate the heavy lifting that John did with this book.

More huge thanks to my agent, Stephen "They're coming to get you" Barbara, for his friendship, advice, and support. I'm so lucky to have him on my side.

A thousand and one thank-yous to my amazing editor, Jennifer Brehl. She helped make this the best book it could be. I'd never be able to fully explain how much her belief in me and this book means. (Everyone, put down the book and clap for Jen, please.)

Big thanks to Camille Collins, Pamela Jaffee, Ashley Marudas, Andrea Molitor, Kelly O'Connor, Caroline Perny, and everyone at William Morrow for their support, enthusiasm, and hard work. I'm so proud to be working alongside all these great people.

Thank you to two of my best friends and co-conspirators, John Langan and Laird Barron, for listening to me whine, agitate, complain, pontificate, and fret my way through this book, once a week by phone (and too occasionally in person).

Thank you to friends and colleagues who've supported, inspired, and helped keep me sane: Karen Brissette (the real one!), Ken Cornwell, Brett Cox, JoAnn Cox, Ellen Datlow, Kurt Dinan, Steve Eller, Steve Fisher, Andy Falkous and Future of the Left, Geoffrey Goodwin, Brett Gurewitz and Bad Religion, Page Hamilton, Jack Haringa, John Harvey, Stephen Graham Jones, Sandra Kasturi, Matt Kressel, Michael Lajoie, Sarah Langan, Jennifer Levesque, Kris Meyer, Stewart O'Nan, Brett Savory, Mark Haskell Smith, Simon Strantzas, Dave Zeltserman, and Your Pretty Name.

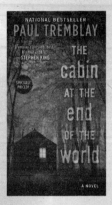